THE WORRIED MAN

Q.C. DAVIS BOOK 1

LISA M. LILLY

SPINY WOMAN PRESS

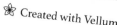 Created with Vellum

CONTENTS

It takes a worried man to sing a worried song,
It takes a worried man to sing a worried song,
I'm worried now,
but I won't be worried long.

- Worried Man Blues, Traditional

1

THE FIRST TIME I MET MARCO, WE TALKED ABOUT DEATH. HIS. The police asked a lot of questions about that later.

We met the night The Harmoniums, the three-person a cappella group I belong to, sang at Kensington Pub in Lincoln Square. I noticed a guy with all his hair–dark, curly, and a little on the long side—walk in during our second set.

I guessed him in his late thirties, which meant he brought down the average age of the audience by a decade or two. Most Kensington patrons are from the Old Town School of Folk Music across the street. Lots of baby boomers with gray hair and ponytails (the men) or silver hair and gauzy skirts (the women). The Harmoniums don't sing traditional songs, but we do a mix of Simon & Garfunkel, Indigo Girls, blues, gospel, and anything that lends itself to good harmonies, so we appeal to the same audience.

Our last song was *California Dreamin'*, a guaranteed crowd pleaser during late fall when the trademark gray skies and icy winds of Chicago's winter threaten. After we finished, I stepped away from the corner that we used as a stage area and hunted around for my charcoal blazer. I'd taken it off when it got too hot with three of us crowding around one microphone.

As I straightened from retrieving the blazer, which had slipped under a table, a smartphone was thrust under my nose.

"I figured it out," the guy with all the hair said. "You're Q.C. Davis."

He smiled, showing teeth that looked bright white against his caramel-colored skin. He wore jeans and a short-sleeved T-shirt that looked like he'd pressed it.

No body art that I could see, which was good. My first boyfriend was inked everywhere and it's a bad association. Not fair to all the great guys with major tattoos that I shy away from, but I can't get past it.

I brushed dust bunnies off my blazer. "Quille."

"What?"

"My name. It's Quille."

"But you're *the* Q.C. Davis." He pointed to the phone. It showed an old profile from early in college when I was still acting. "Aren't you?"

Despite my abhorrence for the name, I was impressed he'd found it. I'm thirty-two, but I've had a couple of career changes already. Because of that, and through some serious effort on my part, "Q.C. Davis" comes up on Page 3 at the earliest in search results. Q.C. belongs to a different part of my life, one I'm finished with.

"You're a good Googler," I said.

He laughed. It made his eyes bright and brought out little lines around them. Maybe he was forty?

"Me and everyone else. I'm pretty sure I saw you in *Token Woman* at Northlight Theater when I was in med school." He held out his hand. "I'm Marco. And it's nice to know you can actually sing really well."

His grip was warm and not too tight.

"Thanks," I said.

Playing a character modeled after notoriously bad real-life soprano Florence Foster Jenkins had been one of my favorite roles. It had also been my last, and the end of my life as Q.C. Davis.

I pulled my black zipper sweatshirt over the blazer, and my fleece-lined jacket over that. Layers are important to survive winter in Chicago. To survive at all in Chicago.

Joe, who sings bass, had his long cashmere coat and gloves on. He and our alto, Danielle, stood near the door talking with some of our regular fans.

Slim and tall, Joe towered over everyone, so it was easy for him to catch my eye. He arched one heavy, dark eyebrow and tilted his head, silently asking if everything was all right. A lot of men come up to talk after shows. It's not that I'm so attractive. I can appear striking with the right make up, but day-to-day I'm only a little prettier than average, mainly because of my hair, which is long and dark and wavy.

As any performer will tell you, though, the instant you step on stage you become ten times more appealing, if not a hundred.

Most people who talk to you after a show are nice, but now and then you get someone who raises red flags, so the three of us watch out for one another.

"Excuse me," I said to Marco, who had his back to Joe. I waved to Joe that everything was fine.

Marco glanced toward the door. "I don't want to keep you from anything."

I put on my fuchsia scarf and gloves. In my day-to-day life I'm a lawyer, and my wardrobe is mostly black, gray, and white. I use bright-colored accessories for variety, and because I'm less likely to overlook or forget them. Daley Center courtrooms swallowed up dozens of black umbrellas before I figured that out.

"Why don't you come with us?" I said.

I hoped he'd say yes. I hadn't met anyone I really liked in a long time.

Outside, we stepped between parked cars, inching out to check traffic. Wind and sleet hit my face as I watched for cabs and bikes riding too close to the parking lane. You wouldn't think people would cycle in the dark and the sleet—I wouldn't do it—but they do. Sometimes wearing dark clothes with no bike lights.

Café Barcelona, the tapas restaurant next to the Old Town School, is laid out like an L with a bar on the short side. There are always nice people there, and the mixed drinks don't cost an arm and a leg. Marco and I chose seats at the end of a long table near Joe and his girlfriend.

Marco returned from the bar with a whiskey sour made with rye for me and a bottle of San Pellegrino for him.

"So what kind of doctor are you?" I said.

"Ah, I'm not a doctor anymore. Too much stress."

I sipped my whisky sour—made just as I liked it with egg white foam on the top and fresh-squeezed lemon juice—as I turned that over in my mind. A non-alcoholic drink on a Friday might not mean much. If he were driving, he might avoid alcohol. But that plus a defection from medicine suggested issues.

"What kind were you?"

"Surgeon," he said.

"And now?"

He ran his hand through his hair. It looked just past where he ought to have gotten it cut. He had flyaway ends along his part. I liked that. It offset his pressed T-shirt and kept him from looking too clean cut or rigid.

"Insurance adjuster," he said.

"Do you like it?"

He grinned. "Thanks for not yawning. It's fun. And sometimes frustrating. I investigate medical fraud."

I ate a few black olives from the shared bowl. "Like stalking people who might be faking injuries?"

"I focus on medical care providers," Marco said. "Mostly clinics."

Joe had ordered a plate of oven-baked goat cheese, tomato sauce, and toast points with garlic for the table. Marco reached for it with his left hand. No ring. Something I ought to have looked for at the outset, but I'm only now getting used to checking.

In my twenties, almost no one I met was married. Now it's kind of a toss up, especially when I date guys older than me.

The conversation segued into politics. Marco joined in without mentioning his own views and yielded the floor when someone else jumped in.

I liked that. Having been around entertainers since I was five, I've had my fill of people who always need to be center stage. A guy like that can be a lot of fun for a couple dates, but what he wants in life is an audience, not a partner.

I get tired of being the audience.

On the other hand, I'd veered too far in the opposite direction with my boyfriend during law school. Now I look for someone who can hold his own in a crowd. Someone I can leave alone for a few minutes at a party without worrying that he'll be lost.

So, basically, I want the Goldilocks of men when it comes to sociability.

When there was a lull, Marco offered to get me a second drink, and I said I'd have what he was having.

He frowned. "If you're thinking I'm an alcoholic, you're right. But you can drink around me. It's fine."

"It's not that," I said. "One's my limit."

One drink helps me relax. Two and I start feeling depressed. Not a place I want to go with my mother's history.

I offered to buy this round, but Marco stood. "I'll get it."

I took it as a good sign. Some guys buy one drink to be polite. Two means interest.

"Could I ask you something?" Marco said after he'd settled in his seat again. "If you can't answer, it's okay. You probably hate when people ask you legal questions."

My stomach dipped and my shoulders sagged. So the drinks were for free legal advice.

"I don't hate it," I said, keeping my tone steady to hide my disappointment. "But I might not be able to answer."

"It's about a will," he said. "I made one the year I got married, and I never updated it. My ex-wife's a good person, but if something happens to me I want any money I leave to go right to my son. He's thirteen."

I smiled at him not trashing the ex. I'd met guys who on the first date couldn't refer to an ex-girlfriend without saying "that bitch." Which ruled out a second date, as I had no interest in being the next bitch.

I texted Marco the names of three good estate attorneys I knew.

"So the two drinks," I said. "Was that just in the hope of free legal advice?"

"No," he said. "I want to ask you out. But obviously I'm really bad at it, or I would have asked already."

I squeezed the lime into my sparkling water, considering. Ex-surgeon, non-drinking alcoholic, possibly-too-recently-divorced Marco waved a few red flags.

"You know," I said, "most people wait until at least the third date before confessing their dark secrets. I'm a little worried."

"Me too," he said.

"Why?"

He smiled. "You haven't told me any of yours."

Marco and I saw each other all through that winter and into early spring. When his lease was almost up, we decided to move in together.

The evening before the move I paused in the tulip-filled courtyard of the aging apartment building where Marco lived. I checked my phone again. Still no response to any of my texts or calls.

It was a rare perfect mid-April evening. Warm, light breeze, sun, the smell of fresh grass. I wore a brand new sleeveless green dress that had a flared skirt. We'd been packing for the last couple weeks, so I'd lived in jeans and T-shirts or sweatshirts. Tonight I wanted to look pretty for our last dinner at his place.

Also, this week I hadn't been much help to Marco. I'd been slaving over other people's taxes and simultaneously trying to settle a lawsuit between two business partners. But two of my friends, both of whom built sets at Chicago Shakespeare for a living, had reinforced the loft above my bedroom. Now instead of storage it could be used as a sleeping space for Marco's son when he stayed over.

It had been finished late last night. I'd texted Marco a photo, but he hadn't responded.

I pressed the third buzzer from the top.

No answer.

Marco had said he had an important meeting today. Maybe it had run long.

I used his entry code and let myself in. The vestibule felt cool and smelled of lime disinfectant. Marco was three flights up. The carpeted steps sagged under my feet. As I reached the second floor a smell like boiled chicken bones overpowered the disinfectant.

I shifted the paper bag from Dinkel's bakery as I climbed. I'd bought flourless chocolate cake—I was thrilled to have found a man who loved dark chocolate as much as I did—and cherry Coke. In the five months I'd been seeing Marco, I'd discovered a lot of fun non-alcoholic drinks.

Inside the apartment the window air conditioning unit blasted frigid air through the kitchen and dining area and into the hall.

The odor, worse in here than on the stairs, assaulted me. It smelled, literally, like shit with an undertone of ammonia. The smell of a poorly-run nursing home. Or maybe of the apartment of someone with bad stomach flu.

"Marco?"

The apartment was laid out in what my grandmother called a shotgun arrangement. Three rooms jutted out from a long interior hallway that ended with a small bathroom. I dropped the Dinkel's bag on the scratched kitchen table and hurried down the hall, my flats clicking on the hardwood.

Stacked and taped cardboard boxes stood along the far wall of the deserted bedroom. The double bed was made, its comforter smoothed out and pillows squared, the desk bare. It was something that unnerved me about Marco. I'd never dated a guy neater than I was, but I figured living with a neat freak would be better than someone who left dirty dishes in the sink and clothes on the floor.

I checked the bathroom. It, too, was empty. Its hexagonal tiled floor looked clean and dry.

A wide archway opened onto the living room. Marco's flat screen TV sat on a low table, the original box and Styrofoam inserts on the floor near it. The sofa, its back to me, faced the TV.

A can of Diet Chocolate Fudge Soda, a glass tumbler, and a bottle of Bacardi Rum stood on the end table. A prescription pill bottle lay next to it.

A wave of dizziness hit as I hurried around the sofa. I put my hand to my mouth and grabbed the back of the armchair.

I couldn't process what I was seeing.

What looked like a mannequin of Marco, dressed in khakis and a long-sleeved collared shirt, lay on its side on the bright green couch. The face was the color of chalk. One of his arms wedged beneath him. The other pointed out and slanted down.

I leapt forward and pressed my fingers to Marco's throat, but jerked away at the feel of cold, rigid flesh. I tried again. No pulse.

I tried to shift him onto his back to start chest compressions. His body was too stiff to move. CPR was impossible. I dialed 911.

As I spoke to the dispatcher, I dropped onto the hardwood floor, knees to my chest, arms around them. The stench filled my nostrils, but it didn't matter.

In a movie, the director would make the actress playing me scream or cover her eyes or sob uncontrollably because that's how women act in movies.

But I felt still and too silent, too focused, for screaming and crying. As if the world had narrowed and I was looking through a telescope that made things small instead of large.

That made Marco small.

2

THE DETECTIVE SAT ACROSS FROM ME AT THE WORN KITCHEN table. His tan suit jacket was large and too boxy for his frame, but his tie was knotted in a perfect half-Windsor. Between that and his silver crew cut he looked ex-military despite the ill-fitting jacket.

"What was your relationship with the deceased?"

During the time it had taken the police and paramedics to arrive I'd pulled the armchair close to the couch and sat. I couldn't leave Marco alone, and I couldn't look at his body. I'd scrolled through photos of him on my phone over and over.

It seemed like I sat on that chair in my new green dress for days. It also felt as if only seconds passed before lights and voices shattered my last moments with Marco.

A policewoman had led me out of the apartment and taken down everything I said. When she brought me back in, she gave me a glass of water and introduced me to the detective, whose name I couldn't remember.

The glass sat in the thin layer of fingerprint dust that covered the scratched wooden table.

"Ms. Davis?" the detective said.

"We were about to move in together," I said. In my head, my voice reverberated and sounded too loud, but the detective scooted his chair closer as if to hear me better. "He was moving in with me. Tomorrow."

Some of Marco's things had already migrated to my place, just as mine had made their way into his. Last weekend to make space for his clothes I'd filled paper bags with skirts, tights, and dress pants I hadn't worn during the last twelve months to donate to a local women's shelter. Marco and I had rearranged my bedroom and living room areas to clear space for his chest of drawers and armchair, the only furniture he was bringing. We'd bought a futon for the loft for Eric.

"I should call his son," I said. "Or should I? Telling him on the phone, I don't know."

"You didn't call him yet?" the detective said.

"I wanted to give him a little more time. Even a few minutes. To still have a dad." I wound a section of my hair around my fingers, twisting the strands into a braid that I immediately unwound. "We just made a place for him to stay."

I opened my phone and found the photo of the loft with the new futon against the interior brick wall. I handed the phone to the detective.

He put on silver-framed reading glasses, looked at the photo, and handed it back. "How old is he?"

"Thirteen. He lives with his mother. In Lincoln Park."

"We'll send someone in person to tell her. Better to let her talk to him. Mirabel Ruggirello, correct?"

I set the phone on the table and ran my finger over the photo. The image shivered. I started to swipe to look at the next photo but realized the detective had asked me a question.

"Yes. Mirabel. I don't know if she still uses Marco's last name."

I'd spoken to her once on the phone about plans for a weekend with Eric, but I'd never met her.

"Is there someone we can call for you?" the detective said.

I rubbed my hands over my bare arms, which were covered in goose flesh. "Someone's coming."

I'd given the policewoman Joe's information. I hadn't called anyone myself. To do that was to make it real. To admit Marco was dead.

The detective set his phone on the table face down. "How long had Mr. Ruggirello been divorced?"

I stared at the Dinkel's bakery bag. It had been shifted to the top of some boxes near the back door. All we'd had left to pack was the kitchen.

That thought kept coming back to me. Marco couldn't be gone, he couldn't have relapsed to drinking or started taking pills, because all we had left to pack were pots and pans and dishes.

"They've been divorced about nine months," I said.

Marco and Mirabel had been married seventeen years counting three years of separation, but they'd dated since high school. A long time.

A uniformed officer came into the room. Embroidered on the right shoulder of his short-sleeved shirt was a white flag with six-pointed red stars sandwiched between light blue bars. He whispered something to the detective and left, camera in his hands.

He must have been taking photos of Marco, the couch, and the end table with the rum and soda and clear amber pill canister.

"The pill bottle, the label. What did it say?" I asked.

I'd looked at it without touching anything right after calling 911. I hadn't been able to see the label. I couldn't believe it was Marco's.

The detective tapped one finger against the side of his chin. He looked like he'd just shaved despite that it was early evening. "It's still being processed. When did you last talk to Mr. Ruggirello?"

"About six," I said. "Last night about six."

"What did you talk about?" the detective said.

"It was a text. Some texts. About tonight. Dessert for tonight."

I sipped some water. The glass shook, so I gripped it with both hands. My fingers felt like ice.

I wanted to leave, to go home, except that home was a place with empty closet shelves and the King-sized bed I'd bought around Christmas when Marco had started sleeping over most weeknights.

"You still have the text?"

I keyed open my phone again, entering my passcode three times before I got it right, to double-check. "No. I clear them every day. So if I lose my phone, no one who finds it sees any messages about my cases."

"Did he seem upset about anything?"

"He sent a smiley face and a soda emoji. Said he loved me and we'd talk later."

My fingers tangled in my hair and I unwound them one by one. I wondered if I would have known something was wrong if we'd spoken rather than texted. If we'd talked, maybe it would have changed everything.

The detective made a note on a small yellow pad. I hadn't noticed him holding it before. I stared at the pen as it moved across the paper. It made a scratching sound. "Did you worry when you didn't hear from him?"

"Not at first. I was working late. I'm a lawyer. A litigator. But I file taxes, too, for theater people I know. I figured Marco was leaving me alone to finish. It only seemed strange when I didn't hear from him today."

I'd been so worried about getting the filing done on time, about the scanner working properly and my calculations being correct, that my heart had kept racing after I clicked the last few keys. I'd made herbal tea and sat in my office for a few minutes staring at the street below to unwind before walking home. Now it seemed insane to have been so concerned about filings. About things that could be fixed.

While I'd been sipping tea to feel calmer, Marco might have been drinking or taking pills. He might already have been dead.

The detective leaned back in his chair, crossed one leg over the opposite knee, and asked if I'd been alone in my office.

I told him yes, that I'd been sitting on the floor of the reception area, crinkled receipts, 1099s, and scraps of paper spread around me. A new client had brought them to me in a literal shoebox on April 13.

As I spoke, it hit me why he was asking.

I sat straighter. "You're thinking murder? You're asking me for an alibi?"

"We need to look into all avenues."

I'd grown up hearing from my parents about police investigations. All their warnings flooded my mind.

My pulse pounded at my temples. "Could you tell me your name again?" I said. "And could I have a card?"

3

DANIELLE, THE ALTO IN THE HARMONIUMS, IS ALSO A LAWYER. We share an office she leases in a larger suite. But she was out of town this week, and the other tenants kept pretty easy hours and had been out the door by six the night before.

After I told Detective Sergeant Beckwell that, he walked me through whether Marco's apartment door had been locked when I arrived, and what I'd done when I'd entered. He asked more questions about Marco.

When I told him Marco didn't drink, the detective pushed his chair back a few inches from the table and shifted sideways, angling his body more toward me. As if we were on a talk show together. "He didn't like alcohol? Or he had an issue with it?"

"He was a recovering alcoholic."

"For how long did he have serious problems with drinking?"

"Six years. Maybe seven." It felt like I ought to remember exactly how long it had been but too much was whirling in my brain. "He lost a lot. His profession—he was a surgeon—his marriage. His investments. But he's been sober for years. Over three years. That's why it's, why I can't—why it's hard to believe he started again."

I rubbed the back of my neck where my muscles had knotted. All of this felt unreal. Impossible. But the sight of Marco's body on the couch, burned into my mind, told me otherwise.

The detective flipped a page of his notepad. "How were his finances? If you know?"

"What does that—" I shivered. My thoughts flew over everything the detective had said so far.

All avenues. Murder, yes, and also suicide. Not an accidental overdose but suicide.

"No." I shook my head. Drinking Marco might have hidden. People relapse. But if he'd been so despondent he'd commit suicide, I would have known. "No. He'd been struggling a little with the separation and divorce, but that's normal. He wasn't depressed."

I gripped my phone with both hands, holding it in my lap. That feeling of unreality grew, as if I were in one of the hundreds of plays I'd acted in. In a second the curtain would fall. I'd take off my make up, dress in my street clothes, and find Marco waiting for me at the stage door.

"How long had you known Mr. Ruggirello?"

"Five months," I said. "But it felt longer. We just—clicked."

I had no other words to explain how everything had felt with Marco. I'd felt like myself. Not like Q.C. the actress or Quille the accountant or lawyer. Like myself. And he'd said the same about being with me. It was why we'd thought moving in together could work though we hadn't known each other long. It all felt right in a way we'd never experienced before.

Plus it wasn't like we were kids. He was forty-two, I was thirty-two.

The detective leaned toward me, elbows on the table. "He'd also lost his medical license, correct?"

Pressure built behind my eyes. I inched my chair back a

little. "He left his practice voluntarily. And he has a good job now. Had. With an insurance company. He's a supervisor. And he owns some income property. It's not doing great, but it's okay. He's okay. He was."

"Had he given anything away recently?" the detective said.

It took me a minute to follow the shift in questioning. Giving things away was another sign of suicide. I remembered that from somewhere. Maybe a college psychology class or an article I'd read.

"Furniture. But that's because of the move. Next week, a few people are—were—coming to get furniture he wouldn't need. The Salvation Army is picking up the rest by the end of the month." My pulse pounded in my head. "Excuse me."

I fumbled in my purse for my mini-bottle of Ibuprofen. Taking three at the first sign usually heads off a migraine, but I need to do it right away. If it's further along, I try Imitrex. But that helps only half the time, and nearly all the time makes me feel dizzy and nauseated to the point of vomiting.

Though I already felt that way, so maybe it didn't matter.

I struggled with the cap. It stuck fast no matter how many times I flicked it with my thumb. Each flick sent a jolt of pain through my entire head.

The detective took it from me, turned the cap a centimeter, and popped it off.

"Thank you."

As I swallowed all three pills in a gulp, two uniformed women carried out a zipped black bag on a stretcher. I watched until they made it out the door.

"Did he have a will?" the detective asked.

Marco's questions the night we'd met flashed through my mind.

I didn't want to answer. Police always take the obvious route. That's what my father says. Maybe the Chicago police would be better than those in Edwardsville where my parents and sisters had lived before I was born.

But maybe not.

Still, I had to tell the truth. "Yes."

"When did he make the will? If you know."

Hair fell into my eye and I pulled it away and wound it around my fingers. "He signed it last week. He hadn't changed it after his divorce. Everything still went to his ex-wife, and she was the executor. He wanted everything to go to his son, directly to his son."

"Is the ex-wife still the executor?"

"No," I said. "I am."

4

THE DETECTIVE TOOK OFF HIS GLASSES AND STUDIED ME. "AREN'T there rules about attorneys who write wills?"

I suspected Detective Beckwell knew a lot about wills and was pretending he didn't to see what I'd say.

"An attorney can't write a will and be a beneficiary. But I didn't write it, and I'm not a beneficiary," I said.

Normally I'm more apt to feel too warm than cold, but I couldn't stop shivering. I got up and shut off the blasting air conditioning unit.

The apartment fell silent. I sat at the table again.

The technicians were gone. The only people remaining were the detective, the policewoman leaning against the kitchen counter and taking notes, and me. The policewoman gave me a faint smile when I shut off the air. She'd probably been freezing, too, or maybe she felt I needed some support.

"But executors control whatever money the deceased person left, correct?" Detective Beckwell said.

"Not really." My entire head throbbed from crown to jaw. "Is this—can some of this wait until tomorrow?"

He held up his hand. His heavy gold wedding band caught

the light from the hallway. "Almost done. Help me out—I'm not a lawyer. I don't know anything about wills. So you don't have control?"

I felt as if I'd never leave this kitchen or this apartment with the boiled chicken bone smells and my pounding head and the too-bright hallway light the technicians had left on. And I never would leave it, not really, because I'd never return to a life with Marco. The pressure in my brain weighed my head down, making it feel too heavy on my neck. I rested my elbows on the table and my chin on my hands.

"The court oversees everything," I said, forcing the words through the fog in my brain. "Especially with a minor. Assets can't be distributed without court approval. The heirs can object to the executor, try to get someone else named."

Marco and I had discussed all this with his attorney. I'd insisted he find someone on his own, unrelated to my recommendations, if he wanted to name me.

"And you don't inherit?"

My chest felt tight, as if an elephant sat on it.

I squared my shoulders. I could get through this. I'd treat it as a play. Forget who was listening, who was watching, and say my lines.

I told him I didn't inherit anything except a lot of work. I'd been an executor for one of my uncles a few years ago, so I understood the process, knew the responsibilities I'd have.

Marco hadn't wanted his ex-wife to be the executor because she'd shouldered so many burdens when he'd been drinking seriously, and she was still angry. He'd felt it wasn't right to ask her to do it. His brother and nieces and nephews lived out of state, his father had died decades ago of a heart attack, and he thought his mother, already in her late seventies, was unlikely to outlive him.

"His mother," I said. "Does she know yet?"

The first time I'd met Marco's mother she'd made us a

three-course meal and said how pleased she was Marco was dating again. The second time she'd taken me aside and whispered that she'd never seen him so happy.

"A patrolman notified his ex-wife," the detective said. "Would she have told her mother-in-law?"

"I—yes, I'm sure," I said. "They're close."

I wrapped my arms around myself. I didn't want to lose control in front of the detective. He might expect it, it might be normal, but I could almost hear Gram telling me to hold it together. To not be like my mother.

"But you'll get fees," Detective Beckwell said. "For doing the work?"

"An hourly fee. Less than I make in my practice."

I hadn't wanted any fee, but Marco had insisted. I'd finally said okay because I figured once his son reached his twenties or thirties, Marco would change the will to make him executor. Or go back to Mirabel as executor if things had become more relaxed between them.

I started to tell the detective all of that, but I stopped myself. Even if I hadn't heard about my parents' experience from the time I'd been a kid, you can't share an office with a criminal defense attorney—which I did—and not know that if detectives or uniformed officers "just want to ask a few questions" about possible criminal activity, you shouldn't talk to them. They are not your friends.

They are not trying to help you out, and they are not your friends.

I wanted to help the police find out what had happened to Marco, but volunteering facts that had nothing to do with his death about things I hadn't been asked wouldn't help. It would make me look defensive.

"When did Mr. Ruggirello ask you to do this?" Detective Beckwell said.

It had been after Valentine's Day, but not long after because we'd been eating pieces of a giant mint-chocolate heart he'd bought me.

"The last week or so of February," I said. "But he mentioned it when we met."

I told him about the conversation we'd had. The detective tilted his head toward me, listening.

"So it wasn't about a suicide plan or being depressed," I said. "It was about his divorce."

The detective folded his glasses and tapped them on his notepad. "I don't have any theory about how or why he died right now."

I rubbed my forehead above my eyebrows. I'd taken the Advil too late. My head felt as if a vise had clamped around it and was gradually tightening. My shoulders and neck ached from sitting straight and listening carefully to each question despite another part of my brain going over and over the moment of finding Marco and the feel of his rigid flesh under my fingers.

"Then shouldn't you be asking if anyone wanted to harm him?" I said.

"Did anyone?"

"Everyone liked Marco." I shifted so my neck was straight and tried to think past the pain radiating from behind my eyes. "There was a malpractice suit. A few years ago, before he—it's what made him leave medicine. The patient, a woman, needed two extra surgeries because of his mistake. And it couldn't be fixed."

I'd been shocked when he'd told me. It was after we'd been seeing each other for a couple weeks. He said there was something I needed to know about why he'd left medicine. I expected him to tell me about a malpractice case, but something with a bad outcome, one that wasn't anyone's fault, and the doctor got sued. Or one where there was a minor error.

But that hadn't been it.

Marco had been hung over and still slightly buzzed, and he'd removed the wrong breast. He'd said others had made mistakes too, that more than one person at a hospital has to drop the ball for anything like that to happen. But he should have known, would have known had he been sober. Instead, a single mastectomy became a double, as the correct breast had to be removed in a later surgery.

The detective wrote another note, his handwriting staying neatly within the lines on the yellow pad. "You know the patient's name?"

"No."

"We'll find it."

After getting a list of Marco's friends from me, the detective finally said he was finished for now.

Joe had texted that he was waiting in his car. He'd been taking a client out but had cut it short.

I paused in the vestibule. Beneath the lime disinfectant smell, the odor from the apartment lingered, making my stomach roll. I didn't know how I had missed it when I'd walked in.

Head throbbing, I leaned against the wall and fumbled out my phone. Voicemails and texts had come in from my oldest sister and Gram. Joe must have called one or the other. But needles of pain jabbed my head, and I couldn't bear answering their questions about what had happened, so I ignored them.

I wanted to check on Eric, but it was only nine in the evening. He might be at a basketball game or out with friends. His mom might not have told him yet. She, too, might have wanted to give him a little more time.

I couldn't risk encroaching on that, especially when at least half my motive was selfish. I wanted to know how he was and offer support, true, but I also desperately wanted to talk with someone else who loved Marco.

———

Gray morning light crept across my condo.

I lay in my King-sized bed, the mattress stretching half-empty across most of the bedroom alcove. Joe was sleeping on my couch.

Beneath my neck and shoulders, the ice packs he'd fetched for me during the night had turned slippery and warm.

The jackhammers pounding my head and my struggle not to vomit in the leather-smelling interior of Joe's Lexus had nearly blotted out everything else on the ride home. The pain followed me all night through confused dreams where I found Marco's body over and over.

Now it was gone, and I had that curious floating feeling my whole body gets the day after a migraine. As if my body weren't really touching anything around me.

I pushed aside the sheets and sat.

Light from streetlights and other buildings' windows filtered through the glass sliding doors at the far end of the condo. Neither Joe nor I had shut the blinds.

My hair, damp and sweaty, hung over my face and in my eyes, but I felt cold. I pulled the comforter around me and stared at the empty space on the exposed brick wall where Marco's chest of drawers was meant to stand.

If I didn't want a repeat of last night's migraine I needed to move, drink some water, and take some preventative Advil.

First, though, I shuffled to my walk in closet. I went through the hanging wire bin until I found what I wanted.

The University of Chicago sweatshirt Marco had worn the last time he was here. I slid it over my head and breathed in.

It was there. Faint, but there.

A hint of his citrusy aftershave and his skin.

I inhaled the scent until I couldn't smell it anymore, then stood with my head pressed against the edge of an empty shelf.

Finally I pulled on sweatpants, got a glass of water, and stepped outside barefoot.

The wood deck felt cold under my feet. The east half of the building where I live—a paper warehouse converted to loft condos in Printers Row—stands seven floors tall. The west half is ten floors, the result of an oddity of Chicago building codes. I live on eight west, so I have a semi-private rooftop deck I share with five other units.

The uplights beneath my next door neighbors' potted plants and trees came on when I exited. The vegetation cast jagged shadows on the brick wall of the building to the south. They merged together when the lights blinked out.

I sat on a heavy wrought iron bench at my patio table, drew my knees to my chest, and put my head on them. I'd forgotten the Advil, but it felt like too much effort to go inside again to get it.

The sliding door groaned. The lights came on again as Joe stepped out.

He set a plain white mug in front of me, a small bottle of generic Ibuprofen next to it. Steam rose, smelling faintly of licorice and honey. He's seen me through lots of migraines back stage, on stage, and off.

His buttoned-down shirt, open at the collar and wrinkled hung untucked over his pinstriped pants. He left the theater world years before I did and went into finance. Now we send each other clients.

"You're awake," he said.

I wrapped one hand around the mug and shivered. I hadn't realized how cold I was until I felt its warmth. "Yeah."

Joe covered my free hand with his. "I'm sorry."

5

JOE DROPPED ME OFF LATE IN THE MORNING AT MARCO'S mother's home on the northwest side of Chicago. I still wore Marco's sweatshirt, but I'd pulled on jeans and a heavy leather jacket and had brushed my hair.

The temperature had dropped to the forties overnight, and a north wind rattled tree branches that were still mostly bare. The sky was gray and overcast, more like November than April.

Marco's son, Eric, sat on the concrete front steps of his grandmother's brick bungalow. He wore jeans, a sweatshirt, and no coat. A skinny boy, his broad shoulders made him look off kilter, as if the rest of his body hadn't caught up yet. Marco's eyes, almond-shaped and brown, looked out from his son's face under dark, curly hair.

Eric stood as I got out of the car. I ran to him and hugged him. He hugged me back. We hung on as if we were both drowning.

When we let go, my arms hung at my sides. I had no idea what Mirabel had said to Eric. Until this moment, he and I had exchanged only texts with photos of Marco without writing anything.

"How much did your mom tell you?" I said.

"Dad's dead because he started drinking again. Is it true?"

I zipped my jacket higher against the wind. If Eric were my son, I'd tell him everything about my discussion with the police and my own doubts, but it wasn't my call. "There was a rum bottle there."

"He didn't drink rum," Eric said.

Marco had told me his drink of choice had been craft beer. He'd seen himself as a connoisseur, not a drinker. Not an alcoholic. Beer had seemed harmless. He later realized those were all rationalizations, but he'd clung to them for a long time.

"It doesn't make sense to me either." The bungalow stood at the end of a row of nearly identical brick houses with cement steps and dormer windows. Wind howled around the corner. "You coming inside?"

Eric shook his head. His hair, in loose curls so much like Marco's, swayed. "My friend's on the way."

He was shivering. I thought about telling him he should wait in the house, but if he was out here, he wanted to be alone, cold or not. I'd bring him his jacket.

I squeezed his shoulder and headed up the stairs.

Inside, Marco's mother, Rosa Ruggirello, sat on the overstuffed sofa talking on her phone. She wore a long purple sweater with snags on one arm and looked ten years older than when I'd last seen her. Her salt and pepper hair hung loose around her face, gray springing from her part. Creases lined her wide forehead, and her eyelids, naturally a bit droopy, hung heavy.

Eric's jacket lay over the back of one of the two recliners that angled toward the TV. When I returned from running it out to him, Rosa had finished her call. She wrapped her arms around me, smelling of vanilla and perspiration.

We sat side-by-side on the sofa. Across from us the TV, a boxy old model playing an all-news channel, flickered. Its sound was turned down but I stared at it, holding one of the throw pillows in my lap. I read the headlines running beneath the talking heads automatically. News items that would have had me jumping to my feet the day before meant nothing.

Marco's ex-wife appeared from the kitchen. I recognized her from photos I'd seen on Eric's Facebook page.

Her dress was navy with faint gray stripes, subdued but fashionable.

She brought over a plain white saucer with a muffin on it for Rosa, who introduced us.

Mirabel's fingers were long and slim, her nails rounded and polished, but her cuticles looked ragged. "You should eat, Mom."

I held the pillow close against my stomach. It hit me that Rosa Ruggirello would forever be "Mom" to Mirabel, and Eric would always be her son. I had no tie to either of them outside of Marco.

Mirabel turned to me. Her face had the flawless, finished look that comes from applying primer, moisturizer, foundation, and highlighter in the exactly correct order. "You found him."

"Yes," I said.

"Don't take it too hard," she said.

I blinked. "His death?"

She smoothed the skirt of her dress. "That you found him. He must have known it would be you. I'm sure it wasn't personal. Marco was thoughtless."

I didn't know if Mirabel was trying to make me feel worse or she was just angry, as any mother whose son's father left him might be. My mother had always told me everyone grieves differently.

"Did the police say it was suicide?" I said. Maybe they'd called Mirabel first, being Eric's mom.

Rosa waved her hands. "No, no," Rosa said. "They're still investigating. And my son would never—it's a mortal sin."

Marco wasn't religious, something he hadn't told his mom because Catholicism mattered so much to her. It was another reason he couldn't have taken his own life. He would have known his mother would be afraid he'd spend eternity in hell.

"What else would it be?" Mirabel said.

"Accidental," I said.

I couldn't bring myself to suggest murder in front of Marco's mother, and in this bungalow with its gray carpet and worn cloth-upholstered recliners it seemed ludicrous. Marco had been a regular person. Not someone mixed up in drug trafficking or crime.

Mirabel shrugged. "It amounts to the same thing, doesn't it?"

"What?" I said.

Her seeming flippancy made me want to shake her, though I'm not normally quick to anger. I pressed my elbows against my sides.

One hand rose to her hip. "He drank for years. He didn't care what it did to me or Eric. Or himself. If it was 'accidental,' it only meant it took longer to kill himself."

Despite not liking the way she was acting, I saw her point. An accidental overdose meant he'd been drinking and had added pills, knowing he could accidentally die. But I refused to believe that's what had happened.

When Mirabel went into the kitchen later to fetch a bottle of soda, I followed her.

The Formica kitchen table with its yellow top and chrome legs had belonged to Marco's grandparents. An oversized white refrigerator crowded it, almost touching on one side.

I rested my hands on the back of one of the chairs. The vinyl felt slippery under my fingers. "What if someone tricked Marco into drinking? Planted the pills."

I'd been thinking about it while Mirabel and Rosa had talked about burial plots, headstones, and coffins, things I couldn't connect with Marco. I still expected him to call or text or walk in the door laughing about the huge misunderstanding.

Mirabel sighed and twisted off the plastic bottle cap. Her anger seemed to have faded, and her eyes looked weary. "Who would do that, Quille?"

"He said he had an important meeting at work Friday. What if someone didn't want him to be there?"

"At a meeting about insurance?"

"He was a fraud investigator."

She drank a swallow of Diet Coke. "Not criminal fraud."

"Sometimes," I said. "There are fraud rings. It's big business. Attorneys recruit people to say they were in a car and got injured and get doctors to fake medical records and bills."

She squeezed my arm. Through the sweatshirt sleeve I could feel how warm her fingers were. "I think you're in denial. But if you're right, the police will figure it out."

My parents' experiences suggested otherwise.

6

Rosa Ruggirello was shocked that my parents didn't come to the wake. She knew about my family's history, but she thought my mother needed to try harder.

It's a five-hour drive from Edwardsville, where my parents live, to Chicago, and my mother suffers from claustrophobia in automobiles. She also gets panic attacks when she's home alone. My aunt, who stays with my mother when my dad needs to be out of town, had the flu, so my dad couldn't be at the wake.

My grandmother, though, had been at my condo with my oldest sister first thing in the morning, Gram looking as sharp as always. She wore a mauve blazer, and the green and rose scarf around her neck set off the white, gray, and black hues in her hair, which she keeps in a short, layered cut. Her age—seventy-eight—and her grief showed only in the deepening of the fine wrinkles crisscrossing under her eyes and the vertical lines between her eyebrows.

Frowning at the sweats I'd been wearing since I'd gotten home from Rosa Ruggirello's a day and a half before, she told me to get cleaned up, and that I needed to look my best. It would make it easier to get through everything. She chose a dark brown blazer, olive pants, and an off-white silk T-shirt for me to wear to the wake.

After I showered and dressed, I stared at myself in the mirror, the tools and supplies that had gotten me through so much of life arrayed on my bathroom sink counter by Gram. No one but she would care how perfect my make up was, but it was easier than arguing with her.

I smoothed on primer and a little more foundation than usual so I looked polished, the way I did for court appearances. I lined my eyes with charcoal pencil after applying understated off-white shadow in the corners. I had to redo my eyes twice to get it right because my hands shook. Blush took away some of my pallor, and I fashioned my hair into a long, loose ponytail that hung down my back.

At least the effort filled the time until we left for the funeral home.

Gram linked her arm with mine as we approached the coffin. Refrigerated floral scents from rows of bouquets and wreaths filled the funeral parlor. Mirabel had placed a gold Number 1 Dad pin on Marco's lapel, one that I'd never seen him wear.

I held onto Gram. From everything I knew, Marco had been a great dad once he'd become sober, but no matter what their emotional or life issues Number 1 Dads don't abandon their thirteen-year-old kids.

I fled to the tiny kitchen where the funeral director had set out pastries, coffee, and tea for the family. Marco's brother stood inside. An older, heavier version of Marco, he was also a doctor. Not a surgeon but an internist who worked in a free clinic in Juneau, Alaska. He'd flown in late the night before.

After we introduced ourselves I heated water in the microwave for tea, and he poured coffee that smelled as if the bottom of the pot had burnt.

Hector shook his head. "Never thought I'd be burying my baby brother. I can't believe he started drinking again. Did you have any clue?"

I clutched my Styrofoam cup of weak Lipton tea. Hector didn't glare or point a finger or look anything but stunned and sad, but it felt like there was an accusation buried there.

I had no good response.

"No," I said.

He shook his head and stared at the floor. "No. I also must say no."

The service the next morning was held at the graveside. Eric stood between Hector and Mirabel. He'd outgrown the dark wool jacket he wore. Its sleeves ended too high, exposing his wrists.

The north wind swept across the cemetery. Toward the end of the final prayer, a slate gray sky spat icy rain on us all.

Rosa had arranged for lunch at a local banquet hall. As we entered the marble lobby, Eric pulled me to one side.

"I want to hire you," he said.

7

Across from the marble staircase was a small room probably used as a bride's room for weddings. It smelled of too much lilac perfume.

Eric and I sat side-by-side on a mauve-colored couch.

"There's nothing to hire me for," I said. "I'll already be handling your dad's estate."

"It's not that." He hunched forward, elbows on his knees. His black suit hung on him other than the shoulders, emphasizing how skinny he looked from the chest down. "I want you to prove my dad didn't kill himself. My mom said last night you don't believe he did."

"I don't," I said. "But I'm trying to accept that it's possible."

At three-thirty in the morning, wrapped in a fleece blanket in my friend Lauren's guest room, I'd used my iPad to research alcoholism, addiction, and warning signs of suicide.

In my heart I couldn't believe Marco had killed himself, but a tiny voice in the back of my lawyer brain insisted that if I weren't personally involved, if I were an attorney advising myself, I'd point out that Marco met more than one triggering factor—financial challenges, the end of a marriage, and a history of addiction.

Those same things also made a relapse likely.

"It's not possible," Eric said. "And I don't care about the note."

I gripped his arm as my stomach lurched. "Note?"

"The police called my mom right before we left," Eric said. "They found a note in Dad's shirt pocket."

The fingers of my free hand dug into the arm of the sofa. The fabric felt scratchy. "What did it say?"

I shouldn't be asking Marco's son this question, but I couldn't stop myself.

The suicide websites cautioned against blaming yourself, saying no one could truly know what led to that decision. But if Marco had killed himself right as we were about to move in together, it had to relate. At the very least, starting a life with me hadn't been enough to stop him.

Eric shifted to face me, his brows lowered. "The detective wouldn't tell her. He said they're still processing it, whatever that means."

He hadn't told me about it at all.

I held my whole body rigid, my mind racing. Not sharing information might mean I was a suspect, which at least meant the police *didn't* think it was a suicide. Or Mirabel was the suspect and they wanted to get her reaction.

Or they'd simply called her because Eric was next of kin and it was exactly what it seemed—they believed Marco had committed suicide.

I swallowed and took a long breath before I spoke. "The police will investigate. That's their job."

I had serious doubts about that, but it wasn't right to infect Eric with my suspicions of law enforcement.

"But they don't know my dad. You do. And you investigate for your cases, don't you?"

I licked my lips, which had become dry and chapped as we stood outside in the cemetery. "It's not the same. I ask questions and research, but it's mostly on paper. And no one's committed a crime. At least, not usually."

Eric frowned. "But there are investigators in your office."

"What? Oh, no, those people aren't in my office." Eric had only been to the suite where Danielle and I have our office once, but he'd sat in the waiting area for a while, and apparently he'd read the signs. "The investigators are in the same suite, but they're separate. They don't work for me. And their work is usually tracking down witnesses or serving papers, not investigating deaths."

The sounds of voices and clattering dishes drifted in from the banquet halls.

"But they could help you," Eric said.

"I'm sure they'd give me advice," I said. "But they don't work free. They charge by the hour."

"I can pay. I've got money from my dad, don't I?"

I twisted my hair around my fingers. The last thing I wanted was for Eric to feel more abandoned than he already did, but Marco and I had talked about finances before deciding to move in together. He'd been meeting his expenses, but barely.

I doubted there would be much money for Eric.

"I don't know," I said. "I'll need to figure that out. But if there is money, your mom will decide how to spend it while you're a minor. Your mom or the court or both. Not me. And if it were up to me, I still wouldn't suggest you spend it on an investigator without a strong reason."

In some ways, it struck me as ridiculous that Eric wouldn't be able to spend his own money. Our world forces people into staying children too long. By the time I turned thirteen I'd been working professionally for five years. I'd averaged only a few thousand dollars per year, but I'd handled my own money with my grandmother's advice.

But my upbringing wasn't a model one.

Eric closed his hands into fists. "How can there be a strong reason if no one will investigate?"

I ought to tell him to put it out of his mind. But as I looked at him slumping on the sofa, with his big shoulders and his skinny body, I couldn't do it, or maybe didn't want to.

I needed answers too. It was a bad reason to go along with him, but I told myself I should at least hear him out.

"What makes you so sure about your dad?" I said.

He met my eyes and lifted his index finger. "First, no matter what my mom says, my dad never let me down, even when he was drinking." He spoke as if he'd rehearsed this, and maybe he had. Maybe he also hadn't slept the last four nights, and he'd spent his three-in-the-morning hours creating an argument against the police and his mom. "He wasn't always there for things, but he never took off for days or didn't call me back or forgot my birthday. So he wouldn't do this. He wouldn't kill himself. He wouldn't leave me."

I nodded, despite remembering what my grandmother often said—life isn't as simple as it appears.

Eric's middle finger lifted to join his index finger in an echo of the old Peace sign. "He also wasn't drinking. I know the signs. I watched for them, and I didn't see them."

That carried some weight. Children of dysfunctional parents become experts in gauging the parent's mood and behavior.

I'd watched my mom's hair. It had always changed before anything else. Instead of blow-drying it, she'd let it air dry, and this cowlick in the back would puff up. Soon after that, she'd skip washing it and it would get oily.

About half the time from there she'd pull herself together again and return to a sort of low key, functioning depression that was her norm. But the other half she'd start skipping her daily showers and end in doing nothing but sleeping and watching TV for weeks on end.

And it always started with her hair.

"Did you ever see alcohol at your dad's place?" I said. "Or prescription bottles?"

Eric shook his head. "No. And I looked. I probably shouldn't have, but whenever I was there alone, I looked."

"Other drugs? Illegal ones."

He rolled his eyes. "No. And he wasn't depressed. He wasn't. He was happy. Excited about moving in with you. He told me he was really glad I liked you because he thought you'd be in our lives for a long time."

I looked at my hands, which lay useless in my lap. "That's how I felt too. That's what I wanted. But sometimes people hide things. Your dad hid from your mom how much he drank for a long time."

"I would have known," Eric said. "I talked to him all the time."

Eric had spent every other Saturday day and night with Marco under the divorce agreement. Mirabel had resisted more than that, saying Eric needed to focus on schoolwork and extracurricular activities.

"Talked or texted?" I said.

His face fell. "Mostly texted."

"It's not easy to read tone in a text. And it is easy for the person typing to hide feelings."

I didn't want to be negative, but I needed Eric to understand that there were no easy answers.

He crossed his arms over his chest and jutted his chin forward. "He texted me twenty or thirty times a day at least. Usually when he was in boring meetings. It drove me crazy."

I couldn't imagine my mother texting me twenty times a day. I couldn't imagine her texting me once.

Despite what I'd said, that Marco had texted Eric often

meant something. If he'd been drinking so much that he'd eventually overdosed or had became so despondent he'd committed suicide, it seemed to me that would affect how well and how often he communicated.

Eric slumped again, staring at the light pink and violet carpet. Hearts bordered its edges. "I didn't always answer him. I should've."

I rested my hand on his back. "None of us is always on top of everything. He knew you loved him."

He looked me in the eyes. His face looked so young, his skin unlined, his complexion pre- adolescent and free of acne. His eyes deep brown like Marco's. "So will you help me?"

My heart raced. I ought to say no. Fixation on death and loss had done no one in my family any good.

"Yes," I said. "I will."

8

My first role in life was that of replacement daughter. The original Q.C. Davis—the "real" Q.C., I said until my therapist in college convinced me not to—lived to be five years old.

Four months after her body was found, my mom got pregnant with me. It was supposed to distract her from her grief. Make her happier.

My father wanted to name me Catherine Quille—an homage to the original Q.C. but still my own name. When my mother filled out the birth certificate, though, she named me Q.C. Davis II.

Q.C. the original was supposed to be the last child my parents had. My oldest sister, Kendra, was born three years after they got married, Q.C. two years after that.

Q.C. disappeared from a cousin's birthday party at a local pizza restaurant. She was playing arcade games in the front with the other kids. My mom and my aunt were drinking glasses of wine in the bar area. My cousin said Q.C. left to use the restroom, which was toward the back of the restaurant, and never returned.

No one actually saw her go into the Women's Room.

The local police spent the next seventeen weeks investigating, mostly my parents. The FBI also got involved. Their efforts eventually led to the discovery of Q.C.'s body.

It was on the other side of the county, buried in the woods with that of another little girl who'd gone missing from St. Louis around the same time. Both had been strangled.

My parents had alibis for when the other girl had disappeared. There was no evidence linking them to either crime, but Q.C.'s killer was never found, and the neighbors' suspicions about my parents never really ended.

My dad had been working as a guitar player and singer in a Bluegrass band that traveled the country. He'd repaired guitars and other stringed instruments on the side. He left the band when Q.C. disappeared so he could be there with my mom and be on hand if Q.C. was found.

A few months after I was born he moved the family to LaGrange, Illinois, where Gram—his mother—lived and worked. Gram owned a four-unit apartment building she and my grandfather had bought before his death. She lived on the second floor.

I grew up in the apartment across from hers. Or, more often, in her apartment or in the lighting store where she worked as a bookkeeper. A friend of her boss got my dad a job fixing copy machines downtown. He was one of those guys you'd see rolling a heavy bag of parts and tools behind him from one office building to another.

Dad hoped a change of scene would help my mother. Everyone said she suffered from post-partum depression. As if my birth and not my sister's death had triggered it. Maybe it had. Maybe I'd been the proverbial straw on my mother's back.

When I was fifteen, my mother announced that she'd been away from Q.C. ("my Q.C.," she always said, which was how I knew she meant the original Q.C. and not me) long enough. She wanted to be able to visit the grave once a week.

My sister Kendra had already gone away to college. I stayed and lived with Gram so I could keep acting in Chicago theater.

If my purpose in life had been to make my mother happy, it was clear to me that I'd failed.

9

I'D PLANNED TO TAKE THE THIRD WEEK IN APRIL OFF SO MARCO and I could unpack his things and settle into living together.

But at home I did nothing but pace circles around my kitchen and living room areas or stare blindly at the T.V. The morning after the funeral I walked the two blocks to my office as faint gray light crept over Dearborn Street. A layer of heavy clouds hung above the city.

A few clients had emailed questions and left voicemails over the last few days. Worried about missing something for lack of sleep, I reviewed the files involved several times to be sure I answered correctly. Then I put my head on my desk and dozed off. I awoke forty-five minutes later not much more rested and with a cramp in my neck.

But I also knew where to start asking questions about Marco.

The people Marco worked with had spent nearly fifty hours a week with him. If you didn't count sleeping, that was a lot more time than I had. Also, work was the only thing in his life I could think of that would cause conflict.

An hour and five minutes later—the extra twenty due to an accident on the Stevenson expressway—I arrived at Hazleton Insurance in Bolingbrook in my friend Lauren's Volvo.

She lives in my building and owns a car but no parking spot, while I own a parking spot but have no car. So Lauren parks in my spot and lets me use her Volvo if she doesn't need it.

I'd called ahead, so Marco's boss, Bob Leonard, met me at the door and walked me through a dark blue and green lobby that smelled of new carpet.

Bob was well over six feet tall, fit, and graying at the temples. He moved with the easy grace of someone who'd been admired his entire life. Framed photos tacked to the cubicle wall behind him—no one seemed to have actual offices at Hazleton Insurance—showed him playing on the University of Arizona's basketball court.

I sat in the padded visitor chair, ankles crossed, arms held close at my sides. Despite that it was still chilly out for late April, I wore a short-sleeved dress with a black-and-white pattern that worked for business and a white lace sweater over it. I'd aimed to walk the line between lawyer and Marco's girl-friend, a combination I hoped would make Bob feel the most sympathetic and so most likely to share.

Officially, I'd come to clean out Marco's cubicle.

"Sorry to call out of nowhere this morning," I said, "but I thought there might be some things here Marco's son might want, and I'd need to do this eventually."

"Of course." Bob's phone was ringing and his laptop chiming, but he ignored both. "Any way I can help. I'm sorry about Marco."

My thoughts felt sluggish from lack of sleep, but I'd made a list in advance of what I hoped to find out. "Was there anything Marco was working on where he might have made enemies?"

I'd tried to think of subtle ways to ask this, but I was too tired to dance around the issues.

"Enemies?" Bob blinked, but his next words suggested he wasn't that surprised by the question. "No one I'd call an enemy."

I listened carefully to how he'd answered, just as if I were deposing a witness.

"No one you'd call an enemy. But some people were unhappy with him?"

Bob frowned. "No one likes what we do. Including our customers. People look only at price when they buy insurance, then they're upset when they can't collect boatloads of cash. So they get angry when we do our jobs. But angry enough to kill Marco? I don't see it."

"What about clinics or hospitals? They must have more money on the line than a single policyholder."

"Generally that's true."

It was a careful answer, and it made me think there was more there.

"Was Marco investigating any clinic or doctor or hospital where there was a serious issue?"

"I can't say. I told the police, and that's all I'm allowed to disclose under company protocol."

So the police had talked to him, and he'd said something to them about an investigation.

I jiggled my knee, feeling both too tired and too wound up to process everything as well as I felt I should. I was a lawyer. It was part of my job to get people to tell me things they didn't want to share, and Bob wanted to help. He felt bad about Marco. There must be a way to get him to open up.

I looked at the notepad on my phone where I'd typed out my topics.

"Marco told me he had a big meeting last Friday. Was it related to whatever you told the police about?" I said.

"We have meetings every Friday. But I can't talk about particular investigations. It's all confidential."

"How about generally?" I said, hoping using his own word from earlier would set him more at ease. "I imagine when you investigate fraud, people get upset."

He raised both hands in twin Stop gestures. "Not fraud. We don't imply to people that their medical providers committed fraud. We look for overtreatment or overbilling."

I rubbed my forehead. Marco had half-laughed at this company line, though he understood the reasoning behind it. I ought to have remembered that it was a hot button word at Hazleton.

"So that's not fraud," I said.

Bob shifted in his chair. "It could indicate fraud. But if we're investigating, it doesn't mean we think it's fraud. That's why it's the SIU. Special Investigative Unit. Not the Fraud Unit."

High-pitched beeps and keyboard clicks sounded from neighboring cubicles. It was eight-thirty a.m. and more employees were arriving.

"Was there anyone specific Marco investigated who might have been angry at him?" I said.

Sometimes asking something a different way gets an answer, but not this time.

"I can't tell you that," Bob said. At least he didn't look angry that I'd asked.

I thought for a minute. "But people being investigated sometimes get mad? I'm not talking about at Marco. Just generally."

Bob sipped his coffee. It was in a large navy blue mug with the company motto—You've Got A Friend—emblazed on it in large silver letters. "It happens."

"Maybe hostile?"

He nodded. "You might call it hostile. Sometimes. We're not involved unless there's an issue."

I inched my chair closer to the desk. I felt myself slipping into the zone I find when I question witnesses or argue at hearings. It was a relief to be on what felt like familiar ground.

"Such as?" I said.

"A customer complains about a bill. Or the computer flags a pattern. Maybe a chiropractor always prescribes twelve weeks of treatment no matter how slight the injury. So we look into it." Bob rocked his chair back and stretched his legs under the desk. His cubicle was larger than any of the others around it, and its walls rose higher, but it seemed too small too contain him. "But Marco was good with people. He had the fewest complaints of any supervisor I ever had."

"Did he still ask the questions he needed to ask?"

Bob nodded. "He did. He was good at asking questions in a non-threatening way so that people talked to him. Really talked. He had a good record of ferreting out fraud."

That didn't surprise me. Marco was easy to talk to. He asked questions and listened to the answers without interjecting his own opinion unless asked.

"What happens then? Is there a criminal investigation?" I said.

"The worst offenders get reported to the National Insurance Crime Bureau. But I've only uncovered criminal fraud a few times in my career, and both were at a different insurance company."

Bob told me that four investigators—called Special Adjusters—had worked for Marco, but he wouldn't tell me their names, which seemed ridiculous. Marco had mentioned a few to me, and I'd met more than one at the wake, though the names hadn't stuck with me. But Bob wouldn't budge, though he did tell me a little more about how complaints were handled.

I asked to be taken to Marco's cubicle. It was around the

corner and down the hall from Bob's, one of six in an area beyond a small combined kitchen and file room.

Marco had been dead less than a week, and it already looked half-vacant.

10

BOB HAD TAKEN AWAY MARCO'S LAPTOP AND REMOVED ALL company property and papers. The cubicle wall to my left had a giant photo collage of Eric, everything from baby photos through junior high, tacked to it.

A magnetic strip of photos of Marco and me from a novelty kiosk at Navy Pier was affixed to a tall metal file cabinet.

In the photos, my hair was a soggy mess. We'd gotten caught in a mid-March rain and ice storm on the way from the restaurant to the Pier. I was laughing, and Marco stood next to me, grinning. Our arms were around each other's waists.

I stared at the photos for a long time without moving. Clearing out Marco's workspace seemed more final than the funeral. Finding his body had been horrible and almost unreal, and seeing him made up and dressed in a suit in the coffin had been horrible and unreal in a different way.

But here he had lived and breathed and worked, and after today there would be no cubicle in this building with his name on it, with a desk and chair and pens and notepads he'd used. Someone else's nameplate would replace his, or the cube would stand empty.

Finally I took down both sets of photos and put them on the edge of the desk, hoping employees passing by might see them and stop to talk to me as I sorted through Marco's things. It was something I'd learned from visiting clients' companies. People say a lot more when they stop to chat than if you drag them into a conference room.

In Marco's upper desk drawers I found a pair of gloves, warranty papers, small white cardboard boxes from electronics items he'd bought long ago, and novelty erasers shaped like bats and pumpkins.

In a bottom drawer I found a phone message pad, the old kind that has a top copy to hand out and the carbon underneath that saves the message. The top copies were all gone. The messages included only the month and date, no year, but it seemed unlikely anyone here used these types of pads. Bob had said everything was recorded electronically.

As I glanced at the faint writing on the carbons, nothing jumped out at me. If it was a Hazleton Insurance business document, I should give it to Bob, but I decided to accept at face value his statement that he'd removed everything confidential. I put it in a cardboard box along with Marco's nameplate.

A woman stopped to say she was sorry about Marco's death. She hadn't worked directly with Marco and didn't know much about his current projects, but I put her business card in my purse.

When the desk was clear and the drawers empty, I closed the box and crisscrossed more shiny tape strips over it than needed.

A tall man with a wide face and faint beard came around the corner and introduced himself as Jerry Hernandez, one of the Special Adjusters who'd worked for Marco.

His cologne had an incense-like sandalwood scent. He lowered his voice. "We should talk. No matter what Bob says, there were two people Marco seriously pissed off."

"What? Who?"

"Not here," he said. "I could get in trouble. But one of them said he'd better be careful crossing the street if she ever drove in his neighborhood."

11
———

CAFÉ BA-BA-REEBA WAS ONE OF THE FIRST TAPAS RESTAURANTS to open in Chicago before the whole small plates dining thing caught on.

I suggested it as a meeting place. It's in Lincoln Park, which is a little ways north of Old Town, the neighborhood where Jerry lived.

I arrived early on purpose, but hesitated in the hall leading to the host stand. Laughter, murmured conversations, and the noise of hundreds of small plates clunking on tables and serving trays filled the air.

Marco had introduced me to Café Ba-Ba-Reeba. Lincoln Park with its mix of college students sporting backwards baseball caps and identically-dressed well-to-do professionals has never appealed to me, so I hadn't been to the restaurant before he brought me there.

Now I loved it, but I didn't want to visit it without him.

I headed for the bar, which is off to one side and has high top tables for overflow seating all around it. Marco knew most of the bartenders. He'd told me he'd never gone there to drink, but he'd often eaten at the bar on the weekends after he and Mirabel separated.

I needed to know if that was true.

I squeezed onto a barstool at the far end.

Rayna, our favorite bartender, saw me and waved. She was almost always there evenings. She was working her way through college and took all the shifts she could get.

Her hair was pulled back into a bun, with a few wisps on the side, a new look for her. Before I could ask if she'd heard about Marco, she said, "Where's my friend? You two didn't break up?"

"No. I—he died."

There must have been a better way to say it, but I couldn't think of one. I can't stand the phrase "passed away," my mother's favorite. It makes me think of someone brushing past me in the hall and hovering nearby, forever unreachable and just out of sight.

Rayna set down the glass of red wine she was carrying. "Oh, no."

"The police say it might be suicide." I hadn't heard any more from the detective, but I wanted to see how she reacted.

Her head drew back, her chin tucked in. "Marco? He was so upbeat."

She said she'd be right back and delivered the wine to someone across the bar. Rayna's reaction struck me as significant given that most people who sat alone at bars shared their troubles with bartenders.

But that was a stereotype I'd picked up from TV. I slouched forward, forearms on the bar. Maybe it had nothing to do with anything.

Rayna returned with a whiskey sour made with rye and said it was on the house. "Figured you might need it. Tell me what happened."

I sipped the drink. There was something comforting about the taste, about something that hadn't changed.

"First I need to ask you something."

"Sure." She reached under the bar for a glass and filled it from a spigot.

"I'm asking because I think the police are wrong, not because I want to check up on Marco. Which I know sounds silly. He's gone, it's not like I can check up on him."

"He wasn't seeing anyone else. Not that I know of."

"No, not that." I wound my hair between my index and middle fingers. It hadn't crossed my mind that Marco might have had another girlfriend, that some sort of angst related to romance had been distressing him. "I want to know if he ever came here without me and drank. Alcohol."

She tilted her head to one side. "Oh, got it. Overdose?"

"Maybe."

She shook her head. "Seltzer with lime."

"You're sure?"

"Always. I notice when people alone don't drink. It's kind of unusual at a bar, but he was one of them. Ever since he started coming here."

"Which was when?"

Marco had told me it'd been three years since he and Mirabel first separated, but I didn't want to prompt Rayna by suggesting that. How people remember things can shift based on what you say to them. If you're cross-examining, that's good. If you're trying to get accurate information, it's not.

She drummed her fingers on the bar. "Couple years at least. I was pretty new, and it was Christmas Eve. He told me he thought he and his wife were divorcing. He looked really sad, but he kept joking, too, you know, like he didn't want to ruin my holiday."

I sipped my drink, which I'd already half-finished. "And he didn't drink?"

"Nope. Told me he'd stopped for two months. I didn't know if he really should be in a bar, but he said it was fine."

Mirabel had kicked Marco out shortly after Halloween, and he'd started a program two weeks later. I wasn't sure how wise it had been for him to go to a bar, either, but maybe he'd figured it was better to be with people than alone.

"Could you ask the other bartenders if they ever saw him drinking?"

"If you think it'll help. But send me a photo. They won't all know his name."

I texted a photo from one of our walks along Lake Michigan in January. The water looked glassy and layers of heavy gray clouds loomed above, but Marco smiled.

Fifteen minutes later, Jerry appeared at the host stand.

"You know it won't really prove anything," Rayna said when she cleared my empty glass. "He could have gone somewhere else to drink, somewhere no one knew him. That's what I'd do."

12

JERRY AND I SAT AT A HIGH TOP TABLE NEAR THE WINDOW. HE worked an early schedule at Hazleton and he'd made it here at 5:15, which meant $7 sangrias, mine red and his peach, until Happy Hour ended at seven.

The small plates were at lower prices until seven as well, which was good since I'd offered to buy and didn't have an unlimited budget.

Jerry gave me the names of the other investigators who'd worked for Marco, though he said he didn't know of anyone being angry. I asked about the woman he'd mentioned threatening Marco.

"She's the billing manager at Vujic Clinic in Elmwood Park. I told the police, and they took her info, but they didn't say much."

That didn't surprise me. Danielle had told me detectives were trained to be careful what they revealed when questioning witnesses. She'd been one of a small number of black woman cops in Chicago for five years before becoming a lawyer, and she'd been promoted to detective a year before passing the bar.

"Why was this billing person mad at Marco?" I said.

"Dr. Vujic is Serbian, and the administrator thought we targeted her because of that."

"Did she say why she thought that?" I said.

I've found it's better to ask people to guess at the motive or thought process of someone accusing them rather than asking directly if the accusation is true. It's instinct to deny that you've done anything wrong or questionable. But if you have to guess why someone thinks you did, you're more apt to share whatever it was that triggered the issue.

Jerry finished what was left of his sangria in one long drink. "We don't target anyone. But another insurance company exposed a Serbian fraud ring a few years ago. It's made us more alert on that front."

"More alert" could be code for targeting by nationality, though I didn't want to think Marco would do that.

A waitress stopped by and Jerry ordered another sangria. I declined. My glass was still half full.

Jerry asked about food. I told him to order whatever he wanted while I looked over my notes. My brain felt fogged and as if it were moving in slow motion. After three nights at Lauren's, I'd decided last night to go back home.

But I'd been unable to sleep in the King-sized bed I'd shared with Marco, or in the futon we'd bought for Eric, and I couldn't lie on the sofa without thinking of finding Marco's body on his. I'd finally layered my comforter and a few pillows on the floor.

"How would they know she's Serbian?" I said after the waitress left.

"They didn't. Not until her administrator started yelling about how we were targeting the clinic because the doctor's a Serb."

"Why were you looking at the clinic?" I said.

"Our computer system looks for patterns. If we see one, adjusters pay more attention, make sure the treatment really happened or the bill is right. Extreme cases are referred to us at SIU."

I drank more sangria. The alcohol wasn't helping me focus, but I welcomed the numb feeling spreading through me. For the first time since I'd found Marco five days before, I didn't feel like my insides were being ripped apart. Maybe that was the draw of alcohol for those who couldn't shake addiction to it.

The background music grew louder. I scooted my chair closer to Jerry's.

"And this Dr. Vujic she's an extreme case?" I said.

"Not her personally. But her clinic charges more than any other clinic in the area. Plus every patient just happens to need the exact number of treatments we'll pay for, and there are three physical therapists who, if their bills are honest, always— and I mean always—work at top capacity."

"Huh."

At the first law firm where I'd worked, and at the accounting firm before that, all our clients had been billed based on time spent on their matters. Those billable hours were what counted when it came to getting raises or good reviews.

But it's hard to work at maximum capacity. It means you never take a personal call or read a text at work, you don't say more than hello to any coworker, and you eat lunch and dinner at your desk while you work or not at all.

If it was the same for physical therapists and chiropractors, everyone at top capacity all the time raised questions.

"So far we don't have enough to prove out-and-out fraud though."

I stirred my sangria. The fruit chunks at the bottom swirled like 3-D confetti. "How long have you been investigating?"

"Two years."

"Long time."

The waitress refilled our glasses and brought over goat

cheese and marinara sauce with toast points. I ate one but had a hard time swallowing the bread. Like almost everything I ate these days, it stuck in my throat.

I drank more sangria to wash it down.

"Yeah, the people at Vujic are not thrilled," Jerry said. "Especially because there're a lot of bills we haven't paid during that time."

The combined alcohol from the whiskey sour and sangria was hitting me. Jerry and the street outside the window behind him looked fuzzy.

"That must make them unhappy," I said.

He grimaced, the whiskers of his beard quivering. "That's not the worst of it. They claim our questions made the patients ask about why they needed certain treatments, and some supposedly went elsewhere. So Dr. Vujic threatened to sue us. That's what the meeting was about last Friday. When Marco missed it, I knew something must be wrong."

"Because?"

"He was the point person on the investigation." Jerry spooned cheese and marinara sauce on a piece of toast. "Though actually he had a pretty good relationship with Dr. Vujic, as much as anyone could. He said they had a lot in common."

He'd never mentioned her to me. "Like what?"

"He didn't say. But the admin person—Cora Smith—calls and screams at us, literally screams. Vujic did her share of yelling too, until Marco went out there a couple times and met with her. Calmed her down."

I typed a note into my phone. My fingers felt clumsy, and when I tried to correct my typos and the mistaken autocorrects my phone supplied, the sentences became muddled.

I set the phone down, hoping I'd remember all this later. "If there was going to be a lawsuit, why would this Cora want to hurt Marco?"

"She said nothing could fix the clinic's reputation or bring back lost business. And she said she'd insist the clinic name Marco in the suit."

It's one thing to sue a company. That happens all the time. But suing an individual employee is a pretty awful thing to do. Being a defendant in a lawsuit can impact a person's credit record and cost a lot in legal fees if the company doesn't hire an attorney for you. I also couldn't imagine it would be good for anyone's job prospects.

All of those things would have weighed on Marco, but he'd never mentioned any of it.

I finished my second sangria. Not much I'd learned tonight seemed helpful.

Worse, Jerry had given me more reasons why Marco might have committed suicide, or at least why he might have turned to alcohol.

13

IT WAS A LITTLE BEFORE EIGHT BY THE TIME I BOARDED THE L. All that was left of the sun was a fiery orange backdrop to the vintage buildings and the elevated tracks.

The train car seemed to revolve around me. I struggled to sit straight, not wanting to appear vulnerable.

While there's no sure way to prevent being mugged or worse when you walk, take public transportation, or hail a ride in the city, the last thing I wanted was to look like low hanging fruit.

Whenever I walk, I keep my purse strapped across my body and my phone hidden away. I never wear earbuds or headphones—both of which advertise that you're not paying attention to your surroundings—and I always do my best to appear alert and able to fight back.

Now, though, I felt myself slumping as I watched the buildings flashing by shift from vintage brick to glass and metal as we neared and then entered the Loop. The sangria, so festive-looking in the restaurant, sloshed in my stomach with each jerk of the train.

I shut my eyes and listened to the train squeal around a

curve. What seemed like a second later, I heard the overhead voice say Van Buren.

I lurched to my feet. My stop was the Harold Washington Library at State and Van Buren.

When I exited onto the platform, though, everything looked wrong.

A set of grimy steps disappeared down into a hulking dark marble building I didn't recognize. The street under the L tracks was dimly lit and had no traffic. The cross street looked too narrow, like an alley. Squished fast food wrappers and other papers littered it.

I pushed my hair out of my face, struggling with a few heavy strands that kept sticking to my lips as I crossed the walkway above the street to the other side. I tried to move confidently, but needed to grip the handrail for balance.

I stared down at a deserted concrete plaza, a heavy chain across it, between two large buildings. It looked vaguely familiar. In daylight—or sober—I'd be able to identify it, but now I had no idea where I was.

I gulped a mouthful of night air. Its diesel undertaste made my stomach lurch and confused me more.

L trains were electric. Diesel meant railroad, but Union Station was near the Quincy stop, and I definitely wasn't there. That was near the former Sears Tower.

I couldn't think of another railroad line anywhere near an elevated track. Exhausted and dizzy, I leaned against one of the metal posts holding up the wooden platforms and tracks above me.

Someone gripped my arm.

14

"HONEY," THE UNIFORMED CTA WOMAN SAID. "YOU ALL RIGHT?"

I started to say yes, but instead words tumbled out my mouth about Marco's death, drinking with Jerry, missing the stop. I wasn't using complete sentences, but she got the idea.

"C'mon." She took my hand and led me upstairs to the enclosed ticket area. "I can't leave, but you collect yourself."

She disappeared into her booth and returned with a bottle of water and a power bar.

I leaned against the wall near the turnstiles, drank the water, and ate the power bar in small slow bites. Two more trains went by and a few people got out, passing me without a glance. The anonymity of the city can be a blessing.

When I felt a little steadier, I approached the ticket booth. Only the woman's face and upper body were visible through the grillwork above her counter.

"Thank you," I said.

"Where you trying to go?" she said.

"Home. On Plymouth Court."

Her forehead furrowed. "Plymouth Court?"

It's a short street that runs only about six blocks north and south. "Near Dearborn," I said, naming the street where my office was, which was only two blocks from my condo. "In Printers Row."

"Oh, sure." She pointed past me. "That way, walk straight ahead a block and you'll be at Ida B. Wells Drive. Cross and turn left."

"What's that building?" I pointed to the tall marble building behind me.

"Options Exchange. LaSalle Street station behind it."

Finally it clicked. Escalators on either side of the Options Exchange building lead to railroad trains above LaSalle Street and Ida B. Wells Drive, explaining the diesel smell. I was at LaSalle and Van Buren. The plaza across the street with the chain across it bordered the Board of Trade. Joe worked right near here, and we'd had lunch at a restaurant with outdoor seating in that plaza.

All of which meant I was more impaired than I'd realized. But also closer to home. I breathed a little easier when I reached Ida B. Wells Drive, a divided six-lane street with lighted planters and lots of foot traffic. The whole time I walked quickly, keeping my shoulders back, glancing left and right occasionally to try to look alert.

At home, I drank a glass of water. When it stayed down despite my urge to vomit, I drank another. It was only quarter to nine, but I took off my jeans and sat for a minute on the edge of the King-sized bed. It looked too wide and too empty.

I unfolded the comforter again, spread it on the rug near my sofa, and curled up on it.

The room spun around me.

15

———

"You should've called," Lauren said.

It was the morning after my challenging L ride home. Lauren sipped a hazelnut latte. She and I started law school together but she left after the first year, becoming a real estate agent instead.

Blond with short bobbed hair, she's two years younger than me, a little taller and curvier, and far more outgoing. She lives in the same loft condo building I do, but a few floors down.

I wrapped my hands around my Earl Grey tea. Rain drove down outside the front plate glass window. "I wasn't thinking very clearly."

Every Thursday barring emergencies, Lauren and I stop at Café des Livres before work.

The café, located on the ground floor of the converted post-card printing factory where my office is located, is all exposed brick, overflowing bookshelves, armchairs, and love seats. It has a reading nook—complete with a fireplace—in one corner, a counter at the back, and a row of small round tables with marble tops near the plate glass window.

The café owner moved to the United States from France in

the early 2000s with her husband. She was the first person I'd told about Marco's death after Joe. He and I had come in for tea, and because I wanted to see her, the morning after I found Marco.

"Did the police give you Marco's things back yet?" Lauren said.

"No," I said.

Two customers exited carrying the trademark black paper cups with the *fleur de lis* designs. Chilly, damp air rushed in as the door swung open.

Lauren buttoned the top two buttons on her cashmere sweater and smoothed her hair. "You definitely should call them. You need to figure out where his financial info is and what's going on with that apartment building he owns."

I nodded, though today I had to deal with the brother of one of my clients. He was threatening to file a temporary restraining order locking my client out of the auto parts store they owned together. The brother had no lawyer, which meant the whole case would take double or triple the time and energy I would otherwise spend, energy I didn't feel like I had.

My phone rang. It was Mirabel.

"You need to do something," she said when I answered.

I'd traded texts with her yesterday, asking her to call me about Eric. I'd told him I would need to talk to her, that I wasn't about to report to him whatever I found without his mother knowing it.

Personally, I felt it was his own business, but as executor I couldn't be hiding things. Mirabel wasn't an heir, but she was his mother, and he was a minor.

"About?" I rested my elbows on the table. My limbs felt heavy and my whole body ached despite the three Ibuprofen I'd taken before leaving my condo to guard against a migraine.

"Our insurance company," Mirabel said.

In my sleep-deprived state, the "our" threw me. I had no insurance with Mirabel.

I realized she meant hers and Marco's.

"What insurance company?" I said.

Lauren cocked her head at me.

"Life," Mirabel said. "I called the company to tell them Marco committed suicide and make a claim, and the man who answered said there'd be a review. What's that mean, a review?"

A preliminary death certificate had been issued so the funeral could take place, and it had listed "pending" for manner of death. I hadn't heard about any final certificate.

I rubbed the back of my neck. "I feel like we had this conversation before. Has there been a finding of suicide?"

"It's obviously coming, and we need the money, so why wait?" Mirabel said.

I took a deep breath and exhaled to stop from saying something I might regret. Why, why do people do things first and ask the lawyer later?

"It's better not to say anything to an insurance company that's not for sure," I said.

A waitress set my chocolate chip scone and bacon in front of me and poured more hot water in the white china teapot.

"You should have told me that before I called," Mirabel said.

My jaw clenched. "If I'd known you'd be calling, or that there was life insurance, I would have."

"Of course there was life insurance. What kind of father do you think Marco was?"

I poured myself more tea and glanced at the reading nook with its fireplace. Today college students had claimed it before Lauren and I had arrived. I wished they hadn't. If I'd been able to sit there, I felt sure I'd have been better able to deal with Mirabel.

To deal with everything.

I reminded myself that Mirabel was grieving, too, and

refrained from pointing out that she was the one who kept saying what a thoughtless, irresponsible person Marco had been.

"Is there a specific reason you need a payout quickly?" I said.

"Eric's tuition bill is due."

"Tuition?" I said. Eric was in his last year of junior high.

"St. Sebastian. It's due by mid-May or he can't start in the fall."

I hadn't thought about Eric needing to pay for high school, and Marco hadn't mentioned it. I didn't have a lot of friends with high school age children, and I hadn't grown up in the city where the options were expensive private school, hitting the perfect combination of luck and high test scores that qualified you for a magnet school, or attending public schools with low graduation rates and high violence.

Still, Mirabel lived in Lincoln Park, a pricy part of the city, in the same house where she and Marco lived throughout their marriage. "Doesn't Lincoln Park have a good high school?"

"We're just outside the boundaries, and it's not that good. Marco told me not to worry, he had the tuition covered. Wrong, as always. Why would they do a review? This insurance company?"

"I don't know right off. I'll look into it. When did Marco buy the policy?"

I made a conscious effort to loosen my jaw, which was starting to ache. I was afraid Mirabel would say sometime in the last few weeks. That would suggest Marco had been planning suicide.

Lauren reached across the table and squeezed my hand.

"Nine or ten months ago," Mirabel said. "As part of the divorce. Marco drained the retirement account when he was drinking and took out a line of credit without telling me, so it was the only way to be sure Eric could get through high school and a good college if anything happened to Marco."

No wonder she was pissed. Marco had told me he'd been hugely financially irresponsible, but he'd left out specifics.

"So Marco planned to pay Eric's tuition from his salary every month?" I said.

Mirabel said she didn't know. When she told me how much the tuition was, I didn't see how Marco could have managed.

Lauren was right. I needed to find out what was going on with the apartment building Marco had owned. I'd had the impression it was more of a money pit than a source of income, but that was the only other place I could think of where he might have expected to have enough to pay the tuition bills.

I asked Mirabel to email me a copy of the policy and decided to leave the topic of Eric for another conversation. One thing at a time.

"Is she in the will?" Lauren said after I'd hung up and relayed Mirabel's side of the conversation.

The throbbing at my temples amplified, but I didn't want to take more Advil, so I took a few more deep breaths before I answered.

"No," I said. "But she'll be the custodian for Eric. She can use the money for his benefit."

The scone crumbled when I bit into it, its texture like sawdust against my tongue and teeth. I tried a bite of bacon. It had gotten cold and felt greasy in my mouth.

Lauren pointed her finger at me. "You need to find out the limits on that. Suppose she starts having a spa day every week claiming it's totally for Eric's benefit so she's a relaxed, happy mom."

"I don't think she'd do that."

Nothing Marco had said about Mirabel suggested she was dishonest or didn't put her son's interests before her own, though as executor I knew I couldn't assume that was true.

"She might," Lauren said.

My head felt heavy. I propped my elbows on the table and my chin in my hands. "I'll watch everything."

Lauren meant to help, but it was overwhelming. I felt relieved when the phone buzzed.

Mirabel had sent the policy. I scrolled to the cover page and stared at the dollars listed.

Lauren finished her latte. "How much?"

"Two million."

The number boggled my mind. I'd made good money at the accounting and law firms where I'd worked, and I was managing to pay my mortgage and other bills now that I was on my own, which was an accomplishment for anyone who'd barely finished the first year of a solo practice.

But two million dollars.

"It's not that much," Lauren said. "Between high school, college, and maybe graduate school."

I nodded, but Lauren and I come from different worlds.

I'd worked my way through college and lived with my grandmother to save money. For law school I'd cobbled together work, scholarships, loans, and savings. My dad occasionally paid for my textbooks and fees and Gram paid for my phone until I finished law school, but that was all they could do.

Lauren grew up in Barrington, a well-to-do suburb where the average net worth was quadruple what my parents could ever have amassed even had my mother kept working. Lauren's parents paid her college tuition and room and board, plus a year of law school while she lived in a luxury high-rise apartment. They put her up there two more years after she quit law school, got her real estate broker's license, and worked toward getting her first major commission.

As a gift to celebrate that, she got her brand new Volvo. Two years later, they gifted her the down payment for the two-bedroom condo she owned two floors below mine.

"You figure thirty thousand a year for high school," Lauren said. "Seventy or eighty a year for tuition and fees at a university with room and board. If he does grad school after that, half that money's gone."

She was right, and maybe as a former surgeon that all seemed far more normal to Marco than it did to me.

All the same, a two million dollar policy struck me as good motive for murder.

16

I found it on the third page of the policy. It was called a suicide clause.

Rather than read on my phone, I'd returned to my office to print the policy. I find it easier to follow complex wording on paper, a trick I learned in law school.

This week I'd needed to read everything, complex or not, three times before I took it in. The moment I'd found Marco kept playing again and again in my mind, and it took all my effort to let it go and focus on whatever I was trying to do.

The clause said if the policyholder committed suicide within two years of buying the policy, no benefits would be paid.

With a little research, I learned this provision was pretty standard in individual life insurance policies. Otherwise people planning suicide could buy a policy a month before and leave a big payout to their families.

I pushed back from my desk and took a small bite of a carrot and spice muffin my friend the café owner had thrust into my hands as I'd left. She'd made a batch special for me. They were light and moist and easier to eat than the scone that

I'd left on my plate. It still took forever to chew, though, and felt like it stuck in my throat when I swallowed.

An insurance investigator, Marco must have known about—and understood—the suicide clause. I doubted he'd have forgotten it or been willing to risk the policy not paying.

I flipped to the next page.

Another paragraph, a contestability clause, gave the insurance company the right to investigate if a death might relate to a pre-existing condition that hadn't been disclosed. An article I found gave the example of an investigation to see if a policyholder who died of lung cancer had been a smoker and hidden that.

That clause seemed bad here if Marco hadn't disclosed his past alcoholism. But he must have known that, too.

After highlighting the most important paragraphs, I texted Danielle. Between her years as a cop and a prosecutor and her decades as a criminal defense attorney she knows more about death cases than I ever will.

I asked if she could stop in after court. She usually goes straight home, so we're only in the office together one or two days a week.

She made it to the office around four, wearing a dark gray pants suit and turquoise blouse, her silver and black hair straightened and smoothed back in a clip.

I set aside a tax appeal I was preparing, having talked the auto parts client's brother off the ledge after I finished reviewing Marco's insurance policy. In the way business is for every solo lawyer I know, I'd veered in a day from quiet to overly busy.

It was almost a relief. Work I could understand. Work I could handle.

Danielle dropped her worn leather briefcase near her desk, which is on the opposite wall from mine. "Unbelievable."

"Bad day?" I said.

She took the clip out and her hair swung around her face as she scribbled a note on her diary. She still keeps one on paper, a habit from when she started practicing.

"One gram of coke and this little boy State's Attorney wants ten years. My guy's a high school senior. About to go into the marines. All over if I can't get it reduced."

"Record?" I said.

"None." She shut the diary. "But how are you? Surviving?"

"I need to ask you about a life insurance issue."

"Hold on." She disappeared and returned a moment later with a cold bottle of water for each of us.

After the first few swallows, I could almost feel my body tissues reviving. I downed half the bottle, took a breath, and let myself settle into my chair rather than perching on the edge.

"Thanks."

"Looked like you needed it." Danielle shut the door, closing out the clicking keys and voices from farther down the hall, then sat at her desk and spun her padded vinyl chair to face me as I filled her in.

"So 'review'—a nice word for investigation?" I said.

"No question."

"What will the insurer do?"

She glanced at her phone, which had buzzed, and set it on the metal file cabinet next to her. "First, order the autopsy report and the medical records. An in-house investigator might also interview family members."

"All of that is the same type of work Marco did. There's no way he'd buy a policy and commit suicide when he knew it wouldn't pay."

"People don't necessarily follow a rational plan when they commit suicide," Danielle said.

I doodled a flower on a pad embossed with my firm name on it—Quille C. Davis LLC.

My former bosses had tried to convince me to use Q.C.

rather than Quille because for numbers and litigation a lot of people are more apt to call a man than a woman. I don't like kowtowing to gender stereotypes, but I might have done it for the sake of business if I didn't have the abhorrence to being Q.C. Davis II. I hadn't had a choice as a child, but I did now.

"That detective seemed to think Marco changing his will suggests he was planning suicide," I said. "That's a plan. Why would he plan that and overlook the life insurance problem?"

Danielle frowned and rocked in her chair. "Good point. Though that doesn't rule out an accidental overdose."

"What if Mirabel did it?" I said. "Staged a suicide thinking she'd collect the insurance money? She knew Marco liked cool soda flavors, so he wouldn't think anything of it if she brought him the Diet Chocolate Fudge. And she probably had old pill bottles with his name on it. If his name was on it."

Danielle held up her hand, palm out. "Hang on a minute. I guarantee Mirabel's the first person the police investigated. Most murders aren't whodunnits. If someone's married or divorced, it's usually the spouse or the ex-spouse."

I slashed black lines over the tulip I'd drawn. "I don't really think she killed him. But two million dollars—I have to consider it."

"I'm telling you the police already did. And it's not like she keeps that money. It's for her son's benefit, and a court would make sure of that. You follow me?"

"I do." It was basically what I'd said to Lauren. "But it seems strange she called the insurance company right away."

"You would too if you had a tuition bill staring at you and no way to pay."

Danielle was a single mom. She and her ex-husband, a jazz musician, divorced ten years ago, and her daughter was two years from starting college, so she knew better than I what it was like to worry about a child's educational expenses.

Still, from what Marco had told me Mirabel had never been

able to get past his mistakes in their marriage and never been able to forgive. It was part of why he hadn't wanted her as executor. He'd felt guilty and hadn't wanted to burden her more.

"I suppose the police must have asked her where she'd been that night and looked into her movements," I said.

"No question." Danielle's chair squeaked as she leaned forward. "You sure you want to stay executor? Seems like it's hitting close to home."

"I'll be fine," I said. "Is it odd the detective didn't tell anyone what the note said?"

"Not if he thinks someone close to Marco might be involved in the death."

"Including me, right? I'm the girlfriend."

She nodded. "And you were alone the night he died. I believe you were here working, but the police might not."

I gripped my pen until the metal clip on it cut into my fingers. Worry about being accused when the police ought to be figuring out who really had done this to Marco mixed with fear that he had really taken his own life, meaning I'd failed him. I felt like screaming and punching the wall, things I didn't do in real life, only on stage.

The only other time I'd felt rage was when I'd been six years old and had overheard my mother bragging about the original Q.C. being the cutest, sweetest, and most talented child in the world. She said those sorts of things all the time, but for whatever reason that day I couldn't stand it. I'd stormed to my room and thrown all my books at the wall.

My mother didn't react. Maybe she didn't notice.

But my grandmother heard. She lived in the apartment across the hall and her living room shared a wall with my bedroom.

She marched over, ordered me to clean up the mess, and warned me that I needed to learn to control myself or I'd be like my mother when I grew up, unable to accomplish anything. But after I put everything back in place she took me to her apartment, gave me a dish of ice cream, and told me to always work hard and do my best and I'd never be second to anyone.

"Quille?" Danielle said. "You all right?"

I inhaled and let my breath out slowly. "Can you be with me if the detective talks to me again? Be my lawyer?"

"I was about to offer. Just in case." She opened her diary and turned to the back pages where she took notes.

"Should I tell him about this?" I gestured at the policy.

Danielle's pen scratched across the page. "Let Mirabel tell him. And if he calls you, if any police contact you, don't say anything. You can listen, that's fine, but don't answer. If they push you, say you're not talking without your lawyer present. Then call me."

"Though that might make me look like I'm hiding something, and I'm not."

My dad had told me one reason the neighbors were convinced he and my mom were involved in Q.C.'s disappearance was that after weeks of police badgering they'd gotten a defense lawyer.

"Some of my clients aren't either. They're not all guilty." Danielle leaned toward me, the faint lines in her forehead creasing. "You follow me?"

17

"ERIC SHOULD NEVER HAVE ASKED YOU TO DO THAT," MIRABEL said.

Danielle had left, as had everyone else in the suite, as it was after six-thirty. I'd called to give Mirabel my take on the policy, and I'd told her about Eric asking me to investigate.

Despite what Danielle had said I also wanted to know where she'd been the evening of Marco's death.

"But you understand why he did," I said. "He can't believe Marco committed suicide. And neither can I."

I shut a metal file drawer. The sound clanged through the empty suite. Danielle and I had a deal that we'd leave the desks and credenzas clear at the end of every day. It made it easier to share the space, and it kept client confidences.

Usually I didn't mind. Neat workspace helps me think. But tonight it felt pointless and exhausting to put away files and pens I'd take out again tomorrow.

"You both share an idealistic view of Marco," Mirabel said.

I slapped a stray legal pad on a stack of papers, my exhaustion turning a corner to irritation. "Is it beyond you to consider that he might have changed?"

"If you'd lived with him for seventeen years, the last ten of which involved him being drunk or absent, it'd be beyond you, too."

My face flushed.

I jabbed the key to close my case management software. Until now, I'd rarely struggled with my temper, but every time I talked to Mirabel I teetered on the edge. Logic told me I was mad at Marco for dying, not at Mirabel, but logic didn't help me stay calm.

And I wanted to. A feud between his mother and me wouldn't be good for Eric.

"Let's stick with practical issues," I said. "The policy is clear. A finding of suicide means no life insurance. You don't want that."

"But what can you do? You can't prove Marco didn't kill himself."

I walked into the reception area and flicked off the Tiffany lamp on the counter. Only the overhead above the suite's exit and the file room lights remained on.

"I don't need to prove it beyond a reasonable doubt like in criminal court," I said. "All I need is enough to threaten the insurer with a bad faith claim."

I'd spent the last two hours researching case law and talking with an insurance coverage attorney. It felt almost soothing to have a concrete problem to work on relating to Marco, something I might be able to solve using my legal skills.

"So who's the prime suspect? Me?" Mirabel said.

In the kitchen, I checked to see if the coffeemaker was off. I was pretty sure I'd checked before, but yesterday I'd left home without locking my door, so I didn't trust myself.

"No," I said. "But it'd help if you tell me where you were when Marco died."

I felt too worn out and frustrated to come up with a subtle

way to question her. Anyway, Mirabel wasn't exactly a model of diplomacy, so she could hardly complain about my lack of tact.

"You're not serious," she said.

I shut the kitchen door. "I'm very serious."

"I hate to disappoint you, but I was at work all day that Thursday and at Eric's basketball game with one of his friend's mothers the entire evening. After that, I took Eric home."

The secretarial desk closest to the door was an empty one, meant for Danielle and me if we needed a secretary, but we both had virtual assistants. It had turned into a floating work-station for anyone who needed to spread out.

I sat on its edge. The light from the hallway through the rectangular window in the suite's front door allowed me to see.

"Thank you," I said. "Can you think of anyone who might have been angry at Marco?"

"Besides me? The police already asked me, and I said no."

That didn't sound like an unqualified No.

"If you had to think of someone, no matter how outlandish, what would you say? Maybe someone who was a little upset with him, or that he was frustrated with?"

I put my phone on speaker, set it down, and grabbed a pen and a pad of paper from the desktop to write notes as I waited for her answer.

"Well," Mirabel said, "last fall Marco mentioned someone at work. Jessie somebody. Said he was tired of her snapping at him when he pushed her to work harder. If Marco pushed her, she must have been a slacker. He hated to come down on employees."

I wondered if she realized she'd said something positive about him at last. I didn't remember the name Jessie from my talk with Jerry Hernandez, but I could text him and ask.

"Anyone else?" I said. "Someone you might not have mentioned to the police because it's so unlikely?"

Her sigh echoed in the deserted suite.

"Mirabel?"

"Hector was mad at him. But he wouldn't hurt Marco."

My pen hung over the notepad. "Hector? His brother?"

"He never really forgave Marco for stealing me away. I dated Hector first. All through high school."

"That's what, twenty years ago?"

As I said it, I realized it must be longer than that. Marco had been forty-two.

"Hector always felt like Marco had everything. He did better in medical school, got a prized residency, had a lucrative practice. And then threw it all away with his drinking. It made Hector mad."

I hadn't gotten any sense of Hector being angry when I'd talked to him at the wake and funeral, though it was all a bit of a blur. I doubted he'd flown in from Alaska to arrange a fake overdose because of sibling rivalry.

I tapped the pen on the desk. "Not really a motive for murder."

"You asked who was angry at him, not who killed him. *I* don't think anyone did."

I rubbed the back of my neck where my muscles had knotted. "You're right. I'll let you and Eric know if I find anything helpful."

"Don't give my son false hope," Mirabel said.

After we hung up, I put on my leather jacket and pulled my black knit gloves from the pockets. Late April and it was still cold outside.

Mirabel wasn't happy, but as in litigation, it wasn't my job as executor to make people happy. It was my job to do my job. I hoped it would lead me to answers about Marco.

18

THAT NIGHT I DUG AROUND IN MY STEAMER TRUNK UNTIL I FOUND my complete DVD box set of Buffy the Vampire Slayer. I'd watched the entire series when it had come out and had viewed it more than once all the way through on the DVDs, though it had been a long time.

I set the first episode playing on my laptop before I crawled into the futon in the loft to try to sleep.

The actors' voices and familiar stories helped me feel less alone without my needing the energy to be around real people. The plots kept my mind occupied, partly short circuiting my ruminations about what signs I might have missed about something being wrong with Marco, though part of me felt that was exactly how I ought to spend my nights. Because one way or another something had been terribly wrong, and I hadn't seen it.

The episodes blurred together as I drifted in and out of sleep.

The next morning I dragged myself out of the futon at seven a.m. I spent the first two hours at the office on my tax appeal, struggling to focus between texts with Jerry Hernandez. I'd been hoping he knew which employee had been mad at Marco, but he didn't. He did promise to try to figure it out, but from what I could read of his tone via text he didn't seem optimistic, and he couldn't talk by phone because he was at Hazleton already.

Around ten-thirty I took a break to call Vujic Chiropractic, hoping it'd be a quiet time there. I figured most people probably fit healthcare visits in before work, at lunch, or right after work.

I asked one of the investigators in my suite about the best approach. He said honesty.

I shouldn't have been surprised.

It's the same in my profession. People think attorneys win cases by browbeating witnesses, tricking the other side, or lying about their own positions. Some might. But I find treating people decently—including lawyers on the other side and their clients—and listening to them respectfully is the best way to get information. We all have plenty of people haranguing us and rushing to trumpet their opinions.

What most people want is to be listened to.

I asked for Cora Smith, the billing administrator, and I was transferred to a woman with a raspy voice.

"Ms. Smith, I'm calling about Marco Ruggirello from Hazleton Insurance." As I spoke, I leaned on the exposed brick ledge of the window by Danielle's desk.

Our office is only four floors up. I watched a CTA double-length bus pull away from the Starbucks and lumber along Dearborn Street below. My forehead pressed against the window. I longed to shut my eyes and drift into the sleep that eluded me at night.

"What's that asshole want now?" Cora's voice, amplified by the speakerphone, jolted me into alertness.

"He's dead," I said.

I hadn't planned on being so abrupt, but Cora's venom had

thrown me. It also jolted me more awake. Unless she was faking, which was possible, the police hadn't talked to her about his death.

"Is this a joke?" she said.

"No joke. I'm the executor of his estate."

"Bully for you. What do you want?"

Given the first thing she'd said about him, I decided not to mention that I'd been Marco's girlfriend. It wouldn't make this woman sympathetic.

I turned away from my computer monitor, which showed the bullet points I'd typed out. Explaining my doubts about whether Marco had started drinking again or committed suicide was honest, but my whole body stiffened at the idea of exposing Marco's vulnerabilities.

"Hello?" Cora said.

I struggled for what to say. Purely as Marco's executor, I couldn't think of any reason for my call. Vujic Chiropractic had nothing to do with handling the estate or distributing assets.

Then my glance fell on a stack of IRS materials on my credenza. A mantra from Accounting 101—one my professor had said we should recite each night before going to sleep—popped into my mind: assets minus liability equals owner's equity.

A lawsuit equaled potential liability.

"I heard something about a lawsuit by your company against Mr. Ruggirello and Hazleton Insurance," I said. "But I haven't been able to find any paperwork on it."

"We haven't filed suit," Cora said.

"Are you planning to?" I said.

"That's between us and our lawyer. You'll find out when you're served."

There was loud click as she disconnected.

I dropped into my chair. I'd made a mistake. There's a six-month publication period after someone dies in Illinois. It restricts creditors to that limited time to pursue claims against the estate. I'd now told Vujic that Marco was dead, so if they wanted to file suit, they'd know to do it soon.

My heart hammered in my chest. I shut my eyes and imagined I was hearing a drum beating a slower, more soothing rhythm. It was a technique I used for stage fright.

I told myself the people at Vujic Chiropractic would have found out about Marco's death in the next few weeks no matter what I'd said. They had on-going issues with Hazleton, and he'd been the contact person. When he disappeared, they'd have asked why and someone would have told them Marco died.

Still, I felt foolish. I'd promised Eric I'd help, but my first duty was to protect the estate and its assets for him. I had to be more careful, pull myself together, and think things through before I acted.

An hour later, I heard from the Chicago Police Department via voicemail, as I didn't answer the call.

They were done processing Marco's apartment, so I could go in to sort through his possessions that night.

If I wanted to.

I didn't, but I would.

19

LAUREN PROMISED TO MEET ME AS SOON AS SHE WAS DONE WITH showing a condo in the South Loop. I decided to talk with Marco's neighbors until she arrived to see if they'd seen or heard anything unusual.

The only one whose name I knew was James, who lived across the hall, but he wasn't home.

I sat on the top stair near Marco's door. I stared at client emails on my phone without really reading them, inhaling the smell of old paint.

James appeared about ten minutes later. He had a square jaw that reminded me of a Disney cartoon prince's, skin so taut it looked like the result of a facelift, and a thin, muscular body that his bike shorts showed off. He was either young looking for his fifties or old looking for his forties.

He said he was sorry about Marco.

I thanked him and asked if he'd ever noticed Marco being intoxicated or smelled alcohol on him.

He draped his jacket over the wood railing. I admired him for biking in this weather. The temperature had barely gotten above forty-five. "The police asked me that."

I got to my feet but rested my lower back against the wall. "What did you tell them?"

"I don't remember ever smelling alcohol on him, but not sure if I'd notice." His voice was deep and his words came slowly, with pauses a fraction too long in between. "Definitely no loud parties. He was a good neighbor. Quiet. Nice."

"Did you see anyone going into his place last Thursday? The night he died?"

"Nope, nothing."

I asked when he'd last seen Marco.

"March 12."

The answer came quickly, a stark contrast to his earlier words.

"You remember the exact date?" I said.

"It's my girlfriend's birthday. Forgot last year. She got really mad. Got to keep the ladies happy." He shook his head. "Or try. It's not easy."

My back ached—too much sleeping on the floor or the futon—and I shifted position. "Where'd you see him? In the hall here?"

"No, no, the other side of the building." James gestured toward the windows in the stairwell. Through them the apartments on the opposite side of the U-shaped building were visible. "A neighbor invited people for coffee. She wanted us to meet some guy running for alderman."

I stood straighter. "And Marco was there?"

I'd never known Marco to be interested in politics. Not that he couldn't have interests he hadn't mentioned in the months we'd been together, but he'd told me he tried to avoid news and political commentary as part of his sobriety. It helped him minimize anxiety and keep a healthy attitude.

"Yeah, he got there late. Right after the guy's wife finished talking about how amazing her husband is. Like that matters.

Every wife's going to say her husband's great if he's running for office, am I right?"

"You'd think," I said. "Who was the candidate?"

Maybe it was someone Marco had known personally, and that's why he'd gone, though it was still odd he'd never told me about it.

"Don't remember," James said, "but he was a Democrat. My girlfriend's big into the Democratic Party in Kane County. She wanted to go to see what the guy said."

"But he'd be running in Chicago."

Kane County included far west suburbs, not the city.

James rubbed the side of his face. "Would he?"

"You said alderman. That's a city council position."

"Huh." The sconce that lit the landing where we stood buzzed, and James tapped it, quieting it. "Chicago's in Cook County, right?"

"Yeah."

"Huh."

Whatever else he was, James wasn't brilliant. I couldn't imagine many residents not being sure what county Chicago was in. With all the taxes Cook County imposes and signs posted all over it's hard to miss.

"Was he maybe running for something else?" I said.

"He was definitely an alderman."

"Right, but could he have been running for another position?"

James stared at me.

"Running to change position?" I said.

"Oh, sure. That could be it."

I took out my phone to type in what he'd told me. "Who was the neighbor who hosted?"

"Dede Ziv. Or Zith maybe. Dede Zith."

I noted the name. If Dede could get neighbors to come to a fundraiser, she must know a lot of them well. Including possibly Marco. I could find out why he'd gone and get her impression on whether he'd started drinking again.

James shifted from one foot to the other, probably impatient to get on with his evening.

"Did you talk to Marco that night? Did he seem upset?"

"Oh, you mean because he committed suicide a month later?"

"Right." I cleared my throat. "If that's what happened."

"I don't think so, but all we talked about was the Bears. He's a big fan, huh?"

I lost my grip on my phone but caught it before it hit the carpeted floor.

If there was anything I was sure of about Marco, it was that sports didn't interest him. We'd joked about it on our second date when we'd gone to a play at a storefront theater in Rogers Park. I thought he'd suggested it to get in good with me, knowing I'd been an actor. He laughed and said no, he really was a guy who loved theater and disliked football.

My chest tightened. Marco had been moving in with me, but I was starting to feel I hadn't known him as well as I thought.

Head spinning, I said, "Why do you say that?"

"He said I must be really disappointed the Bears hadn't been in the Superbowl when they'd come so close. And I tell you, I was. Next year, though."

My neck muscles loosened. My relief was out of proportion, but I felt like hugging James.

The statement was one of those generic comments nonsports people use to be polite when someone else gabs away about the topic. I had my own mental list, though since the Cubs had started winning I could no longer do the sad head shake and say, "Cubs" with a sigh. That perfect all-purpose comment had seen me through college, the accounting firm, law school, and my first several years as a lawyer.

If I talked to Dede, the woman who'd organized the coffee, maybe I'd discover something similar to explain the political connection.

"Did Marco say anything else?" I said.

"Maybe to my girlfriend. I had my earbuds in most of the night so I could listen to the Hawks. At least they had a fantastic season, you know?"

He'd tried to be helpful, and though I felt worn out, I wanted to be polite.

I consulted my list.

"Always good to have a Chicago team in the running," I said.

I headed downstairs and across the courtyard to visit Dede Zith.

20

Marco's code didn't work for the vestibule on the opposite side of the apartment complex, and no one answered when I pressed the button labeled Zith. The first neighbor I tried, though, buzzed me in without checking who it was.

Obviously it wasn't hard to get in whether you lived there or not.

I trudged up the first flight of steps. I didn't feel eager to bang on strangers' doors, but Lauren had texted that she'd be later than she'd expected and I wasn't ready to go into Marco's apartment alone.

Or at all.

I dreaded emptying the boxes he'd packed to move in with me. Worse was the thought of the living room.

We'd played cards with Eric in there only a few weeks ago, lay on the couch watching Netflix shows most Saturday evenings, and watched giant snowflakes drift down outside the ill-fitting windows on Christmas night, blankets wrapped around us against the draft. But now it was forever and always the place where I'd found Marco's rigid body.

Everyone whose door I knocked on was nice to me, but

none had known Marco personally, and one hadn't heard about his death. It was something that surprised me when I first moved to downtown Chicago—the way people didn't know their neighbors despite sharing stairs and halls and elevators.

In LaGrange, the suburb where I grew up, we knew the people next door and above and below us, and some who lived across the street or down the block. But when everyone lives on top of one another, they withdraw a bit to allow some privacy.

Dede Zith answered her door the second time I tried.

She was about five inches shorter than me and wore glasses with funky cat's eye frames and lenses so thin I suspected they were for style rather than function. A streak of silver shot through her nearly-black hair near the front.

Her apartment was larger than Marco's—a two bedroom with a long, rectangular living room, a full dining area, and a separate kitchen. Her own original oil paintings hung on the walls, landscapes featuring oceans with crashing waves, lakefront paths, or winding rivers.

I felt like if only I could step into them, life would be right again.

We sat on her extra long sofa. I accepted a Coke. Dede wasn't a coffee drinker, and I needed the caffeine. She told me the fundraiser had been for a former alderman, Edward Tabacchi, not a current one.

His name wasn't familiar to me.

"What's he running for now?" I said.

Dede sipped from an amber glass that gave her wine an orange cast. "Comptroller."

The Comptroller pays all the bills for the state, and from what I knew it was a pretty thankless job because of Illinois' financial problems. My friends who did legal work for the state had to wait eight or nine months to get paid. Hospitals and doctors were waiting equally long, and some non-profits had closed up shop the last time the legislators had focused on scoring political points rather than passing a budget.

But Comptroller is a powerful position, and plenty of people had probably competed to be the Democratic nominee.

"And Ed won!" Dede said. "Sorry, you're probably not excited about that with Marco's death."

"No. But I'm glad for your candidate." I drank more Coke. The icy cold glass and the fizzing across my tongue helped me feel more awake. "I heard Marco attended, but I don't understand why."

Dede looked puzzled. "I invited him."

"No, I mean why it interested him. He never talked politics."

"Oh, right. A lot of neighbors like my art. They can't afford it, but they like it. So I told everyone it was a great chance to see my latest paintings and meet more neighbors. Plus good food. Tabacchi and his wife paid for the catering. It was a nice spread."

I could see Marco attending something like that. He'd told me one thing he missed about drinking was the social part where people hung out at the same bar and got to know one another. That didn't explain why he hadn't told me about it or invited me, but I'd been pretty busy in March and April at work, so I might have been at the office late.

"Did Tabacchi raise a lot of money?"

"No. It was more Meet and Greet, try to get people to vote in the primaries."

"Did Marco talk to Tabbachi?"

She tilted her head to one side. "Maybe. I think I saw both of them in the kitchen when I went to open more wine."

"Did you talk to Marco?"

"Not really."

I set my Coke on a sparkling mosaic coaster. "So you talked with him a little?"

I'd learned from interviewing clients, taking depositions,

and cross-examining witnesses that "not really" is not the same as "no."

"Yeah. He said something about work. A project he was frustrated with. Something like that."

I asked a few more questions, but she didn't remember anything else. She didn't think she'd seen Marco drinking that night or ever.

As she walked me to the door, she said, "You know, maybe Marco wanted to talk to Edward about that permit issue."

"The what?" I said.

21

DEDE LEANED AGAINST HER OPEN DOOR. "HE OWNED AN apartment building, right? Once when I saw him in the laundry room he mentioned repairs or work—maybe rehab? And permits. Maybe he thought a former alderman could help."

Her comment jogged a vague memory from when Marco and I had talked about finances before deciding he'd move in with me. He'd said he had money set aside for work on his six flat.

If there was an issue about a permit knowing an alderman, even a former one, could be a plus. Things have improved in Chicago since my grandparents' time, but a lot still gets done based on who you know or how much you donate.

"How long ago was this?" I said.

"February? It was one of those warm winter days, you know, when everyone goes out."

I nodded. Once in a while Chicago gets a rare sunny and warm day in January or February and people emerge outdoors, blinking, their moods lifting after weeks of indoor activities and gray skies. Drivers honk their horns a little less and pedestrians smile a little more.

That was all Dede remembered about the conversation, but she promised to call me if she thought of anything else.

I returned to the top step outside Marco's apartment and opened my iPad. His WiFi was strong enough that I got a signal. I navigated to the state board of elections list of political donations. Dede had donated $200 to Tabacchi in March and to about a dozen other candidates in the last ten years.

Over the same ten years, Marco had contributed to one candidate for governor, a Republican, and one United States Senator, a Democrat. He'd made no donations to Edward Tabacchi.

Lauren called as I was searching earlier records. She was outside the building.

I went downstairs to let her in and she hugged me. "Sorry I'm so late. Did you get started?"

I shook my head.

She grabbed my hand. "We'll go in together."

———

I dreamed that after packing Marco's dishes and sorting through boxes of clothes in the bedroom, I went into the living room and found his body all over again.

I awoke gasping. The sheet had wound around my waist, and it took me a few minutes to untangle it. My hair felt damp.

Heart pounding, I crawled out of the futon and down the stairs. As I waited for my tea kettle to whistle, I inhaled to a count of two, held my breath for two, and exhaled for two, then did the same to the counts of four, six, eight, and ten. It was another technique I'd learned as a kid to control stage fright.

Rain spattered the sliding glass doors. Usually I brew tea with loose leaves, timing the minutes for steeping to the second, but it felt like too much effort to get out the diffuser, leaves, and teapot. Instead I poured the hot water over a Sleepy

Time tea bag, then opened the blinds and wedged myself into a corner of my couch to watch the storm, hands around my mug.

The licorice scent and flavor of the tea helped me relax a little until lightning flashed. Thunder boomed an instant later. Something banged against the glass doors, but it was only one of the neighbors' potted trees. The wind must have blown it into my area, and it had pitched over.

I tried not to think about the dream, but it kept coming back to me. As in real life, Lauren and I had stacked boxes of dishes and pots and pans by the door for pick up by a woman at Marco's mother's church who could use all of it for the soup kitchen.

After we'd cleaned, the kitchen had looked almost the way Marco had kept it, every surface annoyingly clear. Not for him the set of knives in a butcher block on the counter or a stray coffee cup on an end table. He put everything away immediately.

He *had* put everything away immediately.

His bed had been made each day, pillow cases smooth and wrinkle-free, unlike my own that I always left in the dryer too long before retrieving. The desk near the wall had been neat, its surface bare.

Bare.

I sat straight, nearly spilling tea all over myself. That was it.

The lack of papers or stray pens wasn't unusual, that was Marco, which made me think he hadn't started drinking again. If he had, I doubted he could have kept everything so orderly. But a plain black laptop usually sat on the desk. Always sat there, as best I remembered.

But it hadn't been on the desk or anywhere else in the apartment tonight. I also didn't remember seeing it the night I'd found him, and the police hadn't listed a laptop on the inventory of items they'd taken.

If someone had taken it, it had to be someone who'd been in the apartment the night Marco died.

22

———

THE NEXT DAY WAS SATURDAY, SO I WAITED UNTIL TEN A.M. TO text Eric. I was at my office to deal with a few matters I hadn't gotten to the day before.

Eric called me immediately. He was on the bus on his way to school for a basketball game. He'd returned to classes the day before.

"You're sure you're okay to be back in school?" I said.

"You're sure you're okay to be back at work?" he said.

I smiled a little. The curve of my lips felt unfamiliar. "I feel better working than doing nothing."

"Me too. Did you find out something?"

I sipped the Earl Grey Tea latte I'd picked up at Café des Livres. "Not really, but I have a question. When's the last time you saw your dad's laptop, the one he kept in his bedroom?"

"Last time I was there," Eric said.

CTA announcements sounded in the background.

On my iPad, I opened a calendar app I'd downloaded separate from my work calendar to create a timeline of events leading to Marco's death. I'd already filled in the fundraiser at Dede Zith's. "Which was when?"

"The week he died. That Monday night. I stopped by to help him pack."

"You're sure the laptop was there? You noticed it?" I wedged the phone between my shoulder and chin so I could type.

"Maybe. Not really. I don't know. But I would have noticed if it wasn't there," Eric said.

I felt less sure of that. The summer I was fifteen, someone had stolen the wicker furniture set from the front patio of my grandmother's building. I'd left in the morning for an early rehearsal, and I hadn't noticed the patio was bare. My grandmother walked out a few minutes later to drink her coffee in her wicker rocker, discovered it was gone, and called the police.

I hadn't been looking for the furniture, so I hadn't seen that it was missing.

"Did you use that laptop?" I said.

"If I wanted to watch something on a bigger screen than my phone."

I tapped my pen on my desk and stared at my own laptop screen. I wanted something that would show a date, proving the laptop had been in the apartment. "What about social media? Would you have posted anything or emailed anyone?"

"Not email." He said it as if that were the most ludicrous thing in the world, and I remembered that high school students don't email. Neither do most of my friends other than for business. "And I post on my phone. But my dad maybe."

"I already checked. His last post was a few weeks ago at your game."

Eric had played well, and the photo showed him on the court driving toward the basket. We'd taken him out for pizza afterwards.

"Do you know if your dad used a backup service for the laptop? Norton or anything like that?"

More background noise, this time honking and shouting. "No."

I paced a circle around the office. "Meaning you don't know? Or he didn't use one?"

I wanted to be sure I had the facts straight before I contacted the police.

"Don't know."

"Okay. Thanks, Eric. I'll let you go."

"You coming to today's game?"

"Absolutely," I said, though I'd forgotten to note it on my calendar. He told me it started at noon, which gave me enough time to finish what I was doing and catch a cab.

Keeping my promise to Danielle not to talk to the police, after ending the call with Eric I typed an email to the detective who'd interviewed me. I sent it only after I read it over the phone to Danielle, who said it was fine. I got an automatic response assuring me my inquiry would be attended to.

I spent the next hour arguing with my auto parts client about the unrealistic response he wanted to make to an offer from his brother to buy him out of the company. Just before I left, a large storage box was delivered. It contained everything the police had taken from Marco's apartment.

It didn't include a laptop.

23

After the game, which Eric's team won, I returned to the office and lugged the box down to the café.

It wasn't quite chilly enough for a fire, but I chose a table near the stone fireplace anyway. The bookcases and armchairs made me feel at home in a way I no longer did in my condo, and the tables near it were among the few that were square, making them better for working at than the round ones near the windows.

Carole Ports, the owner, was behind the counter.

She wore a dark purple flowing skirt and black top with a colorful scarf around her neck. Her short auburn hair framed a triangular face, and her porcelain skin made her look ageless despite crinkles around her mouth and eyes.

"*Chocolat chaud?*" she said.

Hot chocolate was one of her specialties, made with frothed whole milk, 85% dark cocoa, and a drop of vanilla. It was my drink of choice when I planned to go home after working late, as the warm milk helped counter the caffeine.

It was also Carole's way of telling me to go home when I finished.

I nodded, though I'd been planning on ordering Earl Grey. I knew the caffeine I kept ingesting added to my trouble sleeping, but it was the only way I could summon the energy to read a document, make a phone call, or walk from home to the office. Sometimes I stopped at Starbucks just to sit at the counter and gather my energy for the second half of my two-block walk.

With the mug of hot cocoa in one corner of the square table, I sorted through medical bills and records.

Most related to Marco's admission for detox and to follow up treatment. As a former doctor, he'd taken a medical approach to alcoholism, viewing addiction as a function of brain chemistry.

That made sense to me. I'd been given Vicodin after having my appendix out, and I'd stopped taking it as soon as I could. It dimmed pain, but it made me feel unmoored and floaty, as if at any moment I might slip away.

"That's how I felt when I drank," Marco said when I told him about it. "That's what I loved about it."

"That's what I hated," I'd said, though now I felt I better understood the appeal.

I hoped Marco had gathered the documents for the life insurance company. If he'd told them about his past alcoholism, they couldn't refuse to pay on the basis that he'd hidden an addiction problem.

His financial documents included statements for credit cards I needed to cancel and a single Vanguard statement showing a retirement account drained to zero, confirming what Mirabel had said.

The next set of papers was from the six flat. Marco had bought it sixteen years ago and retained it in the divorce. When I'd been in college, the part of the West Loop where it was located had been mostly warehouses. Now office complexes, businesses, and high-priced apartments and condos lined most of the streets.

It must have appreciated a lot, giving me hope there might be a line of credit that could pay Eric's tuition.

The units were all two and three bedrooms, which was why Marco hadn't moved into one of them when he and Mirabel had split. The rent for his one bedroom was lower than what he took in for each rental, and starting this month he would have been paying me half my mortgage payment instead, lowering his monthly outlay further.

I found a few cards from real estate brokers. I wondered if he'd been considering selling the building.

The area behind my eyes ached from squinting at pages of dense small print. I took a break to call my work voicemail and was rewarded with a message from Detective Sergeant Beckwell. I was surprised he checked emails on Saturday.

My pointing out that Marco's laptop was missing hadn't carried much weight, though. Because I hadn't noticed that it was gone the night of Marco's death, the detective suggested I wasn't particularly alert to its presence or absence.

He also said that even if Eric had seen it Monday, Marco could have donated it, thrown it out, or sold it after that and before he died. He did ask if the laptop had a Find My Device function. I doubted it, as it had been quite a few years old, but I made a note to ask Eric and Mirabel if they knew.

I downed two Ibuprofen tablets with a hefty sip of hot chocolate. I'd been taking too much of the anti-inflammatory lately, often on an empty stomach. With a choice between short-term blinding pain in the moment, though, and serious stomach, liver, or heart problems later, I opt to avoid the migraine every time.

I listened to the message again.

Overall, the detective's points didn't ring true. Laptops are hard to dispose of. You're not supposed to throw them in the trash, and Marco was careful about things like recycling and taking old batteries back to the hardware store.

Plus everybody Marco knew likely had a smartphone, a tablet, or both. Who would want an old laptop as a gift? On the other hand, he had been clearing away things he didn't want to move, and the laptop might have qualified.

The rest of the papers were mostly from Marco's work, including meeting agendas with insurance jargon. They had creases in them, as if they'd been brought home after being folded and put in his pockets. None mentioned Vujic Chiropractic.

I dropped the box of documents at my office and sent an email to the general address for the property management company listed on Marco's six flat documents. I didn't have Letters of Office yet—the official papers showing I was the executor—but I needed to start figuring out what to do with the building. I had a call next Wednesday with St. Sebastian to see if something could be worked out about the tuition.

Mirabel was skeptical, but she hadn't argued about my trying.

At home I sank onto the couch, my whole body sagging into the cushions though it was only seven p.m. I scrolled through the numbers in my phone, then calculated the time difference from Chicago to Juneau, Alaska. It was mid-afternoon there. I dialed.

It was time to ask Marco's brother a few questions.

24

HECTOR WAS ON ANOTHER LINE BUT SAID HE'D CALL ME BACK IN fifteen minutes.

I turned on *Buffy* again—I was up to the middle of Season 3 —and let it play as I drank a glass of ice water and unloaded my dishwasher.

Normally I like quiet during weekends and evenings, especially if during the week I've spent a lot of time at court or talking to clients and other lawyers. But since Marco's death, if I had an empty minute I needed background noise.

When the phone rang, I stepped outside onto my deck. It was warm enough to be comfortable wearing my long, fleece-lined cardigan. Motion-sensitive uplights beneath my neighbors' plants clicked on, bathing the deck in warm pinkish light.

On hearing Hector's voice, I dropped onto one of the neighbor's wooden benches, my hands shaking.

In person it hadn't hit me how very much he sounded like Marco because he looked older than Marco, with heavier facial features and a rounded belly. Now, though, it sounded as if Marco were on the other end of the phone asking how I was feeling, his voice warm.

All week when people had asked how I was, I'd said "fine" or "okay" or "I'm managing."

Those answers were certainly what Gram would tell me to say. She disapproved of people—my mom in particular—who answered a rhetorical "how are you?" with a litany of complaints.

But now I found myself telling Marco's brother about lying awake at night imagining dozens of ways things could have played out differently, the nightmares where I found Marco's body again and again, and how I wondered constantly if Marco really had started drinking or committed suicide, and I'd missed all the signs.

"You could be talking about me," Hector said. "It's normal. The guilt, all of it. I've seen patients through it too."

"What do you do? Or what do you tell them to do?"

"That's a better question. Doctors rarely listen to themselves, though we should."

I smiled a little. "Marco said that, too."

"It's true. Sleep is important. You can't make yourself sleep, but it helps to turn off the laptop or the TV. The blue light interferes with sleep. If you need noise, try instrumental music. No voices. Drink herbal tea or water in the afternoon or at night, nothing with caffeine. Buy something with lavender scent. It aids sleeping. Eat what you like. Don't worry so much about eating the right things, go for calories."

"Are you doing all that?" I said.

"Trying."

Wind came around the edge of the building, and I pulled my cardigan closed. "All right. I'll try, too."

"We can check in on our progress," Hector said.

I nodded, but I wasn't sure about that. Hearing his voice made it harder because it was too much like talking to Marco.

"I need to ask you some awkward questions." I took the phone from my ear and glanced at the notes I'd made. "I'm not sure if you heard, but Marco's life insurance is threatening not to pay."

The phone cast faint white light around the bench, highlighting soot and gravel that had blown onto the deck from a construction project on the street behind the building.

"Because it might be suicide?" Hector said.

"Yes. Also maybe even if it was an accidental overdose."

The company hadn't made any official findings, but the adjuster I'd talked to hadn't given me much hope the company would pay without a fight.

"That's horrible," Hector said. "Is Mirabel in a bad way financially?"

"She can't pay Eric's tuition for next year without it."

"Ah, damn. I'd pay it for him if I could. But I work at a free clinic. I never made the kind of money Marco did, and I've got three kids of my own."

"Mirabel mentioned that."

"So what are the awkward questions? If it'll help, I'll answer."

"I need to show he could have died some other way. That it was staged as a suicide. When I asked Mirabel if anyone had a grudge against Marco, she said, uh, she said that you..."

I paused, not wanting to put it into words. This was Marco's brother, and it seemed as impossible as accusing Marco himself of murder.

"That I'm still all broken up over her marrying Marco?" He laughed a little, and I heard Marco again. I hunched forward and pressed the phone to my ear. "I didn't like when she broke up with me. But it's a long time since then."

"So you weren't mad?" I said.

"At the time, sure. I punched him out." Hector laughed again, this time a deep, booming laugh, as if about a fun childhood memory. "He ever tell you that?"

"He said you got along well."

"We did. It was the heat of the moment," Hector said. "We joked about it ten minutes later. And I didn't really punch him out. I look a swing, mostly missed, caught his left cheekbone. He swelled up like a bullfrog. Mom was plenty pissed though. Said she didn't raise us to behave that way. She was right."

I walked to the black iron fence that separated the roof's residential sitting area from the part where the giant industrial coolers stood. They were quiet tonight. It wasn't hot enough to need air conditioning.

"So why does Mirabel think you're still mad?"

"Everyone likes a little drama. And I think it made her feel better when things were so bad with Marco to imagine I still had a little crush on her."

"Did you?"

"No."

I watched a bright light that appeared to move slowly across the sky overhead, a plane on its way to land at O'Hare Airport. The city's ambient light blocked all the stars from view.

Hector might be telling the truth, or Mirabel might be. Or there might be a little truth to both versions.

"Is there anyone you can think of who held a grudge against Marco?"

"There was a malpractice case," he said. "You probably know. A few years ago. But it settled. It'd seem strange for the woman to come after Marco now. What does the autopsy report say? About drugs in his system?"

"There's no final report yet." The detective had told me it might take as long as sixty days to get the final autopsy report with all the toxicology screens and other tests. "Could someone fake an overdose? Make it look like suicide?"

"It's possible. Drugs could be diluted in a drink if it had flavoring that would mask the taste. Or he could've been injected somewhere where it would be hard to find the needle mark. "

I turned my back on the coolers, thinking of the Diet Chocolate Fudge Soda.

I'd never heard of that soda before seeing it on Marco's end table. It might have an undertaste that would mask other flavors. If it had been new to Marco as well, he wouldn't have known how it should taste.

We talked another few minutes and promised to keep in touch, but I wasn't sure how much I would. Part of me longed to listen to his voice again, but I felt that much emptier when I hung up.

Inside, I cleaned my kitchen island and microwave, neither of which needed cleaning. It was after ten when I finished.

Worn out but jittery, I started *Buffy* episodes playing again as I washed my face and brushed my teeth. When I climbed onto the futon, I left the show on, but I closed the laptop lid partway and turned it toward the wall to minimize how much of its light spilled over me.

25

BY FIVE P.M. MONDAY, I STILL HAD NO RESPONSE FROM CHITOWN Property Management despite having left a voicemail follow up to my email early in the day.

I opened an article I'd bookmarked a month ago about proposed changes in the tax law that might affect my creative clients, including one whose complex taxes I was still sorting out after getting an extension. But every siren or horn from the street outside and every ringing phone or raised voice from inside the suite distracted me.

I tried printing the article, as I'd done with Marco's life insurance policy, but this time it didn't help.

I jiggled my knee under the desk and tapped my pen. I felt like I ought to be doing more to find answers for Eric, but I couldn't make ChiTown call me back.

I checked Yelp to see what patients thought of Vujic Chiropractic. Most seemed happy, though a few mentioned being pushed for more visits than they thought were needed.

Three pages in I found a series of posts by someone who used the screen name Dr. X. Dr. X had a lot to say about Dr. Vujic and told patients to boycott the clinic. The hours for therapists were exhausting and the pay was low. In particular, Dr. X was angry about living in a studio apartment and struggling to pay student loans while Dr. Vujic strolled in wearing genuine fur coats in winter and flashing diamond rings everywhere.

Unfortunately, I couldn't figure out who this person was in real life.

I saved every comment in a file and set it aside to run by the investigator down the hall. If it weren't too expensive, maybe I'd pay to have Dr. X tracked down.

In the meantime, I sent an email to another former employee whose comments were less critical but who hinted at being pushed to sell patients on expensive packages of therapy. The comments had been made two years ago, so I didn't have a lot of hope that I'd get an answer.

Feeling frustrated, I went to the suite's galley kitchen where I kept a tin of decaf Caramel Chai tea I'd bought from Café des Livres this morning. I was trying to heed Hector's advice to cut back on caffeine, but I wanted a hot drink. In the week and a half since Marco's death, it seemed like I could never feel warm or even comfortable.

As I measured tealeaves and waited for the water to boil in my electric teapot, I tried to think who else might shed light on anything to do with Marco.

Back in my office, the scent of caramel and spice filling the air, I found the website of Edward Tabacchi, the candidate for Comptroller. It was a long shot, but maybe Tabacchi would remember talking with Marco and whether it had related to permits for the six flat.

Now that he was the Democratic nominee I doubted he'd personally answer a call or an email that didn't relate to a major campaign contribution. If I could attend an event, though, I might get a few minutes of his time.

I found what I needed pretty quickly, but the price was steep. At the end of the week a cocktail party was being held in the Gold Coast penthouse condo of a well-known personal injury lawyer. Attending required a $500 donation, and it was by invitation only, limited to sixty guests.

Even if I could get an invite and the guest list wasn't closed, the price made my palms sweat.

So far my solo practice hadn't been quite as much of a roller coaster as it was for a lot of lawyers, as I had clients with long-term matters that had come with me from my old firm.

All the same, during quiet times I worried that business wouldn't pick up again and during busy ones I worried about getting all the work done and about whether six months down the road things would be slow again.

My family history didn't help.

I knew you could be fine one day and sliding into an abyss the next. My dad's job repairing copy machines had earned him more than being a musician, but my mom never went back to work after the original Q.C.'s death. And after my parents moved back to Edwardsville, leaving me with Gram, Dad returned to the music world. My parents sent money to Gram to help support me until I finished high school, but there was no money for college.

My therapist asked once why my parents didn't stay in the Chicago area so my dad could keep his job. She implied my dad in particular had been irresponsible, at least it felt to me she was implying that, and I'd stopped seeing her.

I thought my dad had enough grief and loss between Q.C., the police suspicions, and the change in my mom. It seemed to me he shouldn't be expected to forever stay away from the music and work he loved too.

But it did mean I'd been aware of money for as long as I remembered.

I decided to first see if I could get an invitation, then decide if it was worth $500 to talk to someone who probably wouldn't remember anything about Marco. I emailed Joe. Working in finance, he'd probably know someone who'd been invited. I also sent emails to lawyers and accountants I thought most likely to be able to help.

I tried ChiTown's general number again, but no matter what menu option I tried the recorded voice simply repeated my choices.

A return to Yelp and a search of other review sites revealed that ChiTown's overall rating was two stars out of five. It was not known for responding quickly. Or at all.

Tenants warned against living in a ChiTown building. Owners said ChiTown had low management fees, but you'd pay for that with your time, as you'd often need to deal with issues yourself that you'd paid ChiTown to handle.

My call with the St. Sebastian administrator about Eric's tuition was in two days. I decided tomorrow I'd visit ChiTown in person. It's hard to ignore someone literally banging at the door.

26

ChiTown's office was in West Town. The walk from the Ashland L stop took me along cracked sidewalks and beneath underpasses scattered with garbage, then through a warehouse district where I threaded my way between closed dock doors and diagonally-parked cars.

The sky spit enough rain to make me feel damp and a bit chilled, but not enough to be worth opening my umbrella given that the wind would probably blow it inside out.

I breathed a little easier when I reached a busier street with a few bars on either side, a restaurant on the corner, and a handful of other pedestrians.

The management company was housed in a solid-looking brick building with a wide storefront window. Through the glass I saw polished desks, honey-colored hardwood floors, and a patterned rug.

Those digs turned out to belong to a law firm on the ground floor. The receptionist directed me to a stairwell that smelled of turpentine. My footsteps echoed on the metal stairs. At the end of a twisting hallway on the third floor I found a heavy gray door on which Suite 308 had been stenciled in black.

I hit the buzzer three times before someone answered. Though I leaned close I couldn't make out the garbled words beneath the static and crackling.

"It's Quille Davis," I said, hoping this was Chi-Town. There was no sign. "I need to speak to someone about Marco Ruggirello's estate."

The door buzzed.

Inside, three or four dozen people at rows of metal desks typed hurriedly, talked on the phone, or both. High ceilings and exposed ductwork amplified the noise. The industrial grade carpet did little to dampen it.

I stepped back, wishing I could cover my ears. Lately I felt easily overwhelmed by loud noises. I took a deep breath and reminded myself that Eric was counting on me.

A pale woman in a dark skirt and a green and blue blouse that tented over her lower half waved me over from the back of the long room. She introduced herself as Charlene Garfield. Her short arms barely extended beyond her body, and her palm felt moist as she shook my hand. Up close, her skin looked doughy.

Her narrow office sported more industrial grade carpet and another metal desk.

Though it wasn't hot outside the air conditioning blasted, as is often the case in Chicago when the late spring weather is cold. Most older buildings shift from heat to air conditioning by mid-April, and chilling the building is the only way to keep air circulating.

With my damp hair, it felt like the arctic. I left my leather jacket on and sat across from Charlene.

"Mr. Ruggirello died?" Charlene's fingers clicked on her keyboard, presumably accessing information on the six flat. "We were unaware."

I'd introduced myself as Marco's executor, leaving out the

personal connection. I'd rather her think of me as a lawyer than as Marco's girlfriend.

To fit the part I'd worn a charcoal pinstriped pants suit with a silk dark gray tank underneath and low heels, and I carried the red Furla shoulder bag I used for court instead of a briefcase. I'd bought it at a deep discount when Neiman Marcus' off-price store, Last Call, in River North went out of business. It helped me feel I projected an image of success.

"I left two phone messages. And emailed."

Charlene licked her lips and gestured toward the busy main room. "We get behind. You see how hard everyone's working."

"Sounds like you need more staff."

She swung her chair to face me. "Unfortunately, that's not feasible right now. But you didn't come to hear my troubles. What can I do for you?"

"I need to know the status of the six flat. What bills need to be paid, what the income is, how much equity there is."

I handed her the will and the papers that had been filed with the court. She barely glanced at them before dropping them on her desk.

"I can't talk to you until you have Letters of Office."

It seemed odd she'd know that term. It's not one most people are familiar with unless they've handled an estate.

Odd or not, though, she wasn't completely wrong. Mirabel had agreed on Eric's behalf not to object to my being the executor, but because he was a minor and I wasn't a family member the judge wanted to see everyone in court and be sure everything was on the up and up before officially recognizing me.

I'd clamped my lips together to keep from snapping at the estate attorney when she'd explained it all. Everything these days felt like it took forever to accomplish, as if barriers were being thrown purposefully in my way.

"Letters haven't issued yet," I said, making a point to keep my voice calm and steady, "but all I need right now is some information."

Charlene folded her arms over her chest so they rested on her belly. "Such as?"

"Did Mr. Ruggirello plan to sell the building?"

Charlene's chin retracted, reminding me of a turtle retreating into its shell. "I don't think I ought to tell you anything that's not public record."

"You can tell me if it's been listed or was listed during the time Mr. Ruggirello owned it. Any real estate agent could check that," I said, kicking myself for not having had Lauren check the MLS before I'd come over.

She frowned. "I suppose that's right. It was listed, briefly, but the listing was withdrawn in January."

"Because?"

She hesitated.

I unclenched my fists, which I'd been holding in my lap, and rested my hands on the desk. "I understand you're being careful. You don't know me. But I'm not a random person calling on the phone asking for a Social Security number or an Internet scammer emailing from an address with a fake name. There's a death certificate that proves Marco died. The will names me executor. I'm a licensed attorney. And I could really use your help sorting things out as quickly as possible for Marco's son."

I fished out my Attorney Registration card and Cook County Sheriff's ID and handed them across the desk.

She looked at them, then studied the will and death certificate. Her lips pursed. "There was snafu. I advised Mr. Ruggirello about it by phone."

Her words set my antennae buzzing.

Unasked, most people don't specify how they communicated unless they expect someone to contradict them. Volunteering "by phone" suggested, at best, that Charlene had never emailed Marco or sent a letter confirming the problem, and she worried that I'd question it. At worst, she'd never told Marco at all.

"What kind of snafu?" I asked.

Sweat glistened on her upper lip. "It came out of an inspection."

"So there was a potential buyer?"

"No, not a private inspection, not for a buyer. For the city, for commercial buildings. The building didn't pass. It had structural issues. It's over a hundred years old."

I folded my hands in front of me, crossing my fingers over one another. "Is that an annual inspection?"

"It's every so many years."

"So is there work underway?" I said.

Charlene glanced to her right, as if looking for cue cards pasted to the wall. "It was supposed to start in March as soon as weather permitted."

"And?"

"You know construction, nothing goes according to schedule."

I felt as if I needed to pull answers from her physically. "So the work hasn't started yet, or it has?"

She shook her head. "It hasn't. The general contractor dragged his feet, and the permit expired. And—well, I won't bore you with the details, but we had to start over with a new construction company."

"I'm an attorney. I like details."

She sighed and her shoulders sagged. "It was my mistake. Mr. Ruggirello was on a budget, and I went with the lowball bid. The contractor did a bad job. We had to fire him."

That might explain her evasiveness. If she'd messed up and there was fallout, whoever her boss was wouldn't be happy. But I didn't want to assume that was the only issue.

"Is there a cash flow problem?" I said.

When in doubt, ask about money.

Charlene shifted in her chair. "All the units are rented," she said, which didn't answer my question.

"So is there a positive cash flow this year?" I said.

"Yes."

I waited, counting to ten in my head and saying nothing. Silence often prompts people to talk.

"Barely," she said.

"And previous years?"

"Some years it's been negative. It depends on vacancies but also on work that needs to be done."

"How far are you from it being ready to sell?"

She looked at the ceiling. It was possible she wasn't deliberately stalling. A lot of people look up when trying to remember something. Singers do it all the time. But her pause ratcheted up my suspicion. It wasn't a hard question unless I was missing something about property management.

"We're working with a new construction company and a permit expeditor," Charlene said.

So there was a permit question.

Permit expeditor, or facilitator, is a polite term for a person in Chicago who knows the local zoning laws back and forth and, more important, has connections that magically help permits get granted. That ChiTown used one probably wasn't unusual, but it still didn't tell me where the work stood or why Charlene was so hesitant to talk.

"I don't know that much about property, and the police have been asking me a lot of questions," I said. "It would really help me out if you'd show me copies of any documents about the work to date and the permit expeditor."

I mentioned the police deliberately, hoping I'd get a reaction, and I did.

Her head jerked back, and the layer of flesh under her chin trembled. "Police? I thought it was a suicide."

"I thought you weren't aware Marco had died?"

She shuffled papers from one side to the other of her desk. "I wasn't. Not until you told me. I guess I just assumed suicide. He's so young, and I knew he'd had a drinking problem."

It was possible Marco had told her that, he was open about being a recovering alcoholic. But I didn't buy it. Something was off.

"The police are investigating the cause of death," I said. "So as much information as you can give me, I'd appreciate. You can send your whole file to a copy service to make a duplicate for me if that's easier."

"No, no, I can't do that. Not now. Send me your Letters of Office when they issue, though, and I'll get you whatever you need."

"I hope so," I said. I retrieved the will from her desk and stood. "If I need to get a subpoena, if that's what your company requires, I will, but I'd rather not waste the estate's resources on court costs."

I wasn't sure this was a situation that allowed for subpoena power, but one way or another I'd get all the documents I needed, and I wanted her to understand that so she wouldn't hold back.

I left convinced either Charlene personally or ChiTown as a company or both were hiding something. My only question was whether it was serious enough to kill over.

27

On the way out, Charlene had agreed to send me the contact information for the permit expeditor.

By the time I reached my office, she had. I called right away. My official purpose was to get an update on the construction project so I'd know how to handle the building as part of the estate. My unofficial one was to learn more about ChiTown and try to find any connection between the building issues and Marco's death.

His outgoing voicemail said he was out of town until tomorrow. I hit zero to talk to his assistant. To my surprise, she made an appointment for me for the following afternoon. Either the permit expeditor wasn't very busy or there was some reason he was eager to talk to me about the building.

I texted Eric to tell him about my progress, what there was of it, and see if I could take him to Salerno's for pizza that evening. It'd require driving Lauren's car through the five p.m. rush hour, but it was his favorite place for thin crust pizza. I hadn't been there since Marco's death.

But he had promised his mom he'd be home for dinner. He invited me to join them, but I felt like I'd be lonely sitting at the table with him and Mirabel. We made plans for Sunday afternoon instead.

When Mirabel called a few minutes later, I thought it might be to reiterate the dinner invitation.

Instead she told me she and Marco had still had a safety deposit box together. She hadn't opened it in years, which was why she hadn't thought of it before, and she didn't know if he had, but it might be worth looking to see if he'd kept any important papers there.

It surprised me that Marco hadn't switched to his own safety deposit box. I was starting to realize that when he'd told me he'd sorted out everything from the divorce, he really hadn't. At least in this case that was a good thing.

———

The main Chase bank in Chicago is housed in a curvy glass building that rises above a plaza with steps on three sides, a mosaic wall by Marc Chagall that portrays Chicago's four seasons, and a fountain with concrete steps on all four sides that's the centerpiece for a beautiful outdoor seating area below street level.

Sliding glass doors beyond the fountain lead to indoor seating for a giant food court. Rectangular boxes of smooth rocks and pebbles bound four escalators to the main floor. The safety deposit boxes are down a long hall that plunges into the center of the underground level.

Thankfully, Mirabel needed to get to work so she left as soon as I was ushered into the windowless six-by-six room.

The heavy door shut behind me, leaving me in silence. The air was flat and smelled faintly of car exhaust. It must filter down from the street into the Blue Line stop that connected to the bank building's basement.

The center island had a granite top that felt cool and smooth to the touch. The overhead air vent blasted cold air.

Marco's box was medium-sized, wide enough to hold letter-sized papers without folding them over. I flipped through his birth certificate, marriage certificate, divorce papers, medical license and other certificates relating to his specialties. There also was a deed to the six flat and a copy of the one to the house he'd owned with Mirabel, as well as the closing documents for both.

The divorce decree showed the house and half Marco's pension had gone to Mirabel, and Marco had agreed to pay alimony for six years. Child support is mandated by the state, including the amount, and Marco paid 25% of his salary to Mirabel for Eric's benefit.

I tapped my pen on my legal pad.

If you set the two million dollar life insurance policy aside, between the alimony and the tuition payments Marco had promised to cover Mirabel had been better off financially when he'd been alive.

Another envelope included papers that related to a malpractice suit. At first I assumed it was the one I'd mentioned to the police. But then I realized there were two cases. The surgery Marco had told me about and another with a court number that showed it had been filed ten years ago.

Two malpractice suits in ten years seemed like a lot. I wondered if drinking had related to this one, too.

I shifted to the opposite corner of the table to get away from the blasting cold air and took out a legal pad and pen to take notes. Ever since law school, I've found I learn new material best by writing by hand. While I could whiz through a tax return or opinion in my sleep, med mal was fairly unfamiliar to me so I wanted to be careful.

According to the settlement agreement, the plaintiff's family physician had referred her to an oncologist, who ruled out malignancy based on the radiology report, which had been wrong.

Marco had one consultation with the patient before the surgery to remove what was supposed to be a benign cyst. The partner in his practice had operated.

So far as I could tell, Marco hadn't been in the operating room, but he'd been swept into the suit with the other defendants. He'd paid $18,000 to settle, and the settlement release only listed him and stated the rest of the lawsuit continued.

The money had come from him personally, not from his malpractice insurance company, and he'd saved a copy of the settlement check, front and back, which surprised me. My bank doesn't send copies of cashed checks. Even ten years ago, I didn't think any of them had, but maybe Marco had requested it or printed it himself from online.

While $18,000 is a lot of money to me and most people, it's next to nothing to resolve a malpractice suit.

From what I'd heard from colleagues, expenses for that type of case run anywhere from twenty to a hundred thousand dollars for experts, technological exhibits, and other costs. The injured person's attorney usually pays for all of that out of pocket and doesn't get it back until years later when the case settles or there's a favorable verdict. If the plaintiff loses, the attorney's almost always out the money. Settling for $18,000 suggested the plaintiff's attorney hadn't thought there was much of a case against Marco.

The box also contained other miscellaneous business records. I took photos of everything so I'd remember what was in it.

Underneath the papers, I found a small velvet jeweler's pouch with a drawstring.

Inside was a sterling silver ring with a citrine stone accented by a diamond chip on either side. I recognized the golden yellow gemstone immediately. It was my birthstone, and it complemented my skin tone perfectly. I'd once told Marco if we ever got engaged, I didn't want a diamond. I found them both too flashy and a little dull. I wanted citrine.

It didn't fit my ring finger, but slid easily over my middle finger. Marco had bought it March 18. The night before we'd been eating carryout at my place, avoiding the St. Patrick's Day drinkers. Over dinner we'd decided that we'd move in together in mid-April.

The receipt showed the ring had cost $1,199.99 plus tax. Marco had never given it to me, so it belonged to the estate, not to me. But now that I'd put it on, I couldn't bring myself to return it in the box.

I left, the ring still on my finger.

The ring flashed in the warm light of my office desk lamp as I emailed Detective Sergeant Beckwell to tell him that Marco must have bought it with the intent of it becoming an engagement ring down the road. To me, that added to the case against suicide.

The detective didn't respond. I also hadn't heard from anyone who could get me an invite to the Tabacchi event. I had one more person to talk to, but I needed to send invoices for work I'd done in March.

It was temping to let the task slide another day, but I've yet to have anyone send me a check when I haven't sent them an invoice, and I had bills to pay, plus I planned to offer to make Eric's first tuition payment if Mirabel and I couldn't persuade the school to give us more time. It'd require me to use my line of credit to cover office bills temporarily, but it was worth it if Eric could start school there in the fall.

As I emailed my last invoice, Jerry Hernandez called in response to a text I'd sent before going to the bank. He was phoning from the Hazleton parking lot where he'd stepped out to smoke a cigarette.

I opened my iPad folder where I'd copied and saved everything relating to the estate.

"Sorry I didn't call sooner," he said. "I thought I might be the employee Marco was mad at. I get a little pissy when supervisors nag me, and the names—kind of similar. Jessie, Jerry."

I scrolled to the notes from my talks with Mirabel and found the part where she mentioned the employee Marco had problems with. "It was a woman."

"Figured that out. But it's not Jessie, it's Kassie. With a K. Frampton."

"You talked to her?"

"No, but she got RIF'd yesterday. Reduction In Force. Gossip is it was because she was so behind. And this time the gossip is true. Her claim files got dumped on me and they're in bad shape. Really bad."

"Do you know her number?"

"Yeah, her home number. She still has a landline. Just don't tell anyone it came from me."

I promised I wouldn't.

I took down the number and thanked Jerry, feeling a thrill of hope at the chance to learn more about whether Marco's work might relate to his death. I feel bad for anyone who gets let go. But as any lawyer knows, if you want the inside information on a company, ask a disgruntled employee.

28

THE LEASE WITH THE BUILDING FOR THE SUITE WHERE I WORK IS held by one person, a red-haired attorney a little older than me whom everyone calls Mensa Sam, though not to his face.

After leaving a voicemail for Kassie Frampton, I headed for Sam's office. It's at the south end of the suite. I don't cross paths with him often because Danielle and I are in the two offices north of the reception area. I hoped he might be able to get me an invite to Ed Tabacchi's fundraiser.

Like Barry Calvin, the prominent lawyer hosting the cocktail party, Mensa Sam handles personal injury cases. Sam's, though, are of the bump-and-bruise variety.

He sends the serious and catastrophic injury cases that might require significant work or a trial to other lawyers and collects a referral fee, which made me think he might know Calvin.

His main sources of business are referrals from his bike riding club and Mensa, one of the High IQ societies.

You can't miss his involvement in either. He wears black spandex bike clothes to work every day even if he has a client coming in, and his Mensa membership certificate hangs in the center of the interior brick wall behind his desk. Framed in gold edging and matted, it's larger than his law school diploma.

Also, the first time he meets anyone, Sam works something about Mensa into the conversation. Thus the Mensa Sam nickname.

Most personal injury lawyers in Chicago are Democrats, not only because the city skews that way but because Republicans usually want to limit how much plaintiffs can recover in lawsuits, which also limits how much their lawyers can earn, as they usually get paid on a percentage of whatever they recover for a client.

That made Sam something of an oddity. His views and the candidates he supported were strictly Republican or Libertarian, and I'd never heard him say anything positive about a Democrat. I wasn't sure he'd be able or willing to help me infiltrate a Democratic fundraiser, but he was the personal injury lawyer I knew best.

He was hunched over his keyboard, typing with his two index fingers.

I paused in his doorway. "Hey, Sam. Do you know Barry Calvin?"

He held up a finger, hit two more keys, and turned toward me, frowning. "Everyone knows Calvin. You can't miss him, the way he trumpets that big verdict against the airlines every chance he gets."

"But do you know him personally?" I said.

Sam wasn't wrong about Barry Calvin. Ten years ago, when I'd still been in law school, Calvin had won the largest verdict ever against an international airline, and he mentioned it any time he gave a talk or was interviewed, much the way Sam always mentioned Mensa.

"He's an ass," Sam said.

I leaned against the doorway. "So you know him?"

"I met him in a CLE." CLEs are continuing legal education

classes that the state requires lawyers to take to keep their licenses. "I was trying to tell him how he could improve his opening statements, and he shrugged and walked away. Because he knows everything. I'm the one who's never lost a trial."

I could imagine how that conversation had gone. When Sam first told me his "never lost a trial" mantra, I'd been impressed. Until Danielle told me he'd never lost because he'd only tried one case—a bicycle accident where the defendant admitted fault and argued only about the amount of damages owed. The jury awarded Sam's client a fair amount. So he hadn't lost, but he wasn't exactly Clarence Darrow.

A good example of how deceptive the literal truth can be.

"That's the only way you know him?" I said, hoping I didn't sound as impatient as I felt.

Whether the conversation took five minutes or ten didn't matter, yet lately I felt as if time were slipping away too fast. Time to help Eric, time to figure out what happened to Marco, and the time since Marco had been alive. It was as if Marco were racing away from me.

"That's as much as I want to know him," Sam said.

I forced my mind back to the conversation. "So that's a yes?"

Sam rolled his eyes. "Yes, that's the only way I know him. Anything else?"

I started to say no, but as I turned to walk away, it hit me he might be able to give me insight into some of the papers in Marco's safety deposit box.

I sat in the single visitor chair on my side of his desk. "If you got sued for malpractice, how long would you save the release?"

"Never had that happen."

"But if it did?"

"Forever probably. In case the person ever came back and said it wasn't a good settlement." He shrugged. "It's not like a release takes up that much space. I'm assuming it's the same in accounting."

My first day in the suite Danielle had introduced me to Sam and mentioned that I'd been an accountant. Since then, accounting had been fixed in his mind as my profession. Short of shaking him and pounding his head against the wall, I doubted he'd ever remember that I was a lawyer.

"What about a copy of the check you paid?"

His eyebrows rose. "I wouldn't be writing a check, my insurance carrier would."

I drummed my fingers on my thigh. "If it were below your deductible, you'd pay personally, though, right?"

"Yeah, I suppose that's right."

"Would you save the release in your office files or scan it to your computer? Or put it somewhere more secure, like a safety deposit box?"

Mensa Sam shrugged. "I'd save it on my computer and keep the original in my office files, but I have my own firm. If I worked for someone else and wanted to be sure no one else found it, maybe I'd put it in a safety deposit box."

"Thanks," I said.

He was typing again before I'd stood to leave his office.

When I returned to my office, I discovered I'd had a piece of luck at last. Someone at my old law firm had emailed that she knew Barry Calvin and had been invited to the cocktail party but couldn't attend. She forwarded me the invite. Without hesitating, I signed up and put $500 on my credit card, ensuring my chance to talk to Ed Tabbachi.

I felt a moment of relief until I glanced at my calendar. Tomorrow morning I had a deposition in my most challenging case and, after that, a call with St. Sebastian about Eric's tuition.

I'd need a lot more good luck to get through that.

29

The next day I dialed into the conference call from Café des Livres half an hour after finishing the deposition. I sat in my favorite spot in a wingback chair by the fireplace.

St. Sebastian's policy was strict. If the initial tuition payment couldn't be made in sixteen days when it was due, Eric would drop off the admission list. I got the sense some exceptions were made, but my hope of getting the life insurer to pay or of discovering income from an aging apartment building didn't qualify.

I sank deeper into the chair. I wasn't doing my best in presenting the reasons the school should give us more time.

It would have been better to schedule the call for a different day. I'd known my brain would feel fried and my body exhausted from the deposition, but I hadn't wanted to put it off.

Questioning a witness requires careful listening to the answers and shifting inquiries based on them. Defending a witness, which was what I'd just done, is equally exhausting, if not more so. You need to listen to exactly how each question is worded and decide whether to object.

You also need to study and analyze your own witness's

expressions and tone of voice to be alert to when the person might be confused or exhausted and need a break, when something doesn't match what the witness told you before the deposition, or when the other side might misinterpret what the witness says, which means you need to clarify when it's your turn to ask questions.

Given our minds' tendencies to wander, even on a good day it's an exercise in concentration to listen carefully to each single word someone says. Doing it while sleep-deprived and struggling not to think about Marco or flash back to the moment I'd found him had taken every ounce of energy I had.

The St. Sebastian administrator told me there were scholarships available, but the deadline was long past. Mirabel hadn't had Eric apply because she'd expected Marco to pay, and now it was too late.

In a separate call between the two of us alone, Mirabel rejected my offer to make the first payment.

"I don't want him to start at St. Sebastian and need to switch to public school after a few months," Mirabel said. "That'd be worse, and that's what'd happen if there's no insurance payment or income from the building. Because even if you could pay going forward, I couldn't accept that."

She was right, and I couldn't afford the entire annual tuition for one year let alone four of them. I clicked off the phone and bent over, arms folded on my knees, head on my arms. I felt both exhausted and angry.

A hand rested on my shoulder and the smells of dark chocolate and bacon filled the reading nook as Carole set a plate with a warmed chocolate chip scone and two slices of bacon, very crispy, on the coffee table. Next to it she placed a mug of dark hot cocoa.

It was my favorite treat, but I hadn't ordered food—or anything—when I'd come in, I'd been so intent on making my call. I also didn't say that the contrasting scents of dark chocolate and salty bacon were making me a little queasy, probably a result of the black tea I'd drunk for hours during the deposition to stay alert.

"You must eat *mon petit chou*. On the house," Carole said.

I sipped the hot cocoa. It felt too thick and heavy in my mouth, and it stuck to my tongue, but I managed to swallow. "Thank you."

"Thank me by eating," she said.

"I'll try."

She brushed my hair away from my face. "You will get through this. *Je promets*."

———

When I stopped in my office the next morning before heading to the permit expeditor's, I discovered a small stationary box was waiting for me on my desk. It held records from ChiTown Property Management, but important information was missing.

I'd like to say my eagle accountant's eyes spotted that despite my exhaustion, but a note from Charlene Garfield told me it was an incomplete file. She couldn't, or wouldn't, turn the rest over until I had official papers as the executor, not merely the will.

The hearing had been set for next Monday. I told myself that wasn't that long to wait. I did a quick review of the pages, stuffed them into my brown accordion estate file, and headed to the permit expeditor's office.

His firm was in a loft building in River North, a trendy neighborhood just across the Chicago River and north of downtown. More restaurants and luxury apartments displace parking lots there every day.

Zacharias Woodruff—who told me to call him Zak— appeared almost as soon as I stepped into the lobby. He wore a starched white shirt with monogrammed cuffs and a charcoal gray suit, but the pants were skinnier than those of most men's business suits, and his chunky black-framed glasses gave him an artsy, fifties-era look. His long jet-black hair was in dreadlocks drawn back by a band of dyed red micro dreads.

According to my research, while his partner had construction experience both as a former contractor and a construction lawyer, Zak's background consisted of fifteen years as an attorney winding his way through the maze of Chicago building codes and regulations. That he also was the grandson of the first Mayor Daley's longtime across-the-street neighbor was the elephant in the room of the permit expediting business.

His corner office featured a long table with narrow legs and a glass top in place of a desk.

An identical table stretched behind Zak, running under the windows. It made the space look larger, as the dark hardwood floor and exposed brick walls seemed to extend everywhere.

Indoor trees in shiny brass pots stood in both corners. The scent of the foliage and the long leaves shining in the sun from the massive windows helped me relax a little after the previous day's deposition and failed St. Sebastian call.

"We're ready to move forward with the repairs on the building if you are," Zak said after we'd talked for a few minutes about the unusually chilly spring, my law practice, and my relationship with Marco.

I'd told him about Marco and me, as holding it back hadn't seemed to help with Charlene Garfield. Maybe sympathy would prompt Zak to be more open.

"What do I need to do?" I said.

Zak folded his hands in front of him. The glass tabletop made his arms appear to float above his lap. "There are outstanding fees that need to be paid before anything else can happen."

"What kinds of fees?"

"My firm's fees, contractor fees."

I frowned. "But the work hasn't been done."

"It was started. The first contractor did $3,000 of work before he was discharged, and it needs to be paid."

In law, fees like that would be owed under a doctrine called *quantum meruit*, and I supposed it applied to tradesmen too. If you're fired, even if it's because you didn't provide good service, you're still entitled to be paid for the value of work you've done.

Zak, apparently less concerned with seeing my official Letters of Office than Charlene, opened his laptop and emailed me his bill and the contractor's, along with a list of the repairs and updates that still needed to be done. I had to flip through multiple screens on my phone to read all the line items.

"Shouldn't ChiTown have paid the $3,000? And your fees? Marco had a repair and maintenance account."

Some of the missing information from the ChiTown file involved that account. I couldn't tell how much Marco had paid each month over the years, where exactly the money had gone, or whether there ought to be a balance left. When I got the complete books, I planned to comb through them to be sure they were accurate.

"The $3,000 went beyond maintenance or day-to-day repairs," Zak said, "so my understanding is Marco needed to pay it separately. He was thirty days late as of April 1st."

Thirty days wasn't that long. Marco might have been planning to pay right around the time he'd died, except that when we'd discussed our finances he'd told me he had less than a few months' rent saved. He might have meant after he paid that bill, but I couldn't get into his accounts to find out until I had the Letters of Office.

"Any chance I could just sell the building? Disclose the issues, discount the price, and leave it to the new owner to deal with?"

Zak took off his glasses. "Unfortunately, the city put a lien on the building. Even if you found a buyer right away, no bank will issue a mortgage on it."

"How much will the work cost? Total?"

"Charlene didn't tell you? The middle bid—by the contractor who's been retained—was $335,000."

I drew in my breath, and my shoulders grew rigid.

The accountant in me had already feared the building was too old and needed too much work to fetch a sale price high enough to cover whatever Marco owed on it or to be a source of income for Eric if it were kept. But $335,000 just to get the building up to code—in my worst moments, I hadn't imagined that scenario.

Unless I could get the life insurance to pay or Marco had a line of credit I didn't know about, the estate would need to default on the mortgage and let the bank take the building.

Zak was too far away to touch my arm, but his hand extended across the desk. "Sorry to be the bearer of bad news. It's possible you could find a cash buyer."

"Is that what Marco was planning?"

He shook his head. "Not that I know of. He planned to go ahead with the work. It might have been in the back of his mind."

I set my phone on the glass desk. I couldn't imagine what Marco had been thinking letting the situation get this bad.

30

Maybe ChiTown had hidden things from Marco. Or maybe Zak had.

I exhaled and shifted in the chair, consciously dropping my shoulders and relaxing my mid-section to try to ease my anxiety so I could think better.

Mirabel was working. Eric wouldn't starve. And he was smart and motivated. He'd make his way in the world regardless. But I wanted to do more for him, to do something to help this boy as he grew to an adult without his dad.

"Is this unusual?" I said. "The contractor delays, the permit issues, the trouble with the city?"

Zak rolled his chair back a bit from the table. "Not exactly."

"But?"

He put his glasses on again. "Here's the thing. ChiTown wasn't the best choice to manage the building. Cheap, but not the best. My guess is Marco—Mr. Ruggirello—went for low price rather than good service, and he paid for it."

"Didn't ChiTown bring you in?" I asked.

It seemed odd for Zak to speak negatively about a company

that sent him business. He could be pointing a finger at ChiTown to avoid attention on him.

He gave a half smile. "Yeah, I ought to be telling you how awesome they are so you'll recommend them to people. They do send us a lot of work. But our client is the owner or the condo association, not the management company that recommends us. I try to keep that in mind."

"Did you ever tell Marco ChiTown made a bad choice with the contractor?"

Zak tapped his fingers on the arm of his chair. "If he'd asked, I would have, but we only spoke once and it didn't come up. Usually we communicated through Charlene."

I opened my timeline on my phone. "When did you talk to him?"

"Late February?" Zak clicked some keys on his laptop. "February 20."

The fundraiser Marco had attended for the former alderman had been in March. The timing added to the idea that Marco might have gone to talk about the permit process. I felt a little better about the $500 for the cocktail party ticket.

"Did Marco seem worried or upset?" I said.

"If he was I didn't make a note of it."

Zak put his fingers on his keypad and flicked them, and the text on his screen grew larger. He turned the laptop so I could read for myself.

I leaned forward, hoping to see Marco's exact words, as if he were talking to me. But the notes were Zak's summary, not what Marco had actually said.

MR called, asked for time frame on permits, confirmed manager had provided all necessary info and GC on board. Told him if all goes well work could be finished by Fall.

"Manager was probably Charlene. GC is general contractor," Zak said.

"Fall?"

I rubbed the area over my eyes. Maybe Marco's plan had been to make the initial tuition payment, get the work done, and sell the building, using whatever profit there was to pay the rest of Eric's tuition. But he'd been taking a huge chance that the work would be done on time, that he'd find a buyer quickly, and that he'd actually make a profit.

My head started pounding. All these financial troubles supported the detective's point that there was enough stress to cause Marco to drink again or to take his own life.

"I'm so sorry to be the one throwing all this at you," Zak said. "It's overwhelming handling the finances of someone you loved, especially who died suddenly."

"It is," I said.

"My grandfather died last year," Zak said. "It's not the same. It was sad, but it was expected. He lived a long life. But I handled his estate, and it was hard. It took almost a year to sort it out and before I felt like myself again. Everything felt wrong, especially the first month. I remember each morning feeling like there was no way I'd get through that day, get everything done."

I nodded, afraid my voice would crack if I spoke.

I'd been holding myself together without screaming or crying when talking to Eric and Mirabel and my friends. I felt like Eric especially needed to know I was doing well and would be there for him. I didn't want him worrying about my emotional state. With everyone else, it seemed easier to keep everything inside for fear if I let it out I'd never be able to act normally again.

"If there's anything I can do—if you want to talk—or have a cup of coffee or a drink, let me know," Zak said.

I nodded again, unsure if Zak was simply being kind or fishing to get closer to me to see what I knew about Marco's death. Or he might be asking me out, which made me more uncomfortable.

I stowed my phone in my shoulder bag. "I'll be fine, but thank you."

I stood and told him I'd call as soon as I had a handle on the estate's finances. He walked me toward the lobby, pausing at a small kitchen on the way.

"I should have offered you something to drink. Would you like anything for the road? Water? Soda?"

I wondered how bad I looked that people kept offering me food and drink.

"No, thanks," I said.

He grabbed a can of soda from the fridge for himself. "If you have any other questions, feel free to call."

Again I wondered if he were seeking a personal connection. I didn't want that, but it occurred to me there was something he could answer, something the detective would no doubt ask if he'd learned what I just had.

"These problems with the six flat," I said. "On a personal level, how serious are they?"

Zak popped the can open. "On a personal level?"

"Are these the kind of problems a person would commit suicide over?"

"Oh. No. Not to me. But I deal with this type of thing all the time. I suppose it's like if someone asked if you would kill yourself over a dispute with the IRS. You fight them every day for your clients."

We didn't always fight, but I got his point.

"So overall these were fairly routine issues for this type of building?"

"Yes," Zak said. "Though sometimes money does people in."

He sipped his soda. For the first time I saw the can clearly. It was Canfield's Diet Chocolate Fudge. The same brand of soda that had been next to the rum bottle on Marco's table.

31

"I DON'T GET IT," DANIELLE SAID.

She, Joe, and I sat on counter stools around my kitchen island. Joe had picked up fried chicken and biscuits from the Popeye's a few blocks away on Wabash. The scent of the extra spicy pieces filled my condo.

This was our first time meeting for dinner and to rehearse since Marco's death.

Danielle and Joe had offered to put The Harmoniums on hold for a while, but singing with my friends was the one thing I still felt good about.

As Danielle had set out the food, I'd told them about meeting Zak and how shaken I felt that he'd had Diet Chocolate Fudge Soda in his office fridge.

I took a small bite of mostly breading from the wing on my plate. "It's the same soda that was on Marco's end table."

Danielle slathered butter on a biscuit. "So it upset you. It reminded you of finding Marco. But why does it make you wonder about this Zak guy?"

"Because I never heard of that soda before that night," I said as Joe retrieved the pitcher of water from my fridge and refilled our glasses.

He topped off everyone's wine as well. "But Marco drank interesting sodas. He was a connoisseur."

When we'd had Joe and his girlfriend over for dinner, he and Marco had engaged in a long discussion about flavors, as Joe was looking for what to serve at "cocktail" parties where some of the clients were non-drinkers.

"Right, but you can't buy this one in stores. I stopped at three Walgreens and the CVS on Ida B. Wells Drive. No one had heard of it. I finally found it on Amazon," I said.

According to the Amazon reviews, it wasn't only me—no one could find it in stores, and it had some very devoted fans. It was sold online by the six-pack, making it stranger still that only one can had been at Marco's. It wasn't as if he could have picked it up at the local convenience store on his way home.

Danielle uncovered her mashed potatoes and grabbed a spork from the pile of napkins and plastic utensils in the center of the island. "So it's hard to find. Sounds right up Marco's alley."

"But not Zak's," I said. "He didn't say anything about being a soda fanatic."

I sipped my wine. Danielle had brought it over. It had a faint dark cherry aftertaste I liked, but I was still finding it hard to eat much, so I'd need to be careful not to overdo it.

Joe finished a drumstick and set it on his plate. "And that makes him a murder suspect? Sorry, Q, I'm not seeing it."

Joe had a little trouble switching to Quille. He met me in a production of A Christmas Carol when I was ten, so he'd known me as Q.C. for nearly a decade.

"More people probably drink it than you think," Danielle said. "Like when you buy a car or a designer purse for the first time and suddenly you see that brand everywhere. Or a psychic tells you someone with a name starting with the letter A will be significant in your life, and every time you meet someone with an A name it seems important."

"So you think I shouldn't mention it to the police?"

Danielle shrugged. "You can mention it as long as you get me on the call with you, but I don't think it'll make any difference."

"Any answer about the ring?" Joe said.

I still wore the citrine ring on the middle finger of my left hand. Its amber-colored stone shone in the warmth of the track lights over the kitchen island. Danielle and I had talked to Detective Beckwell about it when he'd called back in response to my email.

"The detective said Marco putting it in the safety deposit box showed he wasn't planning on giving it to me soon. Also keeping the receipt meant he might be unsure, thinking of returning it. And that it's not an engagement ring because it's not a diamond. He didn't listen when I told him that's what I'd asked for if we ever got engaged."

"Hard to say if he listened," Danielle said. "Just because he disagreed doesn't mean he didn't listen."

"He talked right over what I said."

I took another long drink of wine. The detective had also told me if Marco had planned to propose, it didn't prove anything one way or another. He'd investigated suicides where the person had vacation plans or lunch plans or had promised to be at an event the next day.

Joe washed his hands in the kitchen sink and took out his guitar, signaling that we should get started and maybe that I ought to set the wine aside. I'd told him about my confusion getting off the L, and he'd been really worried about me.

On our third song a cappella, we hit that instant where Joe's bass notes reverberated, my soprano trilled, and Danielle's alto wove effortlessly between the two. My whole body hummed, and I felt as if a weight lifted from my chest.

The feeling continued as I walked outside with both of them. I wanted to retrieve some handwritten notes at my office for a hearing in the morning. It was after ten and nearly all the businesses, including the restaurants, on Dearborn Street were closed, but Joe had said he'd walk me there and back before catching a cab home.

We waited at the bus stop outside the Starbucks first with Danielle. She lived in Andersonville, and the No. 22 Clark bus took her straight to her door. Not that she needed our protection.

One time back when she'd been a cop, she'd been riding the Red Line after midnight. She was off duty and not in uniform. A guy pulled a knife and demanded her wallet. She calmly reached into her coat pocket, took out her gun, and said, "Got change for this?"

Then she handcuffed him and radioed it in. Uniformed police were waiting at the next stop.

In my lobby Joe and I signed in with security and I used my keycard to operate the elevator because it was after hours. Only the stairwells are accessible at night—for fire code reasons—without a card.

One side of the fourth floor is home to the office suite of a medical practice, to the Men's Room, and the freight elevator.

"Be right back," Joe said. "Shouldn't have had that last coffee."

He disappeared down the far corridor.

The opposite hall leads to the Women's Room and to the suite where Danielle and I have our office. It seemed darker than usual. The sconces are always dimmed at night to save electricity, but the one nearest my suite was out.

My uneasiness grew when I discovered the suite door was unlocked. I glanced at my phone.

Through the door's rectangular glass window it was obvious no lights were on, so the cleaning people weren't still inside working. They typically finished our suite by nine anyway.

They might have forgotten to lock the door when they left. It happened. But something didn't feel right.

I dialed the security desk. Before anyone answered a figure in black clothes and a baseball cap emerged from a darkened office, veered around the reception counter, and headed straight toward me.

32

I FLATTENED MYSELF AGAINST THE WALL, HOPING I HADN'T BEEN seen.

The door swung open. The burglar's arm shot out and my shoulder slammed against the wall. My body spun toward the door as it bounced off the wall, my nose smacking its edge.

Daggers of pain shot through my face.

I yelled as much from anger as pain. Spots dancing in front of my eyes, I staggered after the intruder. As he reached the door to the main stairwell I dove toward his feet, connecting with his right heel and landing on my belly on the carpeted floor. Air whooshed out of me. I struggled for breath as the world spun around me.

Trying to tackle him had been a stupid move, as stupid as it gets. Everyone in Chicago knows you don't confront a thief. You hand over whatever you have and hope to be left in peace. It's not worth risking your life for money or things, and I'd always thought I'd be too smart to fight.

Fortunately, he was more worried about a heavy-looking bag that had been slung over his shoulder and had hit the floor with a thunk when he went down. He grabbed it and disappeared down the stairs as the elevator doors opened and the security guard burst out.

"Police on the way," he said.

A second later Joe came around the corner.

———

"What the hell?" Joe said after the police left. "What were you thinking, trying to stop that guy?"

The paramedics had pronounced me not in dire need of having my head examined, as I hadn't lost consciousness and was able to touch my nose, which was now stuffed with cotton, and follow a penlight as they moved it around. I signed the forms turning down their invite for a more thorough check in the Emergency Room. I didn't have thousands of dollars lying around to pay, and I hadn't met my hefty deductible yet for the year.

Laptops and tablets, including mine, were missing from at least six offices, all of which had been rummaged through. In mine and Danielle's, though, every piece of paper seemed to be on the floor. As many of Danielle's files had been trashed as mine.

Danielle sat in the middle of the floor, manila folders, photocopies, and accordion files everywhere around her. She was sorting them into two piles—mine and hers.

Her stack was much taller.

Having started her practice twenty-five years ago, Danielle relied on paper a lot more than I did. She knew enough to print a document from her laptop or to scan one to save it or email it, but that was about it.

The detectives who'd come had been from a different division than the ones handling Marco's death. They were polite but I had the definite impression that the chance of recovering anything was near zero, though the security guard was pulling the security videos.

"I just did it," I said to Joe. I sat in my desk chair, rubbing my hands over my arms. My whole body shook, and my mouth tasted coppery from blood. I'd bitten my lip, though I didn't remember doing it.

Joe paced in the hall directly outside our office, as there was no room to move inside. "He could've killed you. Jesus, Q."

"Quille," I said. "And it's not like he pulled a gun."

He made an angry motion with his hand, swatting away my objection. "You didn't know if he had one or not. You can't take chances like that. How long have you lived here?"

"I don't care." I flung a legal pad and it hit a plant that had already been knocked over on my credenza, sending more dirt flying. "I'm sick of this. All of it. The police don't listen. This guy breaks in. I'm getting nowhere for Eric. Nothing I do helps. Nothing makes anything better. I can't take it. I can't. I won't."

Danielle stood and put her arm around my shoulders. "Breathe. You're okay. You're alive. That's what counts. Nobody died, no one got seriously injured. Everything else is fixable."

"Sorry." I pulled away and righted the plant. My hands still shook as I swept potting soil off the credenza and poured it into the pot.

"Don't be sorry," Danielle said. "You've been holding up well. A little too well. You're entitled to lose it now and then."

I tore a few dried leaf ends off the plant. "For all the good it does. But I meant I'm sorry my questions caused a mess for you."

Both our names were listed on plates outside our office door, but there was nothing inside to show whose laptop or files were whose. Danielle used white labels on the outsides of her physical files and I used light green so we could easily tell them apart, but a stranger wouldn't know that.

Danielle folded her arms over her chest. "We don't know

you were the target. But if you were, it's not your fault. You didn't break in and rip everything to pieces."

"It has to be related," I said. "If Marco overdosed on his own, who would care that I was asking questions? Who would break in to find information?"

With everything strewn about the office I didn't know yet if any of my estate papers were missing, but I couldn't believe the break in was a coincidence.

Joe grabbed a paper towel from the roll I'd brought in and wiped the fingerprint dust from the file cabinet near our office door in quick, sharp strokes. "That's what you should let the police figure out. It's their job, not yours."

"So you think this is about Marco, too?" Danielle said.

Joe slammed the bottle of cleaner on the top of the cabinet. "It doesn't matter. People don't like being asked questions. Maybe the clinic Q's nosing around is running a scam. Maybe someone at Hazleton doesn't like her contacting ex-employees. Maybe the woman who hosted that political coffee night is a closet sociopath."

"So I give up?" I turned to face him, half sitting on the credenza with my back to the windows. I felt both wired and wiped out. "Stop trying to find answers?"

"Yes." Joe put down the cleaning supplies and joined me at the credenza. He put his hand on my uninjured shoulder. "It's terrible what happened to Marco, and I'm sorry you're going through this. But you're not an investigator. I don't want anything to happen to you. I've gotten sort of fond of you over the years."

I let myself lean against Joe. My nose throbbed, and I had trouble breathing with the swelling and the cotton stuffed in it.

I understood what Joe was saying.

But someone had killed Marco, leaving Eric fatherless and me without the first man I'd ever wanted to share my life with. Now that same person—or someone related—had broken into my office. If that had been an attempt to stop my investigation or slow it down, it had been the wrong move.

No matter what the police concluded, I wouldn't rest until I found whoever had killed Marco.

———

I got home at ten minutes to midnight.

As if to approve of my decision to keep searching for Marco's killer, I found a brown-wrapped package with the return address of Marco's brother, Hector, leaning against my door. It must have been delivered to a neighbor by mistake earlier in the day, and whoever had gotten it had left it for me. It seemed like ages since Hector and I had spoken, but it had been less than a week.

Before opening it, I sat at my kitchen island and recreated the notes I'd gone to the office to retrieve, an ice pack taped on my shoulder. I'd cranked the heat to compensate and put a blanket over my lap, but I still shivered. I ran through my opening statement twice, then put work aside and opened Netflix to play sitcom episodes as I got ready for bed.

Though I recognized Hector's advice about how to sleep better was good, other than cutting back on caffeine a bit I hadn't followed it. Silence made me want to pace the floor, I hadn't had the chance to buy any lavender-scented items that might help me relax, and I was still sleeping on the futon.

The package Hector had sent sat on the steamer trunk.

Swearing, I struggled with the brown paper and clear, superstick tape and finally got the box open. Inside were vanilla bath salts, a vial of lavender essential oil, and a CD of rain sounds. The CD was a nice gesture, but the only way I had to play it was on my laptop, which would violate his no blue light rule.

A bath, though, might ease my aching body. I poured in the bath salts, filled my soaking tub, and sank into the hot water.

Gradually my body warmed, starting with my feet and legs. I swirled cupped water in my hands and poured it over my shoulders. Hot water droplets coated my face.

In that quiet room—with vanilla-scented steam so thick that had anyone been there to look, I couldn't have been seen— finally, for the first time since Marco's death, I cried.

33

In the morning my shoulder ached and I had bruising around my right eye, but I'd actually slept until six without waking during the night. After reviewing my notes one last time, I put on one of my pinstriped skirt suits and an off-white lace-edged tank and sheer hose.

Conservative is best when it comes to taxes.

Illinois tax law disputes are heard first by an administrative law judge in a hearing that's a little less formal than a trial. Given the circumstances, I probably could have gotten my hearing moved to a different date, but preparing all over again a month or more down the road didn't appeal to me.

Getting ready again later also might be harder.

I didn't know how much of my files I'd be able to reconstruct. Also, I wouldn't be able to bill my clients for the hours it would take to prepare again, as the break in wasn't their fault.

A continuance also would disappoint my clients, a husband and wife who owned a design studio. They were eager to have this resolved.

Two cups of Earl Grey tea and a chocolate chip scone at

Café des Livres with Lauren helped me feel awake and ready to argue my case.

Carole joined us for a few minutes at the table to ask about my bruised eye and swollen nose. Today she wore a black short-sleeved blouse with a scoop neck and a long skirt with swirls of red and orange that made it look like it was in motion though she stood still.

"Ten o'clock!" she said, resting her hand on the back of Lauren's chair. "Yet another reason you should not work so much. *C'est dangereux* to be walking about so late."

"There were tons of students walking around," I said. Columbia College had dorms down the street from me in one direction, DePaul and Roosevelt Universities in the other.

"*Oui*, and they are foolish, too, as young people are."

The hearing was at the Thompson Center, the glass cupcake-shaped building that houses most State of Illinois offices in Chicago.

Normally I walked the mile there. Walking to get places is the main way I exercise, as I'm not a fan of running or fitness classes. But with my aching shoulder, I took the bus with Lauren. It dropped me a block from the center.

The hearing went well. Sympathy might even have caused the judge to be a little more receptive to my arguments. We wouldn't get a decision for another thirty-five days, but I felt sure she'd understood our position.

My opposing counsel, a guy who often represented the Illinois Department of Revenue opposite me, bought me another cup of tea afterward at the Starbucks across the street. It tasted sharper and had less vanilla than at Café des Livres, but I wanted the caffeine for the day ahead. The attorney recommended I get a cheap refurbished laptop at Best Buy to get me through the week, then look for a new one later.

An hour later my IT consultant, a good-looking man about my age with a shaved head, sat in front of the refurbished laptop, accessed my online backup files, and ordered me to leave.

"It won't help to have you hovering," he said.

Danielle and I were planning to talk with Detective Beckwell anyway in an hour. Someone else had reserved the suite's conference room downstairs but Carole said we could use her back office at Café des Livres for the conference call.

I ate a goat cheese and tomato salad at one of the smaller round marble tables near the window as I waited for Danielle. She arrived about ten minutes late. Her half-day trial at 26th and California had run long. She wore an espresso-colored pantsuit that complemented the blue undertones in her ebony complexion and an aquamarine blouse that set off her silver hair.

Carole's office had a wood and metal desk with a cork board above it full of invoices, curling newspaper articles about the café, and old theater tickets, all affixed with green and white plastic tacks.

I put my cell phone on speaker and set it on the desk as I told the detective Danielle was on the line. She'd been on calls with both of us before.

He said that was fine, and that he'd been about to call me when I'd contacted him. I told him about the break in and tried to convince him it was related, but he kept returning to the point that other offices had been trashed, too.

"Yours looked like the worst to you because it's yours. The other tenants thought the same thing about theirs." His voice sounded tinny in the small office.

"But why our suite at all?" I said.

I sat in front of the desk. Danielle sat to one side, nearly wedged into the corner.

"The downside of development. More buildings, more offices, more people with money means more things worth stealing. There's been an uptick in burglaries in your neighborhood in the last two or three years. More muggings, too."

Since I'd moved into the tiny Printers Row neighborhood where I lived and now also worked, luxury apartments had risen around me and many old buildings had been rehabbed and converted to mixed residential and business use.

I'd always thought of it as making the neighborhood safer.

I felt more comfortable walking when other people were out, too, and passing apartment buildings rather than vacant lots, but what the detective said made sense. Thieves go where there's money to be made.

More crime in the neighborhood, though, didn't prove the attack on our suite had been random.

Detective Beckwell agreed when I pointed that out, but he still wasn't convinced the robber had targeted me. He did at least ask for names of everyone I'd contacted recently about Marco.

When I mentioned Zak, I told him about the soda.

"Coincidence."

"Did you talk to him as part of your investigation?" I said.

Danielle was writing notes on her legal pad, and her pen bumped my phone, knocking it off the desk. I caught it before it hit the floor.

"I can't go over every witness with you," the detective said.

"So it's coincidence that my office was broken into, and coincidence that someone connected to Marco drinks this unusual brand of soda?" I said.

His sigh came through the speakerphone. "Here's what I can tell you. We talked to Zak Woodruff about the building Mr. Ruggirello owns, and we checked him out thoroughly. There's no evidence of any wrongdoing on his part. I can't arrest someone for drinking the wrong soda."

"I know," I said.

The scents of cinnamon and Carole's famous blackberry

cobbler drifted into the office, comforting smells that made our conversation feel even more upsetting in contrast.

"There's also no evidence Mr. Ruggirello was murdered. That's why I wanted to talk with you today. We've followed a number of leads. No one was seen entering Mr. Ruggirello's apartment the night of his death. Toxicology showed Vicodin, enough to cause his death, plus alcohol in his system. A note was found in his pocket indicating distress."

"So your finding?" Danielle said.

"Suicide."

I stared at the phone, feeling like one of those window washers in harnesses swinging near the top floor of a tall building but with no scaffold beneath me.

"Tell us about the note," Danielle said.

The note in Marco's pocket, the detective told us, had his fingerprints, and only his, on it. The handwriting also matched Marco's, though when Danielle pushed, the detective admitted it was hard to be certain with such a small sample.

I closed my hands into fists in my lap. "What did it say?"

He'd refused to tell me when I'd asked before. Danielle had told me that was common if the police thought a person close to the victim might have been involved in the death. Now that the investigation was closed, I didn't see why I couldn't know.

"'It's all too much,'" the detective said.

The walls of the small office felt too close.

"That's generic." I rolled my chair away from the desk a few inches, its springs creaking. "A person wouldn't need to know anything about Marco to write that."

"Except there's no evidence of a 'person' involved other than Mr. Ruggirello. The investigation is closed. The best thing you can do is to focus on moving forward," the detective said. "No one knows why Mr. Ruggirello did what he did, and there's no way to know. Dwelling on it will do nothing but make your life miserable. Don't let this take over your life. Remember the good times instead. If he was the kind of person everyone told me he was, that's what he'd want for you."

Danielle asked more questions—about the fingerprints in the apartment, the label on the pill bottle, the history of Marco's prescriptions—scribbling notes as I sat, stunned, in silence.

Outside the office door, voices called to one another and plates clattered as the detective listed possible suicide triggers. In addition to an impending move to my condo—which the detective emphasized Marco could have seen as a happy change but was a change all the same and therefore stressful—Marco had work challenges, significant financial difficulties, and a recent divorce.

The mention of work made me think of Vujic Chiropractic. I asked if the people there all had alibis.

"Ms. Davis, I assure you, our investigation was thorough. We checked into the people in Mr. Ruggirello's life who might hold a grudge against him. We followed every lead. There's simply no evidence that anyone was involved in his death other than himself."

I stood and paced in the small space beyond the desk, causing Danielle to scoot her chair back. "What about his missing laptop?"

"In March his company issued him a brand new laptop at work. Our theory is he discarded his personal laptop at that time or gave it away. It was five years old."

"It still worked," I said.

I came from a household where you didn't throw out something that still had use. Marco's parents had raised him the same way.

"Did it? You said you hadn't actually seen him use it."

"But isn't it strange that his is missing, and now mine's been stolen?"

"Laptops get stolen, just like tablets and smartphones. They're easy to grab, carry away, and sell."

After another ten minutes trying to persuade him to keep the investigation open, I crossed my arms over my chest. "So you're done. It's up to me to figure this out."

"I can't stop you. You're free to hire a private investigator if you like or to keep asking questions yourself, so long as you don't break any laws. But for your own well-being, I sincerely believe you're better off leaving this alone."

Danielle put her hands on the desk. "But the police investigation is over, correct? If Quille keeps talking to people who knew Marco to bolster her arguments with the life insurance company, she won't be obstructing an investigation, because there won't be one."

"Correct. But let me stress, Ms. Davis, that this isn't a TV show. You're not an investigator. You don't have special skills that we lack, and you've got fewer resources. And if you're convinced someone broke in because of your questions, it's another reason to stop your attempts. I don't believe any of it relates to Mr. Ruggirello's death, but you might have made someone mad for a reason you're unaware of. Don't poke the bear."

After we hung up, Danielle stowed her legal pad in her briefcase. "You should listen to him."

"But you defended me," I said.

"Because I don't want you getting arrested on top of everything else. But he's right, there're only two options. There's nothing to find, or there's something, related or not, and you're risking your life looking for it."

34

FOR THE FIRST TIME SINCE BEFORE TAX SEASON I GOT HOME before the sun set on a weeknight. Before leaving my office, I'd called Eric to tell him about the police finding, but he hadn't answered.

Now we traded texts as I sat at my kitchen island, a mug of lemon verbena tea next to a white legal pad. I'd decided to stop all caffeine after two PM in the hope of sleeping better. If I was going to figure this out, I needed to take better care of myself.

Eric said he wanted to talk to me and would call tomorrow.

After making more tea, I started a list of people who might possibly tell me more about what had been happening in Marco's life in the months before his death. I included everyone, whether I'd already talked to them or not.

1. Jerry Hernandez (Hazleton Insurance investigator who mentioned Vujic Chiro)
2. Kassie Frampton (investigator who worked for Marco, fired after Marco's death)
3. Dr. Vujic (Vujic Chiropractic)
4. Cora Smith (Vujic billing administrator)

5. "Dr. X" and other Vujic employees/former employees
6. Dede Zith (neighbor who hosted fundraising coffee)
7. Alderman/Candidate Ed Tabacchi (Did Marco talk to him? About six flat?)
8. James (across-the-street neighbor—nothing else to ask him?)
9. Patients who sued for malpractice?
10. Hector (brother—nothing else to ask him?)
11. Zak Woodruff (permit expeditor—Diet Chocolate Fudge Soda?—asked me out?)
12. Charlene Garfield (property manager—get rest of records after Monday hearing, talk to her again)
13. Other ChiTown employees?

The detective's offhand comment about my having no special skills had stuck with me.

The contrarian in me—the same part that had insisted I could switch from acting to accounting and accounting to law when everyone advised me to stick with what I knew—insisted he was wrong.

But he'd raised an important point. So far I'd been reacting, doing what came to mind in the moment and struggling to evaluate what I learned through a haze of shock and grief over losing Marco, running mainly on caffeine, sugar, and nerves.

If I meant to find something the police hadn't, I needed to draw on whatever resources, skills, and knowledge I had that they didn't. That wasn't going to happen accidentally. I had to plan.

After pacing in front of my glass doors in the afternoon sunlight I wrote a new list, this one of advantages and skills I had that the police didn't.

1. Disguise/acting (make-up, wigs, posture, mannerisms etc.)
2. Bookkeeping/accounting (comb the financials for ChiTown etc.)
3. Legal research (look at County records for six flat? Check Vujic lawsuits? Learn more about running for election/fundraising?)
4. Knowledge (Marco's personality, feelings about drugs, alcohol, money)
5. Relationships (some people will trust me more than police, will be more open if they understand why I'm trying to find answers and that it's personal)

I also thought I was a pretty good questioner and listener given my law practice, but I'd assume Detective Sergeant Beckwell was good at that too, though I didn't feel he'd listened to me.

I'd started thinking about next steps when Shawn, the IT guy, texted me to come back to the office. I'd actually forgotten for a while about my computer issues.

Ten minutes later I stood in my doorway. Danielle had negotiated with Mensa Sam to borrow his clerk if we paid his hours for a couple days, so the floor looked clear now. Five stacks of files stood on the credenza, pages sticking out here and there but looking marginally organized.

Shawn swiveled my desk chair around to face me. "So your back up program? Not working so well."

Not the words any businessperson wants to hear.

———

I'd been running my own practice for less than two years, so my files weren't extensive. Some documents for the last week had gotten lost, though. I had Sam's clerk scan my hard copies and send them to my virtual paralegal to reconstruct. She said she'd work all evening to conform her files to those as well as pull any recent filings off the federal websites. It was one time I was very glad she lived in another state. Had I had a traditional paralegal with an office in my firm, her equipment probably would have been stolen, too.

While everything could be reconstructed, I wasn't exactly devoting many work hours to my practice these days, and now I'd be getting big bills from Shawn and the paralegal, not to mention the credit card statement with two laptops on it. Shawn had helped me pick out a second one with more bells and whistles to use as my main laptop, and I planned to keep the refurbished one as a back up.

If all my clients paid on time, I could cover those bills and have enough left over to pay my mortgage. If not, I'd need to borrow from my business line of credit for the first time.

The electronic notes I'd made about Marco were on my phone and iPad as well as the laptop and so weren't lost to me. The paper estate file looked thinner than I remembered, but when I paged through I couldn't tell what might be gone.

I didn't think there had been much significant there, but it worried me not to know for sure.

35

It was 5:30 Friday afternoon, and my iPhone sat on Marco's empty shelf in my closet.

The probate court hearing had finally taken place earlier in the afternoon and the judge had ruled that I could be the executor. I'd have papers by Monday. When I'd texted Eric to tell him, he'd answered that he wanted to talk with me about the police finding about his dad. I'd told him to phone me by 6:45, when I needed to leave for an event, so I expected a call soon.

For the Tabbachi cocktail party, I wanted to look like someone with a lot of money to donate.

I started with my nicest, and only, Kate Spade dress. It was black with pearl-embellishments and an A-line shape. I added the pearl earrings that Gram had given me for my law school graduation and a bracelet I'd bought myself to celebrate the one-year anniversary of running my own firm.

From the back of my closet, I unearthed my single pair of Manolo Blahnik shoes. I'd put them in a storage bin with my vintage evening bags to make room for Marco's things. The open-backed shoes had pointed toes and wide black and white stripes plus a tiny bow on each, walking the line between elegant and playful.

I examined myself in the full-length mirror on the back of my bathroom door.

My nose still looked swollen to me, but I doubted anyone who didn't know how I usually looked would realize that. With my hair in a tousled up do, my outfit, and my face made up to hide the rainbow of bruises around my left eye, I looked like a successful young professional woman with money to spend. That ought to get me a few minutes with the candidate.

My phone buzzed as I was inserting a few more bobby pins in the back of my hair. But it wasn't Eric, it was the doorman. Eric was in my lobby. He'd taken the bus over.

I hoped my make up work was enough to pass close inspection. I hadn't told him about the break in, and I didn't want to. There was no reason he should worry about it.

"You're not going to stop investigating, right?" he said once he'd taken a seat on the sofa and I'd gotten him a cherry 7-Up, his favorite soda.

He looked skinnier than ever.

His collarbone showed above his tank top and his legs looked like sticks poking from his basketball shorts. Circles almost as dark as my bruises shadowed the areas beneath his eyes.

I sat next to him, angled toward him. It was a cloudy, hazy night, so the outside light was dim, and I'd left only my track lights over the kitchen island and one lamp on, hoping that would hide my injuries.

"I'll keep asking questions," I said. "But the police finding will make it hard to convince the insurance company that there's still a reasonable chance it wasn't suicide. And there's no way I can get a payout in three weeks no matter what."

I wished I could tell him something else, but from Marco and my lawyer friends who dealt with insurance companies, I knew nothing happened quickly. The odds of getting a large payment approved before the tuition due date or even before the fall semester started would be near zero if I had every shred of proof anyone could ever want in my hand, and I had nothing.

Eric set his glass on a coaster on my steamer trunk. "St. Sebastian—that's my mom's thing. The public high school has a better basketball team. But I still want the truth to come out about my dad."

"So do I," I said. "But your mom's right—she wants you to have a good education, and your dad did, too."

His attitude wasn't much different from what mine had been at his age. I'd cared only about getting more experience as an actor and singer and getting parts, not academic credentials.

Fortunately Gram had been determined. Despite working full time, she'd prodded my mother to be sure my high school self-directed study didn't only allow me to pursue acting but put me in a good position to take the SAT and impress college admissions advisors.

"How are you otherwise?" I said.

His drawn appearance worried me. I'd read that children whose parents commit suicide have a four times higher rate of suicide than other young people.

Eric shrugged, his bony shoulders hitching up and down. "Still alive."

"Still going to practice?"

His basketball uniform suggested that, but I wanted to be sure.

"Yeah."

I asked about school and his friends. Eric answered, meeting my eyes, but he didn't sound enthusiastic. My friends probably thought the same about me.

"You're sleeping and eating?"

"Trying," he said, but his entire face, from drooping eyelids to sunken cheeks to downturned mouth said it wasn't going well.

I sipped my water, my questions reminding me of my own resolve to take better care of myself. "When's the last time you had fun?"

Eric frowned. "When's the last time you did?"

"The last time I saw your dad," I said. There was no reason to lie to him. "But let's make a deal. More than anything your dad would want to be sure you're okay. So once a week, you and I will each make sure to do something we used to enjoy, either together or separately, and we'll tell each other about it. Not something we need to do for work or school or practice, but something just for fun."

"Like what?"

I thought for a moment. The idea of fun felt wrong with Marco dead, but I couldn't let his son sink into depression, and I couldn't expect him to make an effort if I didn't.

"I like movies. Maybe I'll go to a movie with one of my friends. Get an ice cream cone. You could come with."

Marco had loved soft serve vanilla cones. I didn't want to go get one without him, but if it'd encourage Eric I would.

"Not into movies." He slumped into the sofa. "I don't know what I'd do."

"Make something up," I said.

It was Gram's answer when I'd been a kid and said I was bored and didn't know what to do with myself.

He glared at me, much as I had with Gram.

"What's something you liked when you were ten?" I said.

I wasn't sure about boys, but for me that had been a pretty optimum age for fun. I'd climbed trees, played hopscotch, and occasionally gone camping with my dad.

"Skateboard," he said after a minute.

"Good. There's a skate park by Roosevelt Road. Or I'm sure

there's one nearer to you. We'll get you a skateboard if you don't still have one."

I had no idea how much they cost. I'd simply need to add it to my growing credit card bill.

"I've still got one. Let's try Roosevelt. I never went there with my dad, so it won't feel so weird without him."

I hadn't expected him to invite me to come with, and I was glad he did. We agreed to meet Sunday to buy ice cream cones and check out the skate park.

Neither of us was turning cartwheels, but it was a plan.

"Aside from the tuition, things okay money-wise?" I said.

I might be overstepping by asking, but if Eric had deeper money worries, I at least wanted to be aware. I knew Mirabel had stayed home for many years while Marco had been a surgeon. She'd gone back to work in medical records when they'd divorced, but Marco had mentioned it had been difficult for her to get a position.

The technology had changed, and she'd faced competition from newly minted college graduates willing to work for less money. She'd been a manager at a university hospital records department when she'd met him. She started over in a more clerical position at a small immediate care facility.

"We're okay," Eric said. "Insurance is going to pay her, just not me."

I stopped in the middle of taking another drink of water. I lowered the glass to the steamer trunk. "Pay her?"

"Yeah. My dad's company had some other type of life insurance. She got that. So we'll be fine."

My stomach tightened. "How do you know?"

"At my dad's funeral lunch, she and her friend from work were talking about it."

That was before Mirabel had called me in a panic about the life insurance for Eric. She hadn't said anything about a policy naming her, but if it was likely to pay without any hitch I guessed she wouldn't have. Being a group policy through Marco's work, it might not include a suicide clause the way Marco's personal policy did.

I wondered if Marco might have been planning to change the beneficiary on the policy paying Mirabel and whether the police knew it existed when they ruled her out.

And I couldn't help thinking about Danielle's point that the most likely suspect in a death is always the spouse. Or ex-spouse, as the case may be.

36

I called Mirabel in the taxi on the way to the cocktail party. I could walk in high heels, but not two-and-a-half miles, the distance to Barry Calvin's condo. Plus this was my one and only pair of shoes with a price tag equal to half a mortgage payment. I wasn't about to wear them out in one evening.

A flattened cardboard tree air freshener hung from the driver's rear view mirror. Its spearmint odor was overpowering, but it wasn't the worst smell I'd encountered in a cab.

"It's a $5,000 policy," Mirabel said. "I can cover the mortgage for the next two months. That's it."

"Oh."

The cab turned off Michigan Avenue and down Pearson Street, a tree-lined street with a large park on one side and stately brick buildings on the other.

"You need to let this go," Mirabel said. "You're only upsetting Eric."

"He wants to know the truth."

The cab had stopped in front of the private residence side of the Ritz Carlton, a soaring forty-story building with scores of windows and private terraces.

I handed a ten and a five to the driver and got out. I'd tipped nearly thirty percent, but it was too hard to juggle my phone and evening bag, which didn't have a shoulder strap, so I didn't want any singles back.

"The police found the truth," Mirabel said.

Her sudden lack of interest in pursuing the life insurance when before she'd been so adamant made me suspicious.

"And Eric's tuition?" I pushed through the revolving door, not wanting to stand on the sidewalk talking. It's like putting on a cab light for muggers. "You were so worried about it."

"I lost my mind a little," she said. "I was angry. But it is what it is. Marco dropped the ball, and I shouldn't have expected anything else."

I wanted to argue with her, but my questions about how Marco had handled money had grown, and he might very well have been much worse when he'd been married to her.

Also, the doorman was shooting me dagger eyes, apparently not happy with an unknown person, however well dressed, chatting in his lobby.

I told Mirabel I'd like to talk more later. She was non-committal.

The doorman checked my ID and walked me to the elevator so he could put in the key that would allow me to go to the thirty-sixth floor.

The gleaming hardwood on the first level of Barry Calvin's condominium extended through an almost entirely open floor plan. It was a corner unit, with floor-to-ceiling windows on both outside walls.

Sleek Art Deco couches and chairs stood near a fireplace at one end, built-in bookshelves, armchairs, and reading tables at the other. A long polished dining table with narrow legs stood along a long inner wall. French doors beyond it revealed a black-and-white tiled kitchen with a marble-topped kitchen island and Sub-zero appliances.

I love seeing how people decorate their homes.

It's the scenery they've chosen for their lives, and tells as much about them as sets in a play convey about the characters who inhabit them. I wished I could climb the curving Lucite staircase to see the second floor of Barry Calvin's home. But that wasn't what I was here for, and it would be rude.

I counted thirty or forty people standing throughout the vast main room when I arrived, most of them men in expertly tailored suits. For whatever reason, the personal injury field draws a lot of men. Or at least the most well known and ostentatiously successful ones seem to be male.

It would make it easy to break into conversations. One advantage of being a reasonably attractive young woman in a room full of older men is they generally turn toward you as soon as you approach.

The downside was that I was conspicuous, though there were a few other women there. One matched the photo I'd seen of Tabacchi's wife. She was plump and pretty and twenty years younger than her husband. She wore a navy blue skirt suit with a string of small pearls around her neck. The Tabacchis' son, a college student who had the physique of a football player, was by far the youngest person there and the only one wearing jeans and a polo shirt.

It also was a mostly white crowd. The only black men were Larry Rogers, a prominent P.I. attorney, and the bartender. I saw no black women, and a few Asian women and men.

From his campaign website, I'd learned Tabacchi was a lawyer, too, though he didn't practice anymore. When he had, he'd had a general practice.

That type of practice—doing a little of this and a little of that—is unusual in Chicago. It's tough to stay current on changes in multiple areas of law, and it's easier to bring in business in any large city if you target particular types of clients or cases rather than everyone and everything.

But Tabacchi's wife was an executive in her family's hotel chain, so once they'd married maybe he hadn't really needed to work and preferred to do whatever suited him at the moment.

He'd served as an alderman for over a decade, but had been redistricted out of his ward. At first it had looked like he'd run again, but a lot of voters were angry over his stance, or lack of one, on a controversial development plan. He'd dropped out of politics until now.

After hanging my wool peacoat in one of the temporary coat racks near the door, I hovered near the bookcases, pretending to study the view. It was stunning and included a stretch of Lake Michigan. From the corner of my eye I watched Ed Tabacchi.

When he detached himself from the three men he was talking to, I stepped into his path and held out my hand. "Q. Catherine Davis, Mr. Tabacchi. It's so nice to meet you in person."

I lowered my voice on the Q and emphasized my middle name as a way of being a little less recognizable on the off chance his conversation with Marco had veered into the personal.

I wanted to take him by surprise if possible. My name was in the guest list, as the law requires you to list your name and profession when you donate over $250 to a politician, but I doubted he'd combed through his list personally.

Ed shook with his right hand as he covered both our hands with his left in one of those weird politician handshakes. His florid face had more wrinkles around the mouth than his website photo, and his hair had thinned and grayed since it had been taken.

The press pictures I'd seen also hadn't conveyed his height and bulk. I'm a little taller than average for a woman and I was wearing two-inch heels, yet he towered over me.

"Pleased to meet you, Catherine." Tabacchi's voice matched

his physique, booming so loud that I stepped back a fraction. He had more than a trace of the South Side accent you hear whenever a comedian parodies Chicagoans.

"I was so sorry I missed your fundraiser at Dede Zith's," I said.

His expression of mild interest and joy at meeting a new potential donor remained solidly in place, which was telling in itself. People's expressions usually change, at least minutely, when they hear the name of someone else they know. It's a quick involuntary reaction that reflects their feelings for the person.

But I might be reading too much into it. Perhaps it was simply the politician's polished control of his emotions rather than a sign Tabacchi was hiding anything.

"You live in Dede's building? She's a great gal."

I blinked. I didn't think I'd heard a man refer to a woman as a gal since my grandfather died. According to an article I'd read, Ed Tabacchi was in his late sixties. That made him older than me by more than three decades, but nowhere near Gram's age, so in my view he had no excuse. Though "gal" was hardly the worst name a man could call a woman.

"I don't live in her building," I said. "I met her through a friend."

"Where do you live? Illinois I hope?"

His laugh sounded too practiced to my actor's ear, though it was a close call. Laughter is hard to fake, maybe because it's an expression that's triggered in an instant and is hard to purposely evoke in yourself in real life.

When I'd been acting, it had been my least favorite thing to do on stage. I'd have rather done a death scene every night than laugh.

"Printers Row," I said.

"Oh, good, good, nice area. Lots of building happening near there."

That was true, but I wondered what pat phrase he'd trot out if I named one of Chicago's low-income areas. But then I wouldn't be at the fundraiser.

"Did you hear about Dede's neighbor, the man who died in mid-April?"

He frowned. "I don't believe I did. That's terrible."

"Marco Ruggirello. He chatted with you at the event. I thought you might remember him."

He shook his head. "Doesn't ring a bell. Someone you knew?"

His eyes shifted, peering over my shoulder, eager to glad hand the next potential donor or to get away from me or both.

I inched sideways to stay squarely in his line of sight. "I knew Marco pretty well. I'm trying to understand what happened. If you could give it a little more thought—did he happen to say anything to you that night about what was happening in his life? Something that worried him maybe?"

I didn't want to mention possible permit questions, as Tabacchi might say yes simply to end the conversation.

He patted my arm and shifted his weight to his front foot, ready to move on. "I'm sorry. You have my sympathy, but I don't remember speaking with anyone by that name."

A younger man in a gray suit and striped mauve and blue tie drifted over, ready to extricate the candidate.

"Maybe if you saw a picture." I unclasped my evening bag and withdrew my phone. I'd locked it onto a photo of Marco. I thrust it toward Tabacchi. "He might have been concerned about some issues with a building he owned."

Tabacchi's lips pressed together, and I felt sure he wanted to refuse, but he took the phone and stared at the photo. "I'm sorry, Catherine, I don't remember him."

He again had that entirely blank expression that raised flags for me. Still, he might only be covering annoyance or fear that I was some sort of obsessed stalker type.

"Thank you anyway, Edward."

I used his first name because it irks me when politicians and salespeople say my name as if it'll fool me into thinking they're my friends.

Feeling let down and a little on edge at the same time, I drifted to the makeshift bar, a long table set up at the far end of the room under an oil painting. I didn't know what I'd expected.

Edward Tabacchi was an actively-campaigning politician. He must meet a hundred people a week. The odds of him remembering Marco if he had no connection with his death were small, even if Marco had asked about permits. People must ask former aldermen about trash collection, potholes, traffic, zoning, and all kinds of issues all the time, just as Marco still got asked health questions and people thought I could answer everything from whether a real estate contract was proper to whether they should sue their neighbor.

And if Tabacchi had done something nefarious, his years of practice as a politician no doubt prepared him as well as my acting had for pretending everything was fine.

I sighed, put two singles in the tip jar, and asked for a Pinot Noir. There was no whiskey on display, but I might as well get some alcohol for my five hundred dollars. Then I'd circulate and see if I could learn anything personal about the candidate.

The bartender poured the wine to the brim. I introduced myself, and he said his name was Ikenna. His resonant voice and perfect posture made me think he might be in theater. Chicago wasn't like Los Angeles, where the majority of service jobs are filled by aspiring actors, but I had met quite a few.

I asked if he worked a lot of parties for Barry Calvin.

He nodded. "For him and others at his firm."

"Side job?" I said.

"Indeed," he said.

It turned out he was an actor, mostly storefront, and we got talking about the Chicago theater scene.

After a while I returned to fact-finding mode. "Does Calvin host a lot of political fundraisers?"

"Oh, yes," Ikenna said. "He's a party bigwig. Plans to be a judge eventually."

"Nice job if you can get it," I said. "I'm a little surprised he's stumping for a Comptroller, though. Seems like an unglamorous position."

"Not at all," Ikenna said. "Judy Barr ran for governor."

I drank a little more wine. "True."

I'd forgotten about Judy Barr Topinka. She'd been the Illinois Comptroller and had run for governor against Rod Blagojevich, who'd later become the fourth Illinois governor to go to prison. My grandmother, a staunch Democrat all her life, had nonetheless loved Judy Barr. When Blagojevich was sentenced, she'd said, "Serves the people of this state right. Judy Barr wouldn't be going to prison."

I shared this story with Ikenna. He laughed and said his aunt, who'd emigrated to the U.S. decades before Ikenna's birth and sponsored his entry to the country, had said the same thing.

Before I left, he gave me a flyer for an upcoming show, and I promised to check it out. I figured Joe might want to go with me. He still enjoyed plays, and his girlfriend wasn't really a fan.

I circulated for half an hour, chatting with other donors, but I didn't learn anything significant. My phone rang on my way out of the marble lobby.

It was Kassie Frampton, the Hazleton Insurance employee who'd been fired. She was willing to meet with me.

37

Once again I stared at my closet deciding how best to dress the part.

Linked In showed Kassie Frampton had worked for over a dozen corporations before Hazleton Insurance, always for less than two years at a time. Her age was probably early sixties based on her photo and experience. She rarely stepped up the ladder to the next position, and there were significant gaps in her resume. All of which suggested she'd been let go or quit more than once under iffy circumstances, leaving her in a bad spot to negotiate for her next job.

For her, I decided I needed to thread the needle between successful enough that she'd take me seriously and looking like enough of an upstart that she wouldn't associate me with anyone who'd fired her.

Fortunately, despite Gram's criticisms of it, my business wardrobe offered lots of options. I'd created a sort of uniform when I moved into the professional world to help me feel less intimidated by the new environment. Also, I wanted the streamlined, default clothing choices men have that minimize time spent getting dressed and ensure fitting in, though I mix and match a bit more.

For formal meetings or court, I wear skirt suits or pantsuits in strong but neutral colors, varying solids with pin-stripes or subtle patterns. Also like men, I switch to blazers when things are a little less formal.

For business casual, now that I run my own firm and have flexibility, rather than men's khakis and Polo shirts I pair the same fitted short and long-sleeved Ts and tank tops I wear underneath blazers and suits with jeans. I add color with the occasional jewel-toned T (rather than my more typical white, gray, and black) or with jewelry and/or brightly-colored accessories.

Oddly, I feel most like myself when I dress for meetings with business clients in jeans, a blazer, and a charcoal or white tank top because I feel the least like I'm wearing a costume.

For the theater clients whose taxes I do, I often feel like I'm dressing to look like an actor or artist, which reminds me too much of when I was a kid. Back then, I thought if I dressed and behaved like the original Q.C. my mom would attend my plays and concerts and brag to my aunts and uncles about me. It took me until college to realize that would never work.

I could never match the memory of Q.C., and my mother would never be the mom she'd been to that little girl. That woman had died with her daughter. The person who visited Q.C.'s grave once a week didn't have a lot left in her heart for those of us who were left.

A buzz from the timer on my phone pulled me back to the present. Lauren was using her car today, so I needed to pick up a Zipcar in fifteen minutes.

I started with the easiest piece of my outfit, a Coach handbag with the trademark Cs all over it.

That bag is my least favorite. I work too hard for my money to spend it on a product that advertises someone else's brand in giant letters. But I'd found a lot of solo entrepreneurs and middle class clients who know nothing else about designers know Coach and think it's a solid brand worth paying extra for. Which means it says success but not so much success they're afraid I'm charging them too much. I hoped it would hit the same balance with Kassie Frampton.

For clothes, I picked a basic outfit of blue jeans with narrow legs, a white tank top, and a black blazer. I tossed a variety of jewelry into the bag.

The drive to Blue Island took about half an hour due to the light Saturday morning traffic heading south. I spotted Kassie through the window as I pulled into the lot at Peet's Coffee, though it took me a few minutes to be sure it was her.

In her Linked In photo, the only one I'd found of her online, she'd looked professional and had mixed brown and gray hair. Now she wore an Army green vest and jeans and her hair blared bright pinkish-red, a shade that clearly wasn't meant to appear natural. Tattoos ran up and down her arms.

Before getting out of the car, I slipped off my blazer.

The white cotton tank top underneath created a more casual look and showed my single tattoo, a measure of sheet music with two quarter notes and one half.

From my bag, I added a pewter thumb ring with an amber stone and a few bangle bracelets. Those went with Marco's citrine ring that I still wore but didn't overdo it. I still wanted to look like a lawyer, but one who was off-duty.

Peet's smelled like dark roasted coffee and chocolate. I got a Jade Green Tea Latte. The green tea was part of my way to ease out caffeine, though I didn't like the flavor as much as black tea. I bought Kassie a second Almond Cold Brew Fog Latte plus a cinnamon apple muffin.

She broke the muffin into pieces. "I don't see how I can help you. I don't work at Hazleton anymore. And the police already talked to me."

"What about?" I said.

"Where I was when Marco died." She rolled her eyes. "As if I'd kill him because he threatened to fire me. Please."

"He threatened to fire you?" I said.

I would have thought he'd have mentioned it, as it had to be upsetting to him.

"He didn't *say* he'd fire me. He said I needed to work on organization and follow through, and everyone else got gold stars. It was the third time he said that in writing, so I could see where it was going. Which is always how it goes. People nit-pick, nit-pick, and then you get fired."

"The law firm I was at was kind of like that," I said. "Vague comments, then they would refuse to promote someone."

I was exaggerating to relate to Kassie, but it was true that no one got an unqualified good review.

There were bad reviews, which meant you were on the way out, or good ones, but those always included a little back-tracking or questioning. A sentence might say "strong client relationships, but unclear whether that'll be true with a wider range of businesses." That way if you were ever considered for partner and someone didn't want you for political reasons, there was an out.

"But you beat them at their own game." Kassie grinned. "Started your own firm."

"I did," I said, though I'd never thought of starting my own practice as "beating" anyone. The firm had been a pretty good place to work, I just didn't like being an employee. I'd been drawn to both accounting and law because they were profes-sions where you could work for yourself and have more control over your career than actors typically do.

"Right on," she said.

"So the police thought you might have held the so-so reviews against Marco?"

Kassie shrugged. It made the eagle on her upper left arm

flap its wings. "Who knows? They said they were ruling out possibilities, and someone told them I didn't like Marco."

"Was that true? I don't mind if it is, not everyone liked him."

I actually couldn't think of anyone who hadn't liked Marco other than Mirabel, but statistically that had to be true.

"To be honest, he wasn't as bad as my last supervisor at Hazleton." Kassie finished the muffin and folded its paper wrapper into a tiny tight square.

Emphasizing how honest or open you are is a little like telling people how smart you are. If you really felt you were, you wouldn't need to say it, so I guessed she had disliked Marco.

"Can you tell me what you worked on with him?" I said. "His boss was pretty close-mouthed."

"Sounds like Bob. He loved to act like we were all cloak and dagger. All I ever did was make phone calls and type data into the computer. It was as boring as when I was a regular adjuster."

"You didn't like that job?" I said.

"All customers did was whine." She blew air out of her mouth in an expression of disgust. "'My car's so special, I took care of it, it's worth more than other cars its age.' Everyone says that. *Everyone.* All the used cars in the world can't be better than the others cars, yet every single owner thinks theirs is. Every single one."

Marco had told me expressing empathy was a big part of an insurance claims adjuster's job, and other departments sometimes shunted those with bad people skills to SIU positions on the theory that a more abrasive personality made for a better investigator. He disagreed, but he hadn't been there long enough for his view to carry any weight.

It sounded like Kassie had been one of the shunted.

The whir of a cappuccino machine filled the air for a few minutes. When it stopped, I asked more about her conversations with the police. She described Detective Beckwell to a T, so I felt pretty sure they'd really checked into her.

If she was in the clear, the best way she could help was to tell me about Vujic Chiropractic. I planned to approach Cora Smith or Dr. Vujic or both in person, but I wanted more background first. I asked Kassie if she'd had anything to do with the investigation.

"Oh, yeah. I wanted to be a fake patient, but Marco said we already knew it was a real clinic and he'd toured it and seen all the equipment. So instead I just got yelled at on the phone by the billing person there. Corrine somebody."

"Cora Smith?"

"Yeah, her. That place was scamming left and right if you ask me, but no one did. That's what happens when you get over sixty. No one listens. No one sees you. You become invisible."

I wondered if my grandmother would agree. She was over seventy and still managed the books for the lighting store she'd worked at for the last thirty years. She'd never complained about other employees not paying attention to her. Then again, I couldn't imagine anyone not listening to Gram.

I set my latte to one side and rested my arms on the table. "Why did you think Vujic Clinic was scamming?"

If I were lucky, her answer would give me something concrete to use to confront Cora Smith, Dr. Vujic, or former employees.

"Every bill, it was $1 higher than our upper limit of what we pay. *Every* bill. That's no accident."

My shoulders dropped. Not a very dramatic answer.

"They couldn't just have set their prices a bit high?" I said.

"By exactly $1 each time? No way. They got ahold of what we pay and jiggered their charges so they could make a little extra on each bill because they knew we'd look bad to patients if we cut off a dollar."

I wasn't so sure of that. If my health insurer paid all but a dollar of each bill, I'd kiss the claims adjuster.

"Did you ever talk to anyone there who called himself Dr. X?"

The investigator in my office suite had determined that whoever it was who'd slammed the clinic on the review site had used a sock puppet account. He hadn't been able to identify the person, but he'd given me a list of current and past Vujic employees that went back five years.

I'd paid for the service out of my own pocket. It wasn't really in my budget, but unless the information actually led to the insurance policy paying two million dollars I wasn't about to charge the estate.

None of the employees' names included the letter X.

Kassie shook her head and a few pink strands fell onto one shoulder of her jacket. "The only doctor there was Victoria Vujic."

"It could be a nickname. Maybe a patient mentioned someone called Dr. X?"

I was reaching. Dr. X probably had chosen a screen name no one would recognize, but I had to ask.

"Most people don't remember their therapists' names. Sometimes we ask what the person looked like or wore. You know, so we can try to piece together if it's really a therapist giving the treatment."

Marco had told me that one way clinics could scam was to have someone with a lower level of training or qualifications perform a service but bill as if someone more qualified had done it. So if a physical therapist called in sick, an assistant might fill in but bill the insurance company as if the therapist had done the work.

"Wouldn't everyone wear the same thing? Some sort of uniform?"

"Not always," Kassie said. "Some clinics are more casual. So the therapist might be required to wear sweatpants and a black T-shirt but the shirt could be any brand or it could have a movie name or school name or something on it."

That gave me an idea. I doubted anyone walked around wearing a T-shirt with a giant red X, but some of Marco's University of Chicago shirts said U of C. It was worth seeing if any of the Vujic employees had gone to a school with a name starting with X.

What was left of my latte had grown cold. The tables around us were filling and the smells of bacon and quiche mixed with the dark roasted coffee scents as it neared lunchtime.

I glanced at the notes I'd made on my phone.

"Did you confront anyone at the clinic?" I said. "About the high bills?"

"Nope. Supposedly Marco was going to, but in the meantime, we didn't pay. That's why I got yelled at. Cora, Corrinne, whatever, she would call and scream at me." Kassie pointed her finger at her own chest. "Plus she hated me. She liked Marco, but she hated me."

I had my doubts about Cora liking Marco given that when I'd called she'd immediately referred to him as an asshole. But I wanted to hear Kassie's thoughts, not share my own.

"So Cora was nice to Marco?"

"Not nice," Kassie said. "She cussed him out, too, just not as often as the rest of us. And she threatened him."

"What did she say?"

Kassie smiled. "He better hope she didn't run into him in a dark alley. I kind of liked her for that, you know?"

So much for Kassie not being angry at Marco.

38

THAT WAS TWO PEOPLE AT HAZLETON, JERRY AND KASSIE, WHO'D heard Cora Smith threaten Marco, which put the clinic next on my list. I decided to drive there Monday rather than calling again. You can't hang up on someone in person.

After skateboarding with Eric on Sunday—or rather, sitting and answering email on my phone while he skateboarded and taking him for ice cream afterwards—I stopped at Café des Livres.

Carole was setting a fresh plate of Madeleines in the glass display case as I walked in.

She swooped out from behind the counter and handed me one of the shell-shaped cake-like cookies on a small square of wax paper. It felt warm.

"Olive oil and sea salt," she said. "New flavor. You'll be the first."

A moment ago I would have said I wasn't hungry, but the mixed savory and sweet scent gave me an appetite. For the first time since entering Marco's apartment that night, I felt like eating something.

It was as good as it smelled. I ordered two plus a dark hot

cocoa. I figured that amounted to enough calories to qualify as dinner.

There was no wind and all day the sun had warmed the streets and sidewalks. I sat outside, my lightweight leather jacket enough to keep me warm.

The café's WiFi signal is strong and Carole had long ago given me the secure password. As I sipped rich, semi-bitter chocolate I read more patient reviews of Vujic Clinic and ran searches on Dr. Victoria Vujic and her clinic in the Illinois Secretary of State website, including the professional regulation section. I also looked at her Linked In Profile.

A few cabs and cars drove down Dearborn Street, and some bikes whizzed by in the bike lane, but mostly it was quiet. Not many people are going to and fro so close to downtown on Sundays.

Vujic Clinic had been around for six years. Before that, Dr. Vujic had practiced for three years with another chiropractor. She'd attended Palmer College of Chiropractic twelve years after graduating college with a Bachelor of Science.

My research gave no hint at what she'd done in between, but the gap didn't strike me as all that strange. I'd started law school two years after finishing college because I'd worked as an accountant during that time. Dr. Vujic could have had another career or taken time off to raise children or traveled the world for all I knew.

Still, I included that in my list of questions for her.

————

In the morning, I put on jeans, a light gray tank top, and a navy blazer. I spent the morning finishing and e-filing a motion and brief in federal court.

I longed to drive straight to the clinic after that, but the stack of client files on the credenza stared at me reproachfully. I sent my cell phone and landline to voicemail, shut off email alerts, and reviewed an expert report in a case where a sister was suing a brother over the management of a heating and air conditioning business the two had inherited. Disputes between business partners can be worse than divorces, and when they involved family, it quadrupled the emotions involved.

By mid-afternoon, my head ached from bending over my desk, but I'd finished.

Two Advil and ten minutes later I was enjoying the smooth acceleration of Lauren's Volvo as Ida B. Wells Drive morphed into the Eisenhower Expressway. I didn't often miss having a car, but every now and then it was nice to surge forward surrounded by a vehicle. Especially one that handled well and didn't shake or rattle, as had the last car I'd owned—a beloved twenty-year-old Cutlass that had seen me through two years of community college.

Ignoring the GPS, when traffic slowed to a crawl I exited at First Avenue and headed north for a more scenic route. Vujic Clinic stood in a strip mall not far from a small theater I'd often worked at in Elmwood Park, so I was pretty familiar with the area.

As I drove under overhanging tree branches and past a wooded forest preserve, I felt my breathing slow.

Much as I loved it, it felt good to get out of the city now and then. I also loved pulling straight into a parking spot. It was so unlike city garages, which are measured to the inch and are as small as city codes allow.

In the waiting area two water coolers, one filled with pineapple chunks and the other with cucumber slices, sat on a teak credenza near long, comfortable couches. The air smelled of eucalyptus and peppermint. The whole place reminded me more of a spa than a clinic, which was great marketing. No one looks forward to a visit to a doctor, but a spa is a treat.

A woman wearing yoga pants and a long T-shirt sat in an

armchair thumbing through a magazine featuring a collie on the cover. Otherwise, the area was empty, which confirmed the Yelp comments that they got patients in and out on time. It was fifteen minutes to closing.

I approached the counter. A young woman with long, oval-shaped fingernails finished typing and looked up.

"I'd like to speak to Cora Smith," I said.

I hadn't made an appointment, figuring the element of surprise was better, but had verified over the phone that both Cora and Dr. Vujic were in that day.

"Is she expecting you?" the receptionist said.

"She's not, but I'd really appreciate it if you'd get her. It's about Hazleton Insurance."

I figured that would get a response, and I was right. She disappeared through a louvered door. A muscular woman with a sharp chin emerged a few minutes later.

"What's this about?" she said. I recognized the raspy voice from the phone.

"I need to talk to you—and Dr. Vujic—about Marco Ruggirello. We spoke before on the phone. I'm the executor of his estate. I was also his girlfriend."

Cora's shoulders stiffened. She glanced toward the woman in the yoga pants and stifled a frown. It left her mouth in an odd sort of grimace with teeth showing below the flat line of her upper lip. "Sorry for your loss, but he was no friend of ours."

"I got the impression you got on all right with him personally," I said, "and that it was Hazleton—"

She thrust out her hand, palm forward, long, thick fingers rigid as if resisting the urge to turn the Stop gesture into a fist. "Come back when we're closed, if you want to talk about them."

The patient was watching, her magazine forgotten. She swiveled her head from Cora to me as we spoke.

"I'll wait." I turned to sit down on one of the couches.

"Not here," Cora said. "We need a peaceful waiting room."

"I won't disturb anything," I said.

She glared at me. "You, here, it's disturbing."

It was on the tip of my tongue to say, "Thanks for the sympathy."

I understood Cora didn't like Hazleton, but what kind of person refused to muster a little genuine sympathy for another human who'd lost a loved one?

Still, I bit back the sarcastic comment. It wouldn't make her more likely to talk later. Also, she was the gatekeeper to the doctor.

"Back in fifteen," I said.

39

Outside, I moved a few feet away from the glass doors to a spot where I couldn't be seen from inside. I gripped my shoulder bag against my body, longing for a whiskey sour. I imagined its sweet and tart flavors on my tongue, my tense shoulders dropping, and a pleasant numbness spreading through me.

But I wasn't about to leave for a bar, or risk driving after drinking.

Instead I opened an app and looked at soothing sunset photos a friend on vacation in Aruba had posted for ten minutes, then I went back in. I was afraid if I waited longer Cora would lock the doors on me.

The waiting room stood empty. The receptionist was gone, and Cora sat at the desk, scrolling through something on the computer. Music with chimes and bells played, and the air still smelled of eucalyptus plant, but I felt anything but relaxed.

"Dr. Vujic's finishing with a patient. It'll be at least another half hour." Cora spoke without looking up.

"I'm in no hurry," I said, which was true. If I left before seven to return downtown, I'd sit in traffic for an hour and a half. If I waited until after eight, I could cruise back in thirty minutes. "But I'd like to talk with you, too."

She kept typing.

I rested my elbows on the counter.

"I'm trying to sort through some life insurance issues." Despite Cora's hostility, or maybe because of it, I'd decided I might as well be candid. Nothing I told her was going to make her more willing to talk, so I might as well make the conversation less complicated and simply say what I wanted. "They don't want to pay."

Cora's fingers kept moving on the keyboard, but her lips stretched into a rubbery looking half-smile. "Not so fun when the shoe's on the other foot."

I leaned in, forearms on the counter now, encroaching a little more on her space. Usually I take a laid back approach to questioning to put people at ease so they'll talk more. But with bullies, you need to get in their faces.

"There's nothing fun about any of this. You don't like Marco. I get that. But this won't hurt him, and it won't hurt me, it'll hurt his son. He's thirteen, and he just lost his dad, and now the policy Marco got to protect him might not do that."

Cora stopped typing and peered at me over her monitor screen. "Sorry about that. I have a son, too. But what's any of it got to do with us?"

"Did you ever meet Marco in person?"

She hit a key and nudged the keyboard a fraction of an inch to the side. "Twice. He came here for a site visit. Said he'd set things right, but he didn't."

"The other investigators seemed to think you preferred dealing with Marco over them."

Her chin jerked. "Sure, the way you prefer a gnat to a mosquito. They're both pests, but at least the gnat doesn't bite you."

I wasn't sure what to make of that comparison.

"So Marco was less annoying because ...?"

"At least he didn't accuse us of fraud. Not like that bitch Kassie Frampton."

That helped explain why Kassie had been fired. I was pretty sure investigators weren't supposed to accuse people of fraud unless or until they could prove it.

"How about Dr. Vujic?" I said. "What did she think of the people at Hazleton?"

"She put up with way too much. Only got mad when they started questioning our patients. Then she finally let Marco have it, told him what he could do with his investigation."

I opened the calendar app with the Marco timeline on my phone. "How long ago was that?"

"No idea."

"More than a month ago?" I said.

"No. Less."

"More than two weeks?"

Cora shrugged. "Maybe. But what's this got to do with life insurance?"

It was May 3 now, which made the conversation the first week or two of April, so possibly right before Marco's death. Maybe the threats both Jerry and Kassie said Cora had made hadn't been just talk.

"The insurer thinks he committed suicide. I'm trying to understand what he might have been dealing with around that time."

I kept my eyes on the phone as I spoke.

There shouldn't be any stigma around suicide, but there is, and I hated that it might make Cora think less of Marco than she already did. But finding out what happened was more important, and it was the only thing I could think of that explained my questions. I couldn't tell her I thought he'd been murdered and I wanted to know if she or Dr. Vujic did it.

"Really?" Her eyebrows, both heavy and dark, rose. "He seemed happy enough. He never yelled back at me."

"Did he ever yell at Dr. Vujic?"

"Doubt it. He acted like he understood her position."

"Maybe he did," I said.

She shook her head. "No way. He was pretending. He used to spout some bullshit about how they had a lot in common."

I tapped my fingers on the counter. Someone else had told me something like it, though I couldn't think who. "Because he used to be a doctor?"

She shrugged. "Did he? Maybe that was it. I just thought it was crap."

I asked a few more questions, but Cora refused to talk further, saying she had work to finish.

Twenty minutes later she took me to a small square conference room with a polished round table and a view of the parking lot. I'd hoped to get a glimpse of other employees or the treatment rooms, but the doors on either side of the hall Cora walked me through were shut.

Dr. Victoria Vujic, who told me to call her Victoria, stepped in a few minutes after I sat down. She wore a white lab coat and narrow-legged dress pants.

Diamond studs sparkled in her earlobes. Her lipstick was a bright red that complemented her fair skin. Faint, almost unnoticeable lines around her eyes and mouth suggested she might be a decade or more older than me.

"I was so sorry to hear about Marco." She sat in the chair across from me. Music played in the background, mostly percussion, chimes, and what sounded like a mandolin. "We had our disagreements, but he seemed like a good man."

"I'm not sure Cora agrees with you," I said.

"She's been with me a long time. She's very protective. Like a bull dog."

I might have said pit bull, but I opted not to volunteer that.

Instead, I said, "More than one person told me Cora threatened Marco."

"She can get overexcited," Victoria said. "But she'd never hurt anyone."

I felt less sure about that.

"I understand Marco was heading an investigation of your clinic over issues with billing or treatment?"

Victoria sat with her forearms on the table in front of her. Both hands flashed diamond rings, making me think of Dr. X's complaints about her ostentatious wealth. "Yes."

"That had to be upsetting."

"It was. They never told us exactly what the problem was. They thought my bills were high. Well, they are. I provide in depth attention to each patient. And I spend a lot on décor— and equipment—to have the right environment. I resent the implication that I'm trying to bilk patients out of money."

"Wasn't there an issue about treatments too?"

She waved her hand. "That's nothing. One of our elderly clients got confused about what his treatments were called. We got it straightened out."

Either the Hazleton people or Victoria were skewing the facts. Or both were.

"I suppose the police asked you and Cora where you were the night of Marco's death?"

Victoria nodded. "They did. Cora worked late that night. We were behind in the bookkeeping, and I needed to go over everything for taxes. I went home around seven for dinner and stayed in for the evening. Cora stayed until eleven. We emailed back and forth dozens of times."

Staying at home all evening wasn't really an alibi and neither was working late if Cora had been alone, and Victoria confirmed she had been. I'm no IT expert, but it didn't seem like it'd be that hard to make emails to appear to be sent from a different computer or at a different time.

Motive was tougher.

If Marco had been murdered, it hadn't been in the heat of the moment. Whoever had done it would have needed to get the liquor and prescription ahead of time. The dispute between Marco and the clinic didn't help on that front. There was no reason to think Hazleton Insurance would change its approach to the clinic if Marco were gone. In fact, from what everyone had told me, the whole thing might become a lot more vicious.

I asked about the clinic staff. Victoria told me she, Cora, and the receptionist ran the office. Treatment was provided by Victoria or one of three physical therapists, plus she employed two physical therapy assistants.

I scrolled through my phone as if looking for a note, though I knew exactly what I wanted to ask. "I understand you recently let an employee go, someone who was unhappy here?"

I was fishing, guessing what the story might be regarding the hypercritical Dr. X.

Her body stiffened. "Who told you that?"

"I'd rather not say," I said. "I try to keep what people tell me confidential whenever I can."

She fiddled with one of her earrings. "We had a therapist leave a couple months ago. No drama, though. He quit for a better offer at another clinic."

She refused to give me his name, saying it had nothing to do with Marco and she was only answering any questions at all because she felt sorry for Marco's son.

"I know," I said, "and I appreciate it. I understand you had a lot in common with Marco, but he never said exactly what."

"He spoke of me?" Victoria's head tilted to one side and her fair skin pinkened, which I found interesting. "I suppose it was that he was once a medical provider, too. He felt it gave him more empathy for the providers he dealt with, and it probably did, though I don't think he ever had to deal directly with insurance companies."

"Did he tell you why he wasn't a doctor anymore?" I asked.

"I understand he was a recovering alcoholic," Victoria said. "I worried for him. He told me he didn't belong to AA or a Caduceus group."

"Caduceus?"

"Like AA for doctors. It's tough to stay sober without a support community."

She might truly be concerned, or she might be throwing that out there to hint that Marco had begun drinking again because he hadn't followed a traditional recovery program.

"Marco told me the success rate of AA is actually no better than for those who go out on their own. "

"I haven't looked into the statistics," Victoria said. "But support matters for any type of health issue."

We talked a while longer.

I learned Victoria had grown up in Vermont and between earning her first bachelor's degree and attending Palmer Chiropractic she'd married, had children, and divorced. Nothing she said made me think she'd harbored a grudge against Marco.

Cora's abrasiveness and protectiveness, on the other hand, raised flags and gave me a little insight into why everyone at Hazleton thought she was hiding something or the clinic was running a scam. Her anger and fear seemed out of proportion if there really was nothing going on.

It was only six-thirty when I left.

I stopped for a chicken enchilada at a nearby Mexican restaurant. As I ate, I tried a mental theater exercise, imagining both Dr. Vujic and Cora as exactly the same in personality and demeanor, but as men. It didn't change my perception of Dr. Vujic.

But Cora...if she were a man, I wasn't sure I'd see her as drastically over the top in abrasiveness or defensiveness.

I'd worked with a partner at the accounting firm who became incensed at minor offenses. People saw him as hot-headed, but no one took it as a sign that he was violent or potentially criminal. Maybe all that was going on was that Cora's personality didn't fit the stereotype of the helpful, and female, administrative person.

Whether I liked either woman, though, or didn't, they hadn't exactly ruled themselves out of being responsible for Marco's death. What I needed was to find Dr. X.

40

THREE COPIES OF MY LETTERS OF OFFICE WITH THE OFFICIAL court seal were in my office when I got back that evening, delivered by the estate attorney. I walked a mile to a Fed Ex that was open late to overnight one of them to Charlene Garfield with a request to review all the books relating to Marco's apartment building. I left her a voicemail telling her it was on the way to try to stave off a claim that it got buried under a stack of mail.

I took a second copy to the bank first thing the next morning where I closed Marco's checking and savings accounts and opened a new account for the estate with the money.

It totaled just under $4,000, part of which would need to pay the estate lawyer.

I looked away from the account representative as she clicked keys and transferred funds, studying the tellers across the room instead. I couldn't believe this was all Marco had, but he hadn't taken part in Hazleton's 401(k) plan, and he'd told no one about any other accounts. It looked like there'd be nothing left for Eric.

Danielle was at her desk when I got back. It was a rare day

when she had no court, so she wore jeans and a V-neck T-shirt, her blazer hanging on the hook behind the door in our office in case a client came by.

She had no ideas about finding the elusive Dr. X, but she suggested if I wanted to learn more about Victoria Vujic I should search state licensing boards in Vermont where she'd grown up and in neighboring states.

"She might've been raising her kids after college," Danielle said, "but maybe she had some other business or profession she doesn't tell people about. Might give you insight into her business practices and what kind of person she is."

Her comment reminded me that Marco had once told me almost no doctors lost their licenses due to errors, including ones that killed someone, but they did lose them for drug issues. Given Victoria Vujic's comment on AA, after searching a few state websites I searched for Federal Drug Enforcement actions.

Results popped up immediately.

Crosschecking with state licensing boards I pieced together a post-college history. After earning her Bachelor of Science, Victoria had gone to medical school, done a residency, and become a medical doctor in Ohio. Two years later, she'd been disciplined for prescribing Dilaudid to two patients "under questionable circumstances." Another year after that she lost her license for prescribing controlled substances "without therapeutic necessity."

I wondered if she'd prescribed for herself and that was why she knew about the Caduceus group.

Either way, chiropractic made sense as a career choice. Chiropractors treat patients, so she could use some of her skills, but they can't prescribe medication, so her past wouldn't keep her from working in the field.

If she'd been an addict that could explain why Marco

empathized with her more than anyone else at Hazleton had, particularly with her attempts to start over.

On the other hand, if anyone would know how to make it look like he'd overdosed, either purposely or accidentally, it would be Dr. Vujic.

41

MOST OF THE REST OF THE DAY I WORKED ON TAX ISSUES FOR TWO of my clients—graphic designers who'd recently bought property together. I finished around six.

Some evenings I heard music or sound effects from Sam Williams' office at the other end of the suite because when the weather was cold or rainy, he stayed late to play online games with some of his friends. But today it was in the low sixties and partly cloudy, good biking weather, so he'd disappeared early in the afternoon, and everyone else was gone.

Since the break in, I didn't like staying in the office alone for more than a few minutes, but I didn't want to go home.

The things I'd once liked to do when I had rare time to myself—reading, binge watching TV series, or practicing my singing—now left too much room for my mind to cycle through an endless round of What Ifs.

Most involved what I might have done differently so that Marco wouldn't have been home alone the night he'd been killed, others imagined how our life would be right now or in the future if he were still here. Unless I occupied my brain with something else, I couldn't stop.

I called Joe to see if he could meet me at the café. He had work to do, but he didn't mind bringing his laptop and keeping me company.

We sat opposite each other in oversized armchairs near a row of tall bookshelves. I found the faint musty paper smell of old books calming. Joe studied his laptop screen, noise-cancelling headphones on to block the sounds of other patrons chatting.

The café was busy tonight, filled with high school seniors and their parents who, based on the conversations I overheard, had come to the neighborhood en masse to check out one of the loft buildings on Clark Street that catered to college students.

With effort, I tuned out the buzz of conversation and reviewed the list I'd made after the last time I'd talked to the detective.

I hadn't yet talked to anyone about the two malpractice cases against Marco. I opened the photos I'd taken of the documents in Marco's safety deposit box. In the case that had led Marco to leave medicine, the plaintiff's name was Eleanor Czbrynski.

Using the café's WiFi, I searched the online Cook County court records. It was recent, so all the court filings were available to the public electronically. There weren't many, as it had settled quickly.

One of the documents included a phone number for Ms. Czbrynski, which was lucky, as some lawyers omit that type of personal information in public filings.

She didn't answer my call, so I left a voicemail, making my best pitch for her to call me back, then turned to the other documents from the safety deposit box. Now that I'd talked to so many people, something in them might jump out at me that hadn't before.

I flipped to the release for the older malpractice case, the one based on a misdiagnosis. The law firm Conway and Flaherty had defended Marco. The firm was most known among Chicago lawyers for its habit of hiring conventionally attractive people. You could recognize Conway and Flaherty attorneys on sight.

The men were tall with close-cropped hair and strong jawlines. The women were on the slim side but with hourglass figures, and had small, fine noses and perfectly symmetrical features. One of my law school friends had been really flattered when she walked into a courtroom and another lawyer asked if she were from that firm.

The firm representing the plaintiff had been Johnson and Sandman, not a firm I knew.

As I started to look more closely at the misdiagnosis settlement release my phone rang.

It was Eleanor Czbrynski calling me back.

42

Eleanor Czbrynski's voice sounded low and gravelly, not unlike Cora Smith's. She might be getting over a cough or be a heavy smoker, though that seemed doubtful given her cancer history.

I'd already explained in the voicemail who I was and that Marco had died recently. Now I told her that the official verdict was suicide via overdose.

"I'm not surprised," she said. "I'm sorry to hear it, and I'm not angry at him anymore, but I'm not surprised."

I sipped my tea. It was herbal chai with a too-sweet flavor I didn't care for, but I was sleeping a little better these days and didn't want to upset the balance with caffeine at night.

I set my cup on the tall side table next to me. Joe still clicked away at his laptop, though he'd paused a couple times to ask if I was doing okay.

"Why do you say that?" I said.

"Two nurses told my lawyer they'd seen him hung over on surgery days."

That anyone out-and-out admitted to seeing Marco hung

over when he operated looked very bad for the hospital. No wonder the case had settled so quickly.

"That's awful," I said. "It's no help to you now, but if it makes you feel any better, it made him finally stop drinking. He'd been sober for three years when he died."

"Means nothing," Eleanor said. "My first husband was an alcoholic. Quit three different times. It never stuck. He's the one who recommended Dr. Ruggirello. I should have known better, but what happened—who expects that? Coming out of the surgery with the wrong breast gone? And then I have the police contacting me, thinking that, what, I snuck in and offed him three years later?"

"I'm so sorry," I said. "That must have been upsetting."

"Not as upsetting as cancer, but you bet."

I stood and paced in front of the fireplace. I was grateful for all the people in the café. The murmur of conversation kept my words semi-private. "So they were friends? Marco—Dr. Ruggirello—and your ex-husband?"

"They went to medical school together."

It reminded me of a comment Marco had made when I'd asked about whether he had a longtime friend he'd rather name as executor. He'd said he needed to distance himself from the people he drank with.

"What about your doctor friends?" I'd asked.

"Those were my doctor friends," he'd said, and then smiled, but even then I'd wondered if he were really joking.

Apparently not. Something to keep in mind if I ever again needed surgery.

"When the police talked to you, what did they say?"

"Oh, the usual. I guess the usual, I've never been questioned by police before. When I'd last seen him, where I was the night he died."

I gripped the phone, knowing she wouldn't like the next question. "And where were you?"

"Really? Out with my current husband, my brother, and my sister-in-law for dinner. If that's what you called for, if that's what you wanted, you should've said that right off. I'd've told you and saved the chit chat."

"I'm sorry," I said. "It's not the only reason I called. I'm trying to get a big picture. Trying to understand."

"What's there to understand? Your boyfriend was an arrogant asshole alcoholic doctor who got what he deserved."

"I'm sorry I bothered you."

I hung up and shuddered.

Cora Smith calling Marco an asshole hadn't shaken me, as I guessed she'd say that about anyone who crossed her or questioned the clinic's practices. But this woman's bitterness...I could see why Marco had left medicine. She'd suffered so much because of him, and there was no way to fix it.

43

No lawyer show ever depicts attorneys sitting in court for forty-five minutes waiting for their case to be called, but that's what I did the next morning. It's called a status call. When it's your turn, you tell the judge what progress has been made on the case. Sometimes there's no progress, and you go away and come back again in three months when everyone presumably will have done something.

You can wait outside the courtroom so you can use your phone or a tablet, but once you're sitting in the benches you can't talk or have your phone or any device out.

Now and then the bailiff doesn't say anything if you're not obvious about it, but it depends on the courtroom. Reading legal documents is usually okay, as at least in theory you could be preparing for your time before the judge. Reading a book —nope.

When I'd gotten home the night before, I'd unearthed the message pad I'd found in Marco's desk at Hazleton.

It had been stored in my closet at home, and I'd forgotten about it until I reviewed the safety deposit materials on my phone, reminding me that there had been things I'd brought home from Marco's workplace as well. I didn't have a lot of hope for finding anything in particular, but it gave me something to do while I waited for my case to be called.

I'd put the message pad inside an open manila folder to make it look a little more like case materials if the bailiff glanced over. That also helped ensure people around me couldn't see what I was reading, a good habit for court reading because you never know when an attorney from the other side is sitting next to or behind you.

The pad had three messages per page. I flipped through quietly, pausing every time a new case was called so I didn't miss my turn.

Most messages listed the time and date of the call and the caller's name. Unfortunately, there were no years included. The entire pad covered a span of three months, so whoever had taken the calls must have figured the year was unnecessary.

The messages had to be at least several years old, though, given the use of carbon copies. Also, the notes in the messages related to Marco's medical practice, not to Hazleton Insurance.

Most calls came from patients with questions about recent or upcoming visits or from physicians about patients they'd been referred. Personal messages appeared occasionally, mostly from Mirabel, but sometimes from Marco's mother or brother, and a couple times from someone who seemed to be a nanny or a babysitter.

There were none from Eric, suggesting the time frame was so far back he either hadn't been born or was too little to make calls.

As I neared the end, I saw the name Alafair Halliwell, which I'd just seen on the release from the misdiagnosis case. She'd been the first patient who'd sued Marco, to whom he'd paid $18,000.

The Reason For The Call section said, "You'll know what it's about."

Not helpful. It could relate to her treatment or it could relate to the lawsuit, though it would be odd for a patient to directly call a doctor she'd already sued. I doubted her lawyer would have been happy about that.

I flipped to the front cardboard cover on the pad, hoping for a clue on the timeline. But it contained only an ad for an office supply company.

The back cover showed three small square yearly calendars labeled Last Year, This Year, and Next Year.

Glancing to see that the bailiff wasn't looking my way, I took out my phone and enlarged the photo of the settlement release. The release year was the same as the Current Year on the pad. But the message could be any year near then depending how far ahead the office stocked message pads.

"Spivey v. Spivey," the court clerk said, sounding irritated, and I realized that was the second time it had been called. The plaintiff's attorney already stood in front of the judge.

"Defendant," I said as I stuffed the message pad into my accordion file, grabbed my clutch purse, which had my wallet in it, and hurried toward the front of the courtroom.

"Ms. Davis," the judge said. I'm in her courtroom a lot, so she knows me well.

"Sorry, Judge," I said. "My mind was wandering."

I filled her in on the break in at my office and asked for an extra thirty days to answer the other side's discovery requests. The plaintiff's attorney had already agreed, so it was no problem.

I walked the eight blocks back to my office at double my usual pace.

Alafair Halliwell probably had a different phone number by now, but I was determined to find her. She had to be the reason Marco had saved the message pad all these years.

44

THE FIRST THING I FOUND ONLINE ABOUT ALAFAIR HALLIWELL was an obituary. She'd died two years after Marco settled with her over the cancer that had been missed. She and her husband had lived in Romeoville, Illinois, a suburb near Joliet, and had no children.

According to a reverse phone number look up site, the number on the message pad now went to a fast food restaurant.

These days it's almost impossible not to be found on social media, but nothing seemed to exist for Alafair's husband, Frank. If he were the same age as Alafair, he'd be sixty-three now. Without any kids or grandkids, maybe he'd never been pulled into the world where people share everything about themselves online.

The court file also wasn't online. Had Illinois been ahead of the game in filing electronically, it would have been, just as federal court documents are available electronically. But Illinois and Cook County are awash in debt, not money, and efiling hadn't been done until recently.

Which left paper records, meaning my best bet to find more

information was to return to the Daley Center where I'd just been.

I sighed. It had started raining. Drops spattered the windows over the credenza, and the chill in the glass suggested the temperature had dropped in the twenty minutes or so I'd been inside. But I wouldn't melt.

After emailing the client about the new court deadline and reminding her to get me the documents I needed, I changed out of the skirt and low heels I'd worn for court and into jeans and walking shoes I kept in the office. My suit jacket and silk T looked fine with the more casual outfit, one of the benefits of my mix and match wardrobe.

Before I left, I grabbed the latest records from ChiTown. They'd come in while I'd been in court. If I got nowhere researching Alafair, I could at least comb through these and head to Marco's six-flat to see the building for myself.

The Daley Center closed court files are stored on the twelfth floor. It smells of worn paper and stale cigarette smoke that the oldest files absorbed back when smoking was allowed inside city buildings.

I filled in the case name and number from the settlement release on a form and handed it over with my court I.D.

The clerk disappeared into long rows of metal shelving with a handful of requests. Where the ones other than mine had come from I didn't know, as no one was in the long, narrow room except me. I waited at a table with the green spongy top, a leftover from another era, reviewing the ChiTown documents.

About ten minutes later I heard the thunk of files hitting the counter.

I stood.

"Sorry." The clerk scratched his cheek where gray and white stubble straggled across toward his ear. "Couldn't find yours."

"It's missing?" I said.

He shrugged. "Missing. Misfiled. Can't really say. The conversion to digital is on-going, so you might want to check on Fifteen."

On the fifteenth floor, two clerks at side-by-side metal desks sat in front of more rows of gray metal shelves crammed with accordion files.

As they chatted about a cooking show featuring ten-year-old budding chefs, ignoring me, I practiced counting each breath, a good technique for easing tension and refraining from showing impatience. Tapping your fingers on the counter, raising your voice, or frowning are sure ways to end up waiting longer.

It's hard to blame the staff for engaging in some seriously passive-aggressive behavior. I'd seen too many attorneys scream at them or make cutting comments. Though now and then my understanding reached the breaking point, seeing as no one paid me to sit and chat.

If I didn't work for any reason, I didn't get paid.

After a moment, the taller of the two clerks came to the counter. When I told her what I needed, she directed me to Seven, claiming that cases from Law Division—the department where large personal injury cases are filed—went there to live after being scanned and before being shredded.

"This one hasn't been scanned," I said. "I checked. The computer lists the case, but there are no documents to view."

She chomped a large wad of gum. "You gotta click the page icon."

"I did," I said. "Would you double check for me in case I did something wrong?"

"Might take a while."

"I'd appreciate it. I'm doing a favor for a friend, and I hate to disappoint him."

That the friend was dead was a fact I didn't think I needed to mention.

"Let's see." Her fingers flew over the keys. A second later, she shook her head, muttered something, and typed in more commands. "You're right. Nothing online. Hold on."

She disappeared into the rows of files, on a mission now. But she came back empty handed. "Definitely not here. Try Seven."

The information desk clerk on Seven sent me back to Twelve, insisting that after being scanned, paper files were stored there as a backup. That made no sense, as the point of scanning old files was to save space.

But it was Cook County, so I traipsed back up to Twelve.

"Huh, really?" the grizzled clerk there said. "Wait, let me check something."

My heart beat a little faster when he returned with a slim file.

"It was in the To Be Digitized stack," he said.

Standing at the counter, I pulled out manila folders with their faded labels. They were empty. "Nothing here."

He pulled the file toward him and flipped through the folders himself, as if he'd find court documents where I'd found nothing.

"Looks like it was scanned but the papers weren't put back in the file."

"But it's not on the computer."

"Might be a delay in it showing up."

I clasped my hands together to keep from banging on the counter. "And you said it was in the To Be Digitized stack."

"Things get mixed up."

"Where else might the documents be?"

"I could look in the loose filing bin."

"Please," I said.

I'd seen attorneys leave papers on the table and seen clerks sweep them into the bin to be refiled later.

He disappeared again. I remained at the counter, looking

through the ChiTown file, but the numbers and words blurred in my mind.

It wasn't that strange to find pages missing from a file, but it shouldn't be an entire case. If a folder were returned empty, someone from the court system ought to contact the last attorney who reviewed it. How often that actually happened, I had no idea. It might very well be easy for documents to be carried away in a briefcase without anyone noticing.

It was also possible the papers had been loose and been inserted into the wrong file. If that had happened, they'd never be found again unless someone randomly came across them and handed them to the clerk.

I was pacing in front of the copier when the clerk returned, looking regretful. "Sorry, no luck. You've been so nice about this, I looked everywhere I could think of."

His words confirmed two things I'd always suspected.

One, honey worked better than vinegar for getting the clerks to go the extra mile. Two, for many of them, as with anyone I supposed, in a usual day's work they didn't go the extra mile. Or the original mile, as looking everywhere you could think of ought to be the default when trying to find a court file.

But I was convinced this clerk had checked everywhere he could think of, and I'd ridden the elevators all over the building. If the papers still existed, I didn't see how I could find them.

I'd need to find another way to track down Alafair Halliwell.

45

THE TENANT, WHOSE NAME WAS LARRY, LED ME THROUGH AN unfinished basement with a white painted concrete floor and cement block walls. It housed the furnace and the water heater.

"You're with the owner's estate, huh?" Larry wore a flannel shirt with the arms ripped off and jeans with horizontal holes at the knees due to wear, not fashion.

"Yes, I'm his girlfriend. Was." I'd taken off my suit jacket before ringing the bottom buzzer. I wanted the tenants to talk to me as freely as possible, so I didn't want to look lawyer-like. "Does someone sleep there?"

Next to the furnace stood a twin bed covered by a dark blue comforter with cartoon spaceships dancing across it.

"My son."

Between the bed and a basement apartment I hadn't known existed was a bathroom. It had the cramped, claustrophobic look of an airplane lavatory with a sink basin mounted directly against the wall and a triangular premade shower stall wedged into a corner.

The ChiTown documents showed a small amount of rent for a non-conforming unit, but I'd assumed it was connected to one of the other apartments because Marco had always called the building a six flat, and the closing documents only referred to six units.

When I'd arrived, though, I'd found seven buzzers.

No one had answered any of them, so I'd gotten a very early dinner, scanned another third of the ChiTown file, and returned. This man had answered the bottom buzzer.

Now he pointed to a door next to the water heater with a deadbolt lock.

"Washers and dryers for the whole building are in there. I maintain them, maintain all the equipment, and get money off the rent."

I'd need to go back and check, but I seemed to recall a separate fee for monthly equipment maintenance.

Larry's apartment was a studio, minus a bathroom. A small dinette set sat in front of a kitchenette at one end of the single room. An entertainment center with a big screen TV filled the opposite wall. A dark blue cloth-upholstered sofa and matching arm chair were angled toward the TV.

Larry offered me something to drink. I asked for a glass of water and we sat at the table.

"You're not going to tell me I can't stay are you?" Larry said. He'd retrieved a can of A&W Root Beer from his fridge. It was my dad's favorite drink.

"Why?" I said.

"Some guy, I think the property manager, came by last month. Said there were thoughts about selling and a new owner might not keep us."

It didn't surprise me that someone had said that. You didn't have to know building codes to know a child couldn't sleep next to a furnace.

"Was it someone from ChiTown?"

"Youngish black guy, had hair in those skinny braids. Not sure about the company."

Larry didn't remember a name. It could have been Zak, though I didn't know if a permit facilitator would need to visit the building. Also, Charlene Garfield might have a manager who met that description.

"Had you heard anything about it being for sale before that?"

He shook his head. "Nope."

"Did you ever meet him? The owner?"

"Uh-uh. I thought a corporation owned it. Didn't know it was just a guy."

I showed him a photo of Marco in case he'd met him and not realized he owned the building. The man didn't recognize him.

"How long have you lived here?" I said.

"Six years. Me and my son both."

So he'd moved in a few years after Marco had bought the building, and years before ChiTown had taken over.

I had a few clients who owned property and preferred to let it all be handled by a management company. It avoids middle-of-the-night phone calls from tenants or dealing with late or missed payments personally.

But absentee ownership has perils. As this arrangement showed, it was risky to rely completely on your management company for information. If you owned property, you had an obligation to make it safe. Whether you managed it personally or not, you shouldn't let the electrical wiring erode or fail to repair sagging floorboards. Or allow children to sleep next to furnaces.

Even if Marco had assumed the property management company was properly monitoring the building, it shocked me that he might not have checked once in a while himself. Without direct contact with tenants, he'd only hear about complaints or issues if the property manager passed them on.

And if he had known about the basement unit, that was equally irresponsible.

I tapped my foot under the table. I could almost hear Detective Beckwell's voice in my ear pointing out that no matter how well I felt I'd known Marco, you can only learn so much about a person in five months.

"How long ago did that person come here, the one who mentioned maybe selling?" I said.

"A month or so. Maybe six weeks."

"You're sure it wasn't more recent?"

It would make more sense to me if the conversation had happened after Marco died.

"There was snow on the ground."

The last real snow had been mid-March. There'd been a few dustings since then, but nothing that had stuck.

So at least four weeks before Marco had died, maybe more, yet neither Zak nor Charlene had mentioned the basement unit to me. I didn't know if they'd been hiding it or assumed I knew.

"The bed can't stay out there," I said. "If that furnace over-heats, explodes, your son could die."

"I maintain it myself. It's not going to explode. Anyway, that guy, whoever it was, said maybe we can get a waiver."

That seemed unlikely and made me think it hadn't been Zak or someone from ChiTown, but I couldn't think who else would have come here. There might be some zoning variance that would allow a basement apartment, but not sleeping by a furnace.

I finished the last of my water and set the glass on the table. "Not for the bed. And there's no waiver now. You can store the armchair near the laundry room if you need to make room."

His face stiffened and he crossed his arms over his chest. "Fine."

"I'll come back tomorrow to check."

I didn't know when I was going to fit that in, as I had a deposition in the morning and a brief to finish writing and file in the afternoon, but I'd need to do it. And I'd need to check back periodically, as otherwise I had a feeling he'd move the bed in here for tomorrow, then move it back as soon as I left.

I thanked him and climbed the stairs to see if the two first-floor tenants were home.

What I learned from them was also disturbing.

46

LAUREN CAME OVER THAT NIGHT AROUND EIGHT, AFTER HER LAST showing, which had been in the South Loop about a mile past Roosevelt Road. She brought a pillar candle with her that she put on my steamer trunk and lit.

I sank into the sofa.

The flickering flame, vanilla scent, and spicy flavor of the Shiraz I'd opened all combined to help me feel at home after so long of feeling wrong being at my condo without Marco.

"Of course it does," Lauren said when I told her that. "I'm expert at staging a home."

I'd gotten off the L at Washington and Wabash and stopped at the Pastoral Cheese shop near there to pick up bread, four kinds of cheese, olives, and wine. It was someplace I'd always meant to take Marco, but we'd never gotten there.

I told Lauren about the basement as she unwrapped the cheeses and put them on a serving plate she'd found in one of my cabinets.

"You can't let that boy sleep there," she said.

"I know." I ate a garlic-stuffed olive. "But what about the

apartment itself? The ChiTown documents refer to a non-conforming unit. Is that legal to rent?"

"Definitely not." She set the plate of cheeses on the steamer trunk and sat in the armchair across from me. "Even in-law apartments need a bathroom. And not one in a hall or an unfinished basement. And a bed by a furnace—"

"I know. I can't believe Marco let this happen."

Lauren tore off a piece of bread and spread a thick layer of creamy goat cheese across it. "Maybe he didn't know what the unit was like."

I shook my head. I'd been thinking about that. "All the years he owned it he must have visited the units. I would have."

"So would I. But it's my job to know absolutely everything that can go wrong with real estate. And you make your living on what happens when things go wrong. We're more aware of risk than most people."

"That's not all," I said. "The electricity's been shut off twice in the last year. ChiTown told the tenants it was mix ups with Com Ed, but when the first-floor tenant called she was told the bill hadn't been paid."

I'd never had my electricity mistakenly shut off, though once I'd had trouble getting it turned on when I'd moved to a new apartment that had been vacant for a while.

"Was Marco paying the bills?" Lauren said.

I ate a small piece of crumbling, tangy bleu cheese. "He was paying ChiTown, and the money was supposed to come from there. And I don't buy that Com Ed made that mistake twice. Once in the winter."

Lauren refilled her wine glass and motioned toward mine, but I shook my head. "You need to call them."

"It's on my list," I said as pressure built behind my eyes.

If dealing with Com Ed was anything like my phone company I'd be on hold for hours, but I'd need to try. I didn't know how I was going to fit that in along with my other work and visiting the building. Fortunately, Lauren offered to check the next day to see that the bed near the furnace had been moved. Since the basement was a common area, as the agent of a landlord I was allowed to go there without notice to the tenants, so I gave her my keys.

She also gave me the name of a real estate lawyer she knew well so I could ask about how to check on zoning, fines the city might have levied on the building, and anything else I should know about the history.

I decided to do that before confronting Zak or Charlene, but the next day my deposition ran long due to the witness being late and two of the other attorneys arguing over a point that, to me, made no difference. I ran to my office during lunch, edited the brief that was due while eating a power bar, and saved and set about efiling it. Because I was in a rush, I missed clicking one of the mandatory boxes on the screen and the system rejected the filing.

Normally I don't leave things to the last minute because something like that can always go wrong, but everything had caught up with me this week.

I took a breath, reminded myself that technically I had until midnight to finish the filing, and started over. This time it worked, though it made me ten minutes late to the second half of the deposition.

When I got back to my office at three, I finally called the real estate attorney.

She told me to check zoning and permit records in City Hall as well as what to check online. While I was on the phone with her, a client called in a panic over an IRS notice. By the time I calmed him down and sorted through my other emails, my head was pounding. Despite deep breathing, Advil, and a cold pack around my neck, the migraine that had threatened the night before hit me full force.

I stumbled home, feeling like someone was jabbing ice

picks into my head. I lay in the dark listening to a mix of instrumental music and ocean sounds Hector had sent me.

In the morning, the migraine was gone, but my whole body felt sticky with sweat.

After so many weeks where the temperature often seemed more like March than May, the weather had turned hot and humid. The sun beat down and the air almost dripped with moisture.

My weather app, which I had to set to Northerly Island rather than Chicago to get accurate weather for my neighborhood, said it was already in the high eighties.

With no depositions or court hearings today, at least I was free to wear my office uniform—dark jeans and a grey tank top. At the last minute, I grabbed an off white, half-sleeved blazer to put on inside. City Hall always seemed to be either sweltering or freezing. I needed to be prepared for either.

The building is a classic with heavy doors, soaring ceilings, and marble columns. My stop in the property tax division on the first floor didn't reveal anything surprising. At least all Marco's real estate taxes had been paid, and there were no tax liens.

The permit department required heading down to the basement at the opposite end of the long hall.

It took me hours, but along with information I'd pulled online, I traced the history of Marco's building from when he'd bought it. He'd had a mortgage that he'd paid off early, but then he'd taken a line of credit on the building during the time he'd been drinking most heavily, leaving little equity for Eric.

My first read through of the list of cited violations confirmed what Charlene and Zak had told me about the work that needed to be done. It was also true that the repairs were on hold due to permit delays.

The building was zoned as a six flat with no mention of a non-conforming unit. I didn't see how that hadn't been flagged by the city. Perhaps some networking or pay off had resulted in a building inspector looking the other way, which put former alderman Edward Tabbachi on my list again.

The computer froze often as I paged through screens. It took a lot of self-control not to shout at the monitor, and finally I printed some of the longer documents to avoid the need to scroll. The printer's whirring and squealing filled the small underground chamber.

Sweat coating my whole body—I'd long since slipped off the blazer—I read the first few pages at a wobbly work table as the rest printed.

This year's inspection hadn't been the first time the building had been cited. It had been built in the early 1900s, and it was probably inevitable that there would be issues as it aged. It looked like until recently everything had been handled pretty quickly.

Last year, though, ChiTown had failed to file something called a critical exam review. That failure seemed to have led to an additional inspection, and that had ended with a string of violations.

When I compared the text line by line and word by word and weeded out duplicates it appeared that the information in ChiTown's records, at least the ones Charlene had sent me, wasn't quite right.

ChiTown showed more violations than did the city. It might be typos, as sometimes there were only minor wording differences. But if they were typos, they'd resulted in duplicate payments, seemingly to the original contractor. The same contractor Zak had told me was owed still more money.

The duplicate payments were small amounts each but totaled nearly a thousand dollars. I wondered if Marco had discovered someone at ChiTown was collecting and keeping money he thought he was paying for the contractor.

I thought of all those desks and people in ChiTown's outer office.

If everyone there oversaw twenty properties, and someone figured a way to skim just a thousand dollars from each per year, that'd be over six hundred thousand dollars a year. And if it had been going on for decades, whoever it was had a lot of money on the line and faced going to jail if discovered.

I might have found a motive for murder.

47

ON THE FIRST FLOOR, I PAUSED NEAR THE ROWS OF GLASS DOUBLE doors to outside. It had been sunny and humid when I'd disappeared into the bowels of City Hall. Now the street had turned dark and rain pelted down.

Wide marble steps led to the second floor. I sat on the third step, glad I'd worn jeans so I could wash out the grime. I might as well see if I could get some answers while I waited out the rain.

Charlene wasn't in, so I left a voicemail.

Zak answered his phone on the first ring. "Quille, I was about to call you. The work's gotten started again. ChiTown released some funds that apparently were on hold."

"Good," I said, but his news increased my suspicions. No funds should have been on hold. "How much?"

"Just over $15,000. Enough to get work started while you try to get financing."

I fumbled a pen out of an inside pocket of my shoulder bag. I hadn't replaced my iPad yet, so I scribbled a note on a paper file folder. "Okay."

"I also wanted to talk to you about when you stopped in the

office," Zak said. "After you left, I worried I'd said something wrong."

"Oh?"

A wave of damp air rushed through the hallway as a woman in a suit hurried in and folded her umbrella. Water dripped all over the marble floor at her feet.

"I hope it didn't sound like I was asking you out when I suggested coffee. That's not what I meant. Not that I wouldn't under other circumstances, but I know you just lost your boyfriend. I didn't mean to seem like I was disrespecting you or your loss."

"It did come across a little odd."

I shifted on the stair to lean against the wall. It felt cool against my bare shoulder. I felt like I'd been in a dark underground room for days, and it seemed like months since I'd met Zak, though it had actually been more like nine or ten days.

"Yeah, I thought so. Are we all right now? You accept my apology?"

"Yes, sure," I said.

The rain still splattered the sidewalk outside. Whether Zak had asked me out was the least of my concerns about him now that he might be connected to some sort of ChiTown scheme.

"Great. Thanks. So what were *you* calling about?" he said.

I decided for now to stick with what I'd seen at the building with my own eyes. I asked if he'd ever visited it, and he said he'd been there in February to meet with the contractor so he could understand the façade work that was needed.

"Shouldn't someone from ChiTown have done that?"

"Ideally, yes. But they weren't always on top of things, and I didn't want any more delays. Looks bad for me, too."

The timing of his visit didn't quite fit with the timeline from the tenant, but either one could be wrong about the dates. Or be lying.

"What did you think of the units?" I said. "Inside."

"I didn't go inside. Not my area."

"So you've never been inside the building?"

"Is there a problem?"

Someone was coming down the stairs. I shifted closer to the wall to allow a dark-haired woman in jeans, a T-shirt, and sneakers to pass.

"Did you ever talk with any tenants?" I said. "Tell them they might need to move?"

"No, why would I? Did someone do that?"

"Someone told one of them he might need to move if the property sold."

"That must have been someone from ChiTown."

"Is that something they'd tell people?"

"Possibly. A new owner would assume existing leases, but if anyone's month-to-month or their lease is almost over they might have to move out. Especially if there are plans to upgrade and charge higher rents."

"Did you know there's a seventh unit in the building?"

"What? Hold on, I'm putting you on speaker." I heard keys clicking in the background. "Oh, an in-law apartment. Right. Technically, it shouldn't be rented to strangers."

That fit with what Lauren's real estate lawyer friend had told me. In-law apartments were connected to another apartment and could be used by relatives of the resident. So if a first floor apartment had stairs going down to the basement apartment, those tenants could have their grown adult child or their parents living there. But it still needed its own bathroom.

"This one shouldn't be rented to anyone. Did the zoning inspector say anything?"

"It wasn't that kind of inspection. It was about building integrity."

"Someone else would look at the interior?"

"If there's an issue. Let's say there's a substantial rehab, then you need an occupancy permit and all, like with new construction."

Nothing looked like it had been upgraded recently in any of the units I'd seen. The appliances had outdated white finishes and the cabinetry, flooring, and carpet all looked worn.

"If there's no rehab, no one would check that?"

"Probably not."

I stood and peered out the doors, watching the cars inching along Washington Street in the rain. "Why didn't you tell me ChiTown failed to file the critical exam report?"

He sighed. "You visited City Hall, huh?"

"I'm here now."

"I should have said something. But ChiTown fixed it, and I didn't want to make Charlene look worse than she already did."

"Fixed it? Isn't that what triggered the inspection?"

"No, the inspection was standard. It made negotiations harder because the building already failed to do something, but the façade repairs would have had to be done regardless."

"Why were you concerned about Charlene looking bad?"

"She's had a rough year. Her business partner left ChiTown out of nowhere, leaving her holding the ball. She's been scrambling to keep up. But I'm sorry, especially knowing your circumstances, I should've told you everything."

I wound a thick section of hair around my fingers, not sure if I bought his explanation. He hadn't hesitated to say ChiTown was sloppy. That hadn't exactly made Charlene look good. "Anything else I should know?"

"No. Things are moving along."

After I hung up, I stared at the floor, which was covered with wet, grimy footprints.

I couldn't do anything else here, and I needed to make a stop on Michigan Avenue before the end of the day. But the rain was hitting so hard outside it bounced off the street, creating a spray over the slow-moving cars. It was too windy for an umbrella to be much use, and it'd take forever to get a cab or for a ride service to get a vehicle to me.

My other option was the Pedway, the system of underground walkways beneath parts of downtown Chicago.

It doesn't connect to as much as it used to. A lot of buildings locked down after 9/11 for security reasons. But I could get from City Hall to Macy's and to a mail drop center I used on Michigan Avenue without stepping above ground. I hoped a check from a delinquent client was waiting there for me. He'd promised to send it via Fed Ex, and I could deposit it in the ATM in the same building and hope the money would be available in my checking account by Monday afternoon.

The Pedway wasn't my favorite way to travel on humid days. The smells from the subway stops it linked to could be a little overwhelming. But I decided it was the quickest way to get there.

That it wasn't the safest didn't cross my mind.

48

Any mail I get from the court or from the attorneys opposite me in my cases comes to me at my official business address on Michigan Avenue.

When you walk in, there's a man sitting at a desk who will accept packages. Through a door to his right are a series of different sized boxes for mail, and one of those is mine.

Danielle was the one who'd suggested it. She's had seven different offices in her twenty-plus years on her own and for the one we share, there's no written lease. Rather than having to keep changing her address if she moves, she keeps and uses the Michigan Avenue address.

The only downside is running to Michigan Avenue every other day to check mail, but that builds exercise into my week. And since most things are done via email, text, and phone, if I miss a day it doesn't hurt anything. I don't like to wait longer, though, because checks come by mail, and I need the checks.

Underneath Daley Plaza, as I'd feared, the air hung heavy and damp and smelled of urine from the underground L stations, as did the tunnel running from the Blue Line to the Red Line station under State Street.

As I passed Macy's, the temperature grew cooler and the odor improved. The Pedway opens to the gourmet food section, so there's even a slight scent of chocolate. Beyond that are businesses that only those who frequent the Pedway know are there. Those include a shoe shine shop, a convenience store, and a recording studio with accordion blinds pulled down over its wide window.

My phone rang as I neared the revolving doors to a section with escalators up to the Stone Container Building where my mail drop is. It's a newish building with a diamond-shaped roof that always stands out in the skyline.

I glanced at the phone.

It was Eric. Normally I don't answer when I'm walking, but he and I had been missing each other, and I had too much to tell him to use text alone.

As I hit Accept, I sensed someone behind me. I twisted my head, as I always do to see how close anyone is following. A tall skinny man with a beard and baseball cap lunged for my shoulder bag.

I jerked away and ran for the recording studio, yelling "Fire" at the top of my lungs. Danielle had told me that was more likely to get someone to call 911 than "Help," which leaves people unsure what to do.

The man tackled me.

My feet slid sideways. I closed my left fist with the vague thought of hiding the ring Marco had almost given me. The back of my head cracked against the hard tile wall, sending pain like shooting stars through my skull, and everything went wavy and black.

I came to on the floor amid smells of dirt and urine and spoiled food. The world spun around me. I rolled onto my side in case I vomited.

———

An hour later I sat in a Northwestern Hospital Emergency Room stall, my head pounding. An ambulance had brought me in. Because I'd lost consciousness for at least a few minutes, the paramedics had insisted.

I still had my ring on. My red Furla bag—along with everything in it—was gone.

An employee of the recording studio had seen the mugger run off with my red bag but hadn't provided any more of a description than I had. She'd retrieved my iPhone, which had gone flying across the hall. Its screen was cracked, but it worked.

My vision was fine, and I'd passed the neurological tests. The smells of rubbing alcohol and latex sharpened the pain drilling into my head. I'd been forbidden Ibuprofen because I might have a concussion.

Lauren came in while I was waiting for a CAT scan. She held her phone in one hand and a sheet of paper in the other. After the office break in, I'd made a list of all the important numbers to call and given it to Lauren. She'd done the same with her information.

As we waited, she started making the calls, saying she was me since my head was killing me and I couldn't think clearly. I gave her the security info she'd need just before they took me away for the CAT scan. She also called Eric to tell him I was all right.

By the time I was wheeled back, Lauren had finished.

"You'll have an Am Ex by tomorrow morning," she said. "And your firm charge card should arrive by the afternoon."

"Thanks."

A doctor or nurse, I wasn't clear which, returned to tell us that my CAT scan had been fine. She dimmed the lights and started pain medication through an IV.

Lauren stepped out to make some more calls. I lay flat on the hospital bed, shivering from the chilly room, and closed my eyes. Both the mugger and the burglar who'd broken into the office suite had been tall and thin. I strained to picture the two side by side, but the images blurred and my thoughts kept drifting. My head throbbed from crown to earlobes to jaw to chin.

From the other stalls came sounds of beeping, voices, and squeaking wheels of gurneys. Every one was like someone twisting a knife into my brain. I struggled to breathe evenly, afraid the medication had been started too late to help.

Before Marco's death, I'd seen what had happened to the original Q.C. as an aberration, something tragic and horrible, but not the way the entire world worked. Maybe I'd had the luxury of feeling that way because I hadn't been alive when it happened, despite how much my family's grief over it affected me.

Now, though, I felt as if danger lurked everywhere. I wondered if that was how my mother had felt since Q.C.'s death, if that was the root of her anxiety.

My hands closed into fists.

I made myself relax my fingers as I tried to sort through what had happened and why it had happened. A random mugging seemed as bad as one connected with Marco because it was completely out of my control and purposeless.

But if it had been connected, it didn't mean I was getting anywhere. As Joe and the detective had suggested, maybe I'd dug around and stumbled into underhanded dealings at Vujic Chiropractic or ChiTown, worrying somebody enough that the person broke into my office. And then I'd been mugged because of it or just because I'd violated my own rule about taking my smartphone out while walking, especially in the Pedway.

Either way, all my efforts had proven nothing, except perhaps that I was in deep denial.

Logic said I'd feel better when the migraine passed, if it ever did, and my injuries healed. But in the dark with the frigid air and hospital smells pressing in on me, I didn't believe it.

49

LAUREN GOT ME HOME IN A CAB.

It was after nine at night, but it felt like two in the morning. The medication had finally worked, bringing with it the unmoored floating feeling I disliked, but easing the migraine.

I'd signed on the dotted line that I'd pay, and I'd been warned not to drive for forty-eight hours just in case and to return if I had severe head pain. I had no doubt I'd meet my health insurance deductible this year, and I wouldn't be buying a replacement for the Furla bag or a whole lot of anything else for a while.

Eric sat slumped on one of the upholstered benches in my lobby. He ran over when he saw me and hugged me.

I hugged him back. "Hey, I'm okay. Mostly," I said, though my back ached and my stomach felt hollow and empty. "What're you doing here?"

"I wanted to be sure you're all right." He backed off and studied me. "You look awful."

"Thanks," I said.

I hadn't thought I looked that bad, but my make up had

worn off, and there was still some faint bruising around my eyes from the break in.

Upstairs Eric and I sat at my kitchen island. I called Mirabel, who hadn't known Eric was stopping to see me after his game. She said she'd pick him up in an hour. Lauren headed down to her condo but promised to come back later to check on me.

Glasses of ice water and a plate of chocolate chunk cookies in front of us, we sat with only the light over the sink and my small living room floor lamp on. Darkness feels best post-migraine.

I told Eric what I'd learned about ChiTown and Vujic, hoping the despair I'd felt in the ER wasn't obvious in my voice.

He heard it.

He pushed his half-eaten cookie toward the center of the island. "You think it's hopeless."

"No. I'm just wiped out. Rough day." I sat straighter, one arm on the counter, propping myself up. "I'll figure it out."

His shoulders rounded and his head bent. He spoke into his chest. "What if there's nothing to figure out?"

"You mean what if your dad really did kill himself?" I said.

He looked up at me, eyes hidden by the shadows. "Maybe."

I put my hand on his shoulder, setting aside my own worries. If I didn't help Eric face his real fear it would stay with him whether I unraveled Marco's murder or not.

"I don't believe that's what happened," I said. "But okay, what if he did? It wouldn't change who your dad was. Or how he felt about you."

He jerked away. "Yeah it would. It'd make it a lie. Everything he said about being sober, starting life over."

"Loving you?"

"No!" Eric's chin trembled, and even in silhouette he appeared so much younger than thirteen. "Maybe. It's stupid."

"It's not." I spun the citrine and silver ring around my finger. "Did I ever tell you why I stopped acting?"

He shook his head, too polite to ask what that had to do with anything.

"It's kind of the same reason I started. I always heard about my sister, the one I was named for, having been a great child actress. Plus what a beautiful voice she had, and how she could dance. So when my mom suggested an acting class, I said yes. When she wanted to give me piano and voice lessons, I said yes. Some of the only times she seemed happy were when we sang together, and it was about the only time the two of us spent together.

"But she never went on and on to her friends about me. Not my plays or concerts or anything. Sometimes she came to an opening night, and that was it."

"That had to suck," Eric said.

"It did. My Gram was always excited for me, though, and I liked acting and singing. I was proud of earning money at it. But I still felt second best. Especially when I heard my mom say Q.C. had been a baby model. I never modeled." Q.C. had been round-cheeked and pig-tailed and blond, things I'd never been. "I never had those kinds of looks. And she starred in a musical the summer before she disappeared."

"You could never live up to her," Eric said. "Is that why you quit?"

I drank more water and took more chocolate chunk cookies from the Rubbermaid container.

"In a way. I researched Q.C.'s case for a paper in college. I read local newspaper articles about her and talked to people in town. That's when I found out the truth."

The owners of a local grocery store, a mom-and-pop business five blocks from my parents' house, had been struck by a candid photo of Q.C. during a summer festival in their parking lot and had asked if they could use it by the baby food aisle. That had been Q.C.'s modeling "career."

As for starring in a musical, Q.C. had been in a tiny tots choir that did a revue of songs from different musicals that year, and she had a few lines she sang by herself. Impressive, yes. She was probably the only four-year-old who could truly carry a tune, had a nice voice, and could remember the words. But it wasn't exactly what my mom had told me.

"What did you think?" Gram had said when I told her what I'd learned. "She was five when she was killed. She could hardly have built an extensive resume."

Yet that was what I'd been led to believe, and it made me mad. All my life I'd been competing with a supergirl who didn't exist. Q.C. the star. Gram said it hadn't occurred to her that I'd felt overshadowed by Q.C., and she told me to look on the bright side. The competition was part of why I'd worked so hard and achieved so much.

My mom insisted she'd never lied to me. "My Q.C. would have been a star," she'd said.

When I told Joe my mom's response, he'd said, "Of course." By then he'd left acting, gotten his MBA, and gone into finance, which he loved. "You'll never match Q.C. If you ever win a Tony, Q.C. would have won it three years earlier. If you got the Screen Actor's Guild award for Best Actress, Q.C. would have gotten an Oscar. If you're acting to beat Q.C., it's not worth it. The profession's hard enough if you love it for itself."

"So were you glad?" Eric asked after I told him the story. "That Q.C. wasn't really a star?"

"Yeah." My cheeks flushed. It sounded as petty as I'd feared to hear my thoughts aloud, and I was glad my kitchen area was dim enough that we couldn't see each other's faces well. "Not very kind, is it, feeling jealous of a little girl who got murdered?"

"You couldn't help it," Eric said. "And anyway, it's more

about your mom, right, than Q.C. You didn't even know her."

"That's true. And it was kind of freeing learning more about her. I was nineteen, and for the first time it hit me I didn't need to be Q.C. Davis II."

"So you became Quille."

"Yep." I twisted long strands of hair between my index finger and thumb. "And I tried to forgive my mom for not being there for me. Her grief isn't about me, and she's probably doing the best she can."

Eric ate another cookie. I said nothing, spinning the ring around my finger.

"So if Dad slipped and started drinking again, or if he killed himself, you're saying it wasn't about me. It was whatever he was dealing with—or not dealing with."

"Yes. He loved you—and he loved me—and no matter what the answer is about how he died, it doesn't change that."

Eric nodded. "I guess that's right. It doesn't feel that way, though."

"No." I took the ring off and put it in Eric's hand. "I found this in your dad's things. I think he meant to give it to me down the road, but it's not mine, it's the estate's."

He held it up in the faint light from the lamp, turned it around, and gave it back to me. "I think he'd want you to have it."

"I can buy it from the estate, but are you sure you don't want it? You might like to give it to someone someday."

He shook his head. "It should be yours. I don't suppose it cost enough to cover my tuition? That'd make my mom happy."

"No. It was $1,200. But it's $1,200 you didn't have before."

After Eric left, I showered to get the grime from the Pedway off me and took out the lists I'd made of people to talk to and skills I had. Despite wanting Eric to be okay no matter what I learned or didn't about Marco, there was no way I was letting him go through life thinking his dad chose to leave him.

50

Over the last ten days I'd been to a cocktail party for Edward Tabacchi, visited Vujic Chiropractic, gotten records from ChiTown, hunted for the court file on Alafair Halliwell, and talked with Zak Woodruff about the six-flat.

One of those things had worried someone enough to attack me.

"My money's on Dr. Vujic," Lauren said. "Or her admin."

It was nearly noon on Saturday, and we sat across from each other in a corner table at Café des Livres. Lauren's red and white striped golf umbrella sat on the floor behind her to dry. Outside, rain once again pelted the street, and the gutters were awash with water.

My migraine was gone, but my back ached.

"Because?" I said.

"Dr. Vujic lied about what she had in common with Marco," Lauren said.

I cut another piece of French Toast. Powdered sugar scattered on the marble tabletop. "People lie for lots of reasons."

I'd learned that representing companies. Employees might lie when I interviewed them about something they'd done, but

241

usually it wasn't because they were guilty of whatever the lawsuit alleged. They just didn't want to tell me anything that might make them look like a bad worker or get them in trouble with a supervisor.

Lauren pushed a piece of avocado that had fallen on the plate back into her BLT club. "A lie's a lie. You need to find out more about her."

"I don't think she'll talk to me again."

"Totally not a problem. When my client was late this morning I searched Linked In. One of the other realtors at my firm has an assistant who's connected to a naturopath who runs a health and wellness center in Lakeview. He went to college with Vujic, and guess who's taking him to lunch Monday."

I set down my knife and fork, not sure I liked the idea of Lauren getting involved because of the possible risks. "What'd you tell him?"

"Nothing about Vujic. I told him I wanted to learn absolutely everything about alternative medicine."

"Will he buy that?"

She laughed. "I can sell anything. And he's fifty-five."

Men twenty or thirty years older than her always seem to be drawn to Lauren. I suspect it's partly that she looks a little like Michelle Pfeiffer did in 1980s movies like The Fabulous Baker Boys and Dangerous Liaisons. If anyone could get information from this man without making her goal obvious, she could.

Her BLT club was garnished with homemade frites, the skinny shoestring kind I love. I ate a few. As always, they tasted fresh and crispy. "Careful. If he's a friend of Dr. Vujic and she really was involved in Marco's death, she might have told people she knows to watch out for unusual questions."

"I can be subtle," Lauren said. "Anyway, he knew her a long time ago. That doesn't mean they're friends now."

"They could be. Watch your back."

Joe had agreed to let me bounce thoughts about ChiTown's records off him once I'd reviewed them in depth. He was working from home—he worked more Saturdays than almost anyone I knew—so he asked me to come over to his place. I think he really wanted to see for himself that I was all right.

He lived in the Fulton River District, a neighborhood just west and north of downtown. As the name suggests, he had a view of the Chicago River. The rain stopped by mid-afternoon, but his balcony furniture was soaked, so I sat on his leather couch while he worked in his home office.

First I texted Dede Zith to see if she'd be able to tell me more about Edward Tabacchi and how the fundraiser had come about. I also figured she was my best shot at getting more than a few minutes with him since she'd hosted an event for him.

I wanted to talk to her in person so I could read her expressions. She had a busy week getting ready for an art show, but she was a runner and often jogged along the lakefront early Sunday mornings. She agreed to meet me there.

After that, I turned to ChiTown's statements for Marco's accounts, going through the spreadsheets line-by-line. Rent checks went directly to ChiTown, deposited into an operating account. Money went out for utilities, routine repairs, taxes, and maintenance. Every month, Marco got a statement and every quarter, he either got a check or needed to add money of his own to cover expenses.

I compared every entry to Marco's checking account, which I accessed online, to contractor invoices, and to the city violations and reinspection reports. My specialty wasn't property management, but the figures heightened the suspicions the City Hall records had raised—that ChiTown had billed Marco for more repairs and updates to correct violations than had been necessary over the last few years.

The entries also included a lot of low dollar unspecified "miscellaneous" expenses, something Lauren had told me to watch for. Then there was a lag time in paying bills, such as Com Ed's, that shouldn't have happened given that Marco had kept a decent balance in the account.

A separate column showed nearly $12,000 to cover the work that needed to be done now to satisfy the city, and that was after the original contractor's $3,000 bill was paid.

Marco had to have put that money there before he died, so it made no sense that ChiTown had delayed paying the original contractor. I wondered if Marco had been hoping not all of that money would be needed and that he could draw from it to make up any shortfall for the second tuition payment for Eric.

By the time I'd rechecked my figures the sunlight outside the windows was fading and the streetlamps glowed along the walkway that ran below Joe's balcony and above the river. My back ached from curling on the couch. Having been slammed to a hard floor the day before didn't help.

I stood and stretched. Without seeing ChiTown's own accounts I couldn't be sure, but it looked to me as if someone there had siphoned funds and then possibly put some money back when the problems with Marco's building threatened to make that obvious.

Joe was ready to call it a day as well.

We ordered pizza and opened a bottle of Pinot Noir, and he looked over what I'd found. It left him with the same questions I had. We called Danielle, who'd defended a string of people in real estate fraud cases during the recession in the late 2000s.

She was backstage with her daughter at a high school choir concert. I could hear voices and the sounds of horns and stringed instruments tuning up in the background.

"Ask for a forensic audit," she said. "If the data's as strong as what you're telling me, you can make a case that ChiTown has to pay for it."

The second part I hadn't known, and it was reassuring that I wouldn't need to spend the estate's money. My only question was whether I ought to ask for the audit now, putting the people at ChiTown more on guard than they already were, or wait until I could figure out if any of it related to Marco's death.

"What, you're waiting for someone to kill you next time?" she said.

I didn't have the phone on speaker, but her voice was loud enough for Joe, sitting across the dining table from me, to hear.

"Told you she'd say that," he said.

51

SUNDAY PROMISED TO BE SUNNY AND THE WARMEST DAY SINCE Marco's death. At seven AM, it was already seventy-five degrees. I slid my bare feet into the gray Teva sandals I live in during the summer. They have rubber soles, offering a lot of support for walking on Chicago sidewalks, through the parks, or along the lakefront.

Despite meeting Dede, I had no intention of joining her in anything more than a fast walk.

Running is something I've never understood doing for fun. Or at all. Now that I'm in my thirties and almost everyone I know who runs regularly has some type of knee problem I feel justified. Clearly, our bodies were not meant to run long distances.

I also wasn't thrilled with where she'd chosen to meet, which was in the Museum Campus near the water taxi dock. A mile from my condo, it's where she always paused her Sunday morning runs to take a break, do an about-face, and head north again along the lakefront.

It had been one of Marco's and my favorite places.

It was beautiful even in winter in a stark sort of way with

the columns of the Field Museum in the background and the aquarium jutting into the water to the south. We'd looked forward to sharing early spring and summer mornings there once he moved in with me, watching Lake Michigan turn warmer and bluer as the seasons changed.

The café wasn't open until eight on Sundays, so I made my own Earl Grey and poured it into a travel mug. Normally I'd walk through the leafy streets of Dearborn Park, through the underpass for the Roosevelt Road bridge, and up a side path used only by residents. But it was early enough that other than a few dog walkers the area would be deserted, and the underpass made me uneasy. I felt safer sticking to busier streets.

Despite that it wasn't quite 7:30 when I reached Michigan Avenue people waited at bus stops, and the 24-Hour Jewel grocery store on Roosevelt and Wabash had a half-full parking lot.

A few blocks east and I was in the Museum Campus. It's an area of concrete bike paths, grassy embankments, and walkways that connect the Field Museum, the planetarium, and the aquarium. On the east edge, below street level, it borders Lake Michigan.

I waited on the bench where Marco and I used to sit.

The sun's rays glinted off the lake, turning it from a deep purplish-blue to a silver-tinged aquamarine as the sun rose higher in the sky. The cool breeze and warm sun hit my face. As I inhaled the scent of the tea with its citrus, lavender, and vanilla undertones, a faint it's-almost-summer anticipation flickered in my soul.

For the first time since Marco's death, I felt almost happy.

And immediately felt stricken. I couldn't be happy when Marco would never see spring turn to summer or hear red and gold leaves crunch under our feet next fall or see his son grow into a young man and maybe have children of his own.

I squeezed my eyes shut.

The travel mug felt warm in my hands, and I could still picture the sun's rays rippling off the lake and smell the rich, black tea. I'd told Eric Marco would never want him to spend his life feeling terrible because his dad was gone. If I believed that for him, I had to believe it for me, too. Marco wouldn't want me to shut out everything beautiful.

I opened my eyes again. Dede appeared in the distance a few minutes later. Her muscled tan legs stretched from her emerald green running shorts, and her auburn and gray hair flew out behind her in a long ponytail.

She slowed to a walk and then stopped near the bench. I must have done an excellent job covering what was left of my black eye, as she looked only at my feet. "Those aren't running shoes."

"Uh, no. I'm more of a walker."

She sighed. "Fine. I can cool down a bit."

We got lemon Italian ices from the street vendor near the water taxi station.

"So what else can I tell you?" Dede said. She spoke more slowly than she had when we'd met, a bit winded from her run. "I don't remember anything else about Marco."

I licked my Italian ice. It had a tart flavor that tasted like summer. "Do you do a lot of political fundraising?"

"That one for Tabacchi was my first. I don't mind telling you, I was a little nervous. I know sales, but not politics. Though it turns out they're not so different."

We walked north between the concrete that edged the lake and the stretch of lawn that sloped up toward Lake Shore Drive. A series of abstract red metal sculptures stood in the grass, a temporary exhibit sponsored by Columbia College.

Seagulls wheeled overhead, honking and diving for whatever they saw in the murky lake water lapping at the concrete.

"Sales?" I said.

"It's my day job. I sell software to non-profits."

I shouldn't have been surprised. Earning a living, especially in a city as expensive as Chicago, is a challenge for any artist, even one whose paintings sell for thousands of dollars.

"How did you end up hosting?"

A beep-beep came from behind us, and I moved to the side. A bike whizzed past, then a skateboarder barreled toward us from the other direction. We veered closer to the lake.

"A friend asked. She knows I like to entertain, and she said this candidate wanted to have an event in my section of Lincoln Square."

The sun had gotten hotter, and I took off my blazer. A musky algae smell filled the brisk morning air.

"Did you know who Ed Tabacchi was before that?" I said.

"I'd heard his name, but he was never my alderman. Couldn't tell you who was, really."

Most Chicagoans don't know their alderman unless the person is in the news for scamming or there's a neighborhood problem. If there's a pothole the size of a lake on your street that causes your tire to blow out, or a developer wants to build a high rise in the lot next door and block your view, you find out who your alderman is and complain. Otherwise, you don't need to know.

In that sense, it's a lot like being a lawyer. No one calls you because things are going great.

"Why did he want to meet people in your neighborhood?" I said.

She shrugged. "Something about it being a good demographic."

The wind kept blowing long strands of hair into my mouth, and I brushed them away. "Really? What demographic?"

It couldn't be simply Democrats because that would cover most of Chicago. And if he wanted wealthy donors, Lincoln Square wasn't the place.

Unlike the similarly-named Lincoln Park, which is home to

lots of well-to-do, middle-aged professionals, most of Lincoln Square consists of modest homes or aging apartment buildings, and most of its residents are in their late twenties or early thirties.

Dede adjusted her sunglasses. "Funny, I didn't ask. I was thinking more about whether I could manage it. And whether I might sell a few paintings if Tabacchi got some supporters who didn't know me to attend. Which he didn't."

The clouds shifted, hiding the sun. We'd reached a desolate stretch of the lake where cigarette butts, soda cans, and plastic bags washed in on the tide.

"What about the friend who connected you to Tabacchi? Is she a long-time supporter?"

"No. She met him at the City Club."

The City Club is a business-focused organization, conservative (for Chicago), with a heavy quotient of older white men who still wear their college class rings because they went to impressive universities or belonged to elite fraternities.

It hosts a lunch once a month in the banquet room at Maggiano's in River North. I've no doubt it's great for politicians who need to jump start fundraising.

I don't belong, but I go to most of the lunches. It's a good place to meet potential clients, and Maggiano's food is excellent, especially the crescent lemon cookies for dessert. The speakers are usually interesting people, some of them famous. The program always finishes on time to get people back to their offices.

"What did he say to her?" I asked.

"Something about Tabacchi wanting to have a fundraiser right off the Damen L stop."

The request struck me as oddly specific. He must have asked a lot of people before finding a host. Most of the buildings lining Damen Avenue near the L are commercial, not residential. If "right off" meant within a five or ten block radius, though, that would sweep in a lot of apartment buildings, two and three flats, and single-family homes.

"And she didn't know Tabacchi well personally?" I said.

"She didn't know him at all personally I don't think."

Dede texted her friend to see if she'd mind talking with me. She responded as we passed Monroe Harbor with its yachts and boats with white sails dotting the lake.

"She's good on you calling her," Dede said. "I didn't say why. I'll leave that to you."

52

DEDE'S FRIEND CHATTED WITH ME BY PHONE BUT DIDN'T HAVE much to add. She had no particular in to Edward Tabacchi. She'd connected him with Dede mainly with the idea that it was never bad to have a politician owe you a favor.

After the call, I sat on my deck and looked over Tabacchi's campaign website on my spare laptop, lingering over the names of his staff.

If I questioned one of them, though, they'd almost certainly tell Tabacchi. On the off chance he had anything to hide, I didn't want to tip my hand.

People who'd worked for him when he was an alderman, on the other hand, might not still be in touch with him.

Using a Web archival service, I found an old City of Chicago webpage. It showed a photo of a younger, thinner Alderman Tabacchi with a slightly less ruddy complexion and darker hair. What I couldn't find was a specific website for him as alderman. It seemed impossible that he hadn't had one.

I searched for my current alderman, a woman lawyer who'd won the last election, to see what type of information she included on her site. (It's still called alderman in Chicago even if you're a woman. Because adding that extra "wo" syllable to the word would just be too much work, I guess.)

Her website included a photo, a generic statement about how seriously she took her duties to the people of her ward, and a menu of options to request or complain about city services like recycling fees, garbage pickup, or potholes.

Three neighboring ward aldermen had similar sites. Two of those included signed pledges about serving the ward. Nothing anyone would guess an alderman would need to delete.

I sipped the lemonade I'd made when I'd gotten home. The early afternoon sunlight on the deck was warm, but there was enough of a lake breeze to keep it comfortable.

I returned to more general searches about Tabacchi's aldermanic campaign. Most of what I found was the expected political gladhanding in multiple photo ops.

He'd been a partner at a firm called Somers and Tabacchi. The firm did a little of everything, including criminal defense, zoning commission hearings, slip-and-fall cases, and real estate closings. I cross-referenced Linked In to find other people who worked for the firm.

Before going into private practice, Tabacchi had been an assistant state's attorney—what prosecutors are called in Illinois—for twelve years. His time there hadn't matched Danielle's, and she'd heard little about him good or bad.

After fifteen years, Tabacchi had left the firm. He'd run for alderman six months later, but hadn't been elected until his second try when the second Mayor Daley endorsed him.

I emailed the investigator in our suite asking if he had any suggestions for finding Tabacchi's staff from his alderman days. Stymied in my search for Alafair Halliwell's husband, too, I asked him to check one of his subscription databases. I'd need to pay for that type of search, but he said he'd only charge if he found something.

He did.

53

All the information on Alafair Halliwell's husband had led to the same phone number I'd found, which was disconnected. There was, however, a record of a nephew who lived in Denver.

I traded voicemails with Will Halliwell for a day and a half.

In the messages, I said only that I was an attorney with some questions about his aunt's case. We connected in the late afternoon when I was writing a response to a motion in my case with the brother and sister suing each other over the company they'd inherited.

I shut my office door and put Will on speaker.

His Facebook photo showed a man in his thirties with small eyes, a wide, flat nose, and wire-framed glasses. His voice had a nasal quality. "What's your interest in my aunt?"

I explained about Marco having seen Alafair Halliwell once and that he'd been sued along with her regular doctor for her misdiagnosis. I also told him about my relationship to Marco, that he'd died, and that I was trying to learn more about what led to his death.

"What, was he murdered or something?" Will said.

"I think so." I moved to the window to stare at people hurrying along Dearborn Street below. "The police don't."

"Sorry," Will said. "But I don't see why you're calling me."

"I'm probably grasping at straws. Marco had some papers about the case in a safety deposit box. And when I went to look at the old court file, it was missing. I'm thinking he might have discovered something someone didn't want him to know."

"About my aunt?"

I paced the office. "Maybe. She called Marco after he settled with her or right around that time."

"Are people who sue each other not supposed to talk?"

"They can if they want," I said. "But their lawyers tell them not to. And why call? If your aunt thought Marco committed malpractice, she wouldn't go to him for treatment. I was hoping if I could talk to your uncle, he might remember."

"Yeah, he won't," Will said. "He's in a long term care facility. Alzheimer's."

"Oh. I'm so sorry." I stopped my pacing and half-sat on, half-leaned against the credenza. Sometimes it felt as if there were nothing but bad things in the world. "Is there any chance you know anything about the case?"

"I was in high school. I knew my aunt was sick, but I didn't know there was a malpractice case until you mentioned it."

I wasn't ready to give up yet. "If you had to guess why she might call, what would you say?"

It was a long shot, but once in a while people's speculations are on target. Or they know more than they want to say for fear of getting dragged into something, but are willing to talk if you call it guessing.

A sigh came through the phone. "She was a nice lady. Not much like the rest of my family. Maybe she called to apologize. If it's true your boyfriend saw her once and got roped into a lawsuit, she might have felt bad that he got sued."

It felt good to talk to someone who didn't assume Marco

was a terrible person, but I had my doubts about his theory. However nice Alafair had been, she'd been going through radiation for cancer that might have been stopped early on had the diagnosis been correct.

Also, she hadn't been a doctor or lawyer. She probably would have assumed if her lawyer included Marco in the suit, there was some reason she wasn't aware of.

I glanced at my laptop screen where I'd typed bullet points for the call. "You don't happen to remember who her attorney was?"

If I could find the attorney, I felt sure I'd learn why Alafair had been calling Marco. I'd certainly remember if one of my clients decided to contact someone on the other side.

The settlement release had listed, and the electronic docket for Cook County had confirmed, the firm name, which was Johnson and Sandman. But in Illinois, unlike in federal court, a law firm, not an individual lawyer, officially appears for a client, so that's all that shows on the electronic court record. The particular lawyer's name might be on a court order or on a motion, but since Alafair's paper file was missing I had no way to know it.

I also hadn't been able to find any website for the firm. The lack of an Internet presence made me think the lawyer or lawyers involved were sixty or older—from the generation that didn't have the Internet when they started and still relied on personal word of mouth and referrals.

"Sorry," Will said.

I rubbed my forehead. "Is there anyone in your family who might remember?"

He agreed to ask his mother and let me know if he learned anything, but I didn't feel very hopeful. My concerns couldn't seem that important to him, and it didn't sound like his family had been close with one another.

Frustrated, I returned to the reply I'd been writing, but ten minutes later I took out the list of former employees of Tabacchi. If I couldn't learn more about the Halliwell lawsuit, I could at least find out more about the former alderman.

Before I started contacting people, though, I decided I needed to become someone else.

54

Contrary to how movies, TV, and books depict attorneys, we're bound by a strict code of ethics we swear to uphold, and we can lose our licenses for violating it. The one thing most people at least have heard about is that we can't put a client on the stand to testify to what we know is a lie. If a client insists on lying, we have to withdraw from representing that person, though we're in a weird spot because we can't spell out exactly what the issue is.

We also have what's called a duty of candor to the court.

We can't lie to a judge, but it's more than that. If there's a case out there against my client's position that the judge is required to follow, I need to tell the judge about it even if my opponent misses it.

The ethics code applies outside of court, too.

In Illinois, Professional Rule of Conduct 8.4 forbids a lawyer from engaging in "conduct involving dishonesty, fraud, deceit, or misrepresentation." Nothing in the rules said, though, that I had to risk my life by making it easy to target me.

I created an email address using my last name and Cat, a short form of my middle name. Cat Davis' email included the phone number for the second landline in my office. If someone really hunted, they might discover that line traced back to me, but it wasn't listed anywhere.

Cat needed a reason to talk to people.

I decided I'd gather information for an article to submit to the CBA Record, a publication of the Chicago Bar Association. Anyone can submit an article and hope it gets published. To make my story truthful, I'd write the article, which would be about attorneys running for political office, and submit it.

Cat had blondish-brown medium-length hair because that matched the best wig I could find that fit well on short notice. She wore dramatic make up to accommodate my need to cover what was left of the bruising around my eye and because it's different from my style, which is pretty understated. I added chunky costume jewelry for the same reason.

I also stopped at a Victoria's Secret where the saleslady was more than happy to find me a padded B-cup bra that fit despite that I'm barely an A.

I got one positive response out of six emails. One woman was available to meet that evening, a man said he might be able to talk later in the week, and the others didn't answer.

Before leaving the office, I did what I used to do before a first read through of a new play. I shut my eyes, took a breath, and pictured myself literally stepping into Cat Davis' high heeled shoes.

55

"HE WAS A LUNATIC," JACEY WILCOX SAID. SILVER STREAKS IN HER platinum hair and slight puffiness under her eyes put her at least in her forties. She had a bright, lilting way of talking, though, that made me think of someone younger, particularly the way she turned sentences into questions. "A complete lunatic?"

We sat at a high top table overlooking the river outside Tiny Hat, one of the many bars and restaurants along the Chicago River Walk. Jacey had worked for Somers and Tabacchi over ten years ago. I hoped that meant she didn't still need Edward Tabacchi as a reference.

I'd promised not to quote her directly or name her in the article unless she wanted me to.

"How so?" I sipped my whiskey sour.

It tasted like it had been made with lemon-lime soda rather than real lemon juice and simple syrup, and I doubted an egg white had ever entered the equation. But it was light on the whiskey, which was how I'd asked for it to keep my head clear.

"He always had different women calling him that he'd broken dates with, right, and he'd never take the call."

"Wasn't he married?"

"Not then. This was between marriages."

"Hm. Okay. So women would call?"

I hadn't realized Edward Tabacchi had been married before. His college-aged son must be from the previous marriage. I wondered if Tabacchi had felt being divorced was a drawback and had chosen to purposely make it appear that he'd been with his current wife longer than he had.

"Yeah. This was before everyone texted, and he refused to give anyone his cell number. So they'd call the office, and the receptionist would have to tell them whatever excuse he'd come up with and she'd get yelled at by the woman."

"How long did you work at Somers and Tabacchi?" I said.

"Eleven years? I started a year after the firm formed—it was June Somers, P.C. then—and left three years before it closed."

"Long time to stay with a lunatic."

"They paid really well, right? Not at first, but if you stuck it out. Good raises, nice bonuses if it was a good year."

At the next restaurant over, live music started. It was two guys with acoustic guitars, but they had microphones and amplifiers and were practically banging their picks across the strings. That and their off-key singing made it painful to listen to.

It was one thing I didn't like along the River Walk. The bar and restaurant owners seemed united in the view that any band or singer, no matter how bad, was better than silence.

Gripping the tall table for leverage, I scooted closer to Jacey so I could hear her over the noise. The movement caused a sharp twinge in my back and I drew in my breath.

"What if it was a bad year?" I said once the pain had eased.

"Well, that kind of sucked." She ate the stuffed olive off the cocktail toothpick in her martini. "That meant no bonus. But the good years made up for it. At least, for me."

"Not for other people?"

"Ed liked me because I knew all his excuses by heart, you know? If he wasn't around, I could trot one out on a dime. For clients, his kid, his women friends. I didn't like doing it, but I could."

The waiter brought a stack of curly fries I'd ordered. Tiny Hat made them with a lemon aioli sauce that I loved. "Was that uncomfortable? Lying to people?"

"Oh, I never lied. I always said 'Ed told me' or 'his calendar says...' The women sort of knew it was crap. But they kept calling."

A double decker tour boat went by, and a bunch of people along the railing of the top deck waved. A few people sitting around us waved back.

"What kept them hanging in?"

"Not sure. But he made everyone feel good about themselves, you know? He could turn on the charm. If you were upset, he'd give you his full attention. It was like having a spotlight on you, right, but not in an uncomfortable way? More like here was your chance to have your say. He was never that politician looking for the next more important person to talk to."

Jacey's description made me wonder about how quickly Tabacchi had wanted to move to the next person when I'd met him.

Maybe he'd changed as he'd gone further into politics, become more attuned to fundraising and the need to meet as many people as possible. Or he'd wanted to extricate himself quickly because he had something to hide. To be fair, though, a lot of people are uncomfortable talking about death. That might have been a motive to move along to the next person.

"Why'd he run for alderman?" I said.

Jacey swished what was left of her martini around in its plastic cup. "No idea. I'd left the office by then."

I ate a few fries. The sauce was amazing, as always, and I ate a few more. "You didn't keep in touch?"

"Holiday cards."

I closed the small notebook that lay on the table in front of me. "Your best guess based on knowing him? I won't put it in the article if you don't want me to."

Jacey ate a curly fry. "I think he got tired of private practice. It's really up and down, right? One month you're swamped and can barely find time to breathe, the next you're wondering where the next case will come from."

"Definitely," I said.

Within eight weeks of starting my firm, I'd decided I never wanted to be anyone's employee again, but that didn't mean the roller coaster Jacey described didn't worry me. When I was busy, I worried I wouldn't get everything done, but the first time I left the office by five I felt on edge for fear I'd soon be sitting at an empty desk staring at bills I couldn't pay. Danielle promised me eventually I'd get more comfortable with it.

"Ed especially stressed because he handled the business side," Jacey said. "Bringing in clients, paying the bills, collecting fees. June just wanted to practice law."

I finished my whiskey sour and chewed the ice cube left at the bottom. "Was he good at it? Managing the business?"

"He had lots of clients. Maybe not as great with money. He spent a lot when times were good, and he had a hard time reining it in when they were slow. Whenever we finally settled a big case, he'd pay all the bills, but a lot of times there was nothing left, so the firm went right back into debt."

I made a note to look for lawsuits against Tabacchi or the firm relating to debts. It'd be ironic if the man running to handle money for Illinois had been hounded for bad debts himself.

Jacey didn't have anything else to tell me about the practice, so I asked some general questions, things I already knew answers to, so it would look more like I was getting background for an article.

"Who else are you looking at?" Jacey asked after I'd paid and we walked toward the concrete steps that lead up to Wacker Drive. "For the article?"

I rattled off the names of other lawyers recently turned politician that I'd compiled in case anyone I interviewed asked. Fortunately, most congresspeople at the state and federal level are or were lawyers, and there are tons of local positions where that's also true. When I actually wrote the article in my non-existent spare time, I'd have plenty of material.

We parted ways at street level.

I didn't want anyone to connect me with Cat Davis, so I headed north on Michigan Avenue and slipped through the gold revolving door of the Shops at North Bridge.

After being sure no one was watching me, I ducked into the second floor public restroom outside Nordstrom. I had a large shopping bag from a previous visit folded in my purse. Inside a stall, I stowed the purse, wig, and padded bra in the shopping bag. A few make up remover pads toned down my make up. I fluffed out my hair and emerged as myself, though wearing a T-shirt that was a bit baggy around the top since it was sized for the B cup bra.

Fifteen minutes later I rode the Red Line to my neighborhood to meet Lauren. She'd texted that she'd found out a lot about Dr. Victoria Vujic from her lunch date. Also, since my other attempts were failing, I was hoping she could work her magic to get me some time with Edward Tabacchi.

56

"HERE'S THE DEAL," LAUREN SAID.

We sat at Sociale, a wine bar and restaurant on the corner of Clark and Polk. At the base of a luxury apartment complex, it stands in what had been a parking lot with broken asphalt and tons of gravel when I'd moved into Printers Row.

Café des Livres doesn't serve alcohol, so it was our default when we wanted to have wine with dinner. Or just wine.

Whenever it's warm out, the restaurant's north and east walls fold open to the outdoor seating space. We sat at a tall table on the edge of the divide. It still felt like dining outside, but we weren't breathing as much of the construction dust blowing over from a nearby construction site.

Lauren had ordered a bottle of Pinot Noir before I'd arrived. I might have chosen a less pricy bottle, but this one probably was a good compromise between my preference for fruitier wines and hers for heavy ones like Cabernets.

I started with ice water. Diving into the wine immediately after the whiskey sour seemed like a bad idea.

I hoped Lauren would get to the point quickly, without adding too much drama. Being so careful what I said to Jacey had been more wearing than I'd realized until I'd found myself slumping against the wall during the L ride.

Lauren put our menus back into the holder on the side of the table. "After losing her medical license, Dr. Vujic moved to New York, got an M.B.A., and started a vitamin company with a partner who was still an M.D. They put out this pill, Sober Sooner, as a cure for drunkenness."

I raised my eyebrows. "Nothing cures drunkenness."

"That's completely what the FDA said. The partner left the company. Vujic started a new business without him selling basically the same formula but as an aid to recovering from hangovers."

Our favorite waiter brought the charcuterie plate Lauren had also asked for before I arrived. As Lauren relayed the rest of our order, I noticed a slim guy with a beard playing with his phone at the bar. He looked familiar, and after a second I realized he was roughly the height and weight of the burglar and my mugger. My whole body stiffened.

After the waiter left, I leaned forward and told Lauren in a low voice.

"Let's get a photo," she said, motioning to the waiter to come back.

"What?"

She positioned us so we stood arm-in-arm with our backs to the bar and asked the waiter to take the photo. She asked him to do three different ones, slightly altering our poses. The guy was in the background of two, and in one his face was visible.

By the end, I felt foolish. There must be thousands of slim bearded guys in the city. Maybe tens of thousands.

"Can't be too careful," Lauren said. "Did he seem like he was watching us?"

"Not that I noticed."

Our roasted beet salad had arrived. One eye on the man at

the bar, I asked Lauren what had happened with Vujic's new product.

"She was careful," Lauren said. "The ingredients didn't make it a drug, and she didn't claim it made you less drunk. Which makes it like any other herbal remedy. She could say whatever she wanted about promoting health as long as she put in enough disclaimers."

A young woman with spiky hair joined the bearded guy at the bar. The two moved to a low table near rows of wine bottles that were stored behind glass on the long wall of the restaurant. I relaxed a little, though I still planned to check if he was around when Lauren and I left.

I ate a few small chunks of beet. "I can't believe I didn't find any of this."

"You wouldn't. She was married at the time, to the doctor, and all of it was in her married name. When she got divorced, she went back to her maiden name and went to Palmer College."

I ate some prosciutto and tried the wine. It had deep cherry notes but was a bit on the dry side. "It shows she's a little shady. Maybe more than a little. But it doesn't relate to Marco."

Lauren pointed her fork at me. "Maybe not, but guess who was with her the whole time? Through absolutely every stage of her career?"

"Cora Smith."

"You got it. They're cousins."

I dipped some bread in olive oil and thought about Cora. Definitely great loyalty to Dr. Vujic, but there was no crime in that. Still, Lauren had found good background information, and I was grateful to her.

"You got a lot from the fifty-five year old."

Lauren smiled, showing her perfectly straight white teeth. "Totally. And it was fun. We're going out Friday."

"Catholic?" I said.

She nodded. "And not a CEO, a real one."

Lauren didn't date non-Catholics because she didn't want to marry outside her faith. By Catholic, she meant a man who agreed with the Church on most major issues plus attended mass every Sunday and every holy day. Not a Christmas-and-Easter-Only Catholic.

I spread Camembert on a piece of multi-grain bread. "Did he know Dr. Vujic well?"

"He did, but not any more. I'm sure he won't say anything to her."

The roasted cauliflower arrived, and the waiter poured more wine. As we were finishing it, the bearded guy and his friend paid and left. Despite that, I felt glad that Lauren and I would be walking home together. The man at the restaurant probably had nothing to do with me, but someone who had assaulted me and broken into my office was still out there.

The wind shifted, turning much cooler as I filled Lauren in on what I'd learned about Tabacchi.

I felt like I was leaving out important parts, as the whiskey sour plus the wine had made my thoughts blurry. I shivered, wishing I'd brought a sweater, and stared at my empty wine glass. I knew that the alcohol was part of it, but at this moment I felt like I'd never uncover the truth. Eric and I would be in limbo forever, never knowing why we'd lost Marco.

"Nothing you learned rules Vujic in or out as a suspect," I said.

"No." Lauren covered my hand with hers. Her fingers were warm, and I felt a little better. "But my back's been bothering me. I made an appointment this morning for my first chiropractic adjustment."

57

I drummed my fingers on my desk.

It was early evening the day after my dinner with Lauren, and I'd taken a break from my law work to dig further into Edward Tabacchi's life. His former partner June Somers was retired, and I hadn't been able to find a current address or phone number for her. The other former employees I'd unearthed hadn't gotten back to me yet.

Tabacchi was listed on Avvo, a site that compiles information on attorneys. I've found it mixed as far as reliability goes. It seems to draw from public records to fill in information, then urges people to correct it if it's wrong. It had me listed as an attorney but my employer as the accounting firm where I'd worked for two years after college and before law school. I updated my own information, declined to pay a fee to join, and hunted for Tabacchi.

Before becoming a named partner, he'd been an associate for June Somers, P.C. Before that, he'd worked briefly at a firm that mainly handled white collar crime, which made sense with his prosecuting background. That seemed to be where he'd gone right after the State's Attorney's office.

The timeline was incomplete, though. If Avvo's dates were to be believed, there was a six-month gap after he'd left the State's Attorney's office and a nine-month gap before June Somers, P.C.

The subscription databases Danielle and I belonged to confirmed the Avvo information, but neither filled in the gap.

The Attorney Registration and Disciplinary Commission showed no complaints against Tabacchi, and he'd never been suspended, disbarred, or sanctioned.

On the street below, a siren blared. I pushed away from my desk, frustrated. Ed Tabacchi was probably a wild goose chase, and I had work to do for a hearing next week. But I had the nagging feeling I was missing something.

Restless, I wandered to the galley kitchen along the south wall of the suite. The smell of dead flowers hung in the air. A vase of wilted tulips, a forgotten gift from a court reporter to Mensa Sam for his birthday, sat in the center of the table. I dumped it out and washed the vase, my thoughts spinning.

Maybe I'd been going about this all wrong focusing on Tabacchi's online presence and information.

Tabacchi was a charmer, a glad-hander. As an aspiring politician and an attorney, it had been part of his job to meet people and reel them in. Perhaps the connection was personal, not political.

I returned to my office and made two lists. One included people I'd talked to who knew Marco, and the other people I'd talked to or would like to interview about Tabacchi. I eyeballed the professions and jobs listed next to each person, considering whether the ones on the Marco list could have crossed paths with Tabacchi and vice versa.

Perhaps even a long time ago.

58

THE NEXT MORNING I AWOKE EXHAUSTED, BUT AT LEAST I'D SLEPT. I was finally used to the hardness of the futon, though each time I crawled onto it I heard Gram's practical voice telling me how ridiculous it was that I'd spent so much on a King-sized bed I wasn't sleeping in.

I'd worked at home until ten the night before researching Tabacchi further and preparing for my hearing. I'd also emailed Joe and Danielle with an idea about getting into Tabacchi's orbit. It was a long shot, but both said they'd think about it.

Clutching a giant-sized Earl Grey Crème tea from Café des Livres, I popped into Mensa Sam's office first thing. I was hoping he could help me find someone who might connect the dots between my Marco list and my Tabacchi list. I was leaving Vujic Chiropractic to Lauren for now.

Sam wore black Spandex as usual. He waved me in as he finished a phone call.

After he hung up, he shook his head. "Woman's son walked in front of a car. Against a red light. And she wants to sue the driver because pedestrians have the right of way."

A stack of files covered his visitor chair, so I remained standing. "Did the son survive?"

"Barely. But no way she'd win a lawsuit. There's at least 90 percent contrib. That's contributory negligence."

I sipped my tea, which I'd let steep too long, giving it a bitter taste that overrode the hints of vanilla. "Right. You can't be over fifty percent at fault."

"In Illinois, if you're partly responsible for your injuries, you can still sue," Sam said.

I nodded. "I know."

I debated adding that I'd ridden to work on a purple giraffe to test my theory that he wasn't actually hearing any word I said.

"So if like this woman's son, you're crossing the street, but it's against a light—"

"And the jury finds you're fifty percent or more at fault you can't recover," I said.

Sam waved his hand. "—you'll never recover anything. Because ninety percent—that's way over the fifty percent limit. Get it?"

"Yes," I said, as I not only know the law, I'm not stupid. I didn't say that to Sam though, since I wanted his help.

"So I had to tell her that, and she was not happy," Sam said.

"I'm sure," I said. "Do you happen to know anyone at Conway and Flaherty?"

Conway and Flaherty was the firm that had defended Marco in Alafair Halliwell's case. I'd learned yesterday from the firm's receptionist that the specific lawyer who'd represented Marco was long gone. She'd given me his name, and I'd called him at his new firm, but he'd remembered nothing. Not too surprising. Conway and Flaherty was high volume. He'd probably handled hundreds if not thousands of cases since Marco had settled with Alafair.

My odds of getting any other lawyer at Conway and

Flaherty to research a closed file were slight. The attorneys there billed by the hour and had to bill over forty hours a week to keep their jobs. Which meant they worked fifty to seventy hours each week because not all attorney work can be billed to clients.

Asking one of them to spend time on a legal matter they couldn't bill was like asking them to donate hundreds of dollars. Some nice person might do it, but probably not for a random stranger. If Mensa Sam knew an attorney there well, though, I might have better luck.

"They don't do taxes," Mensa Sam said. "They defend personal injury cases."

I set my tea next to the philodendron with yellowed leaves that straggled across the corner of his desk. It sat directly in the sun that shone through the window behind Sam. "I know that. Do you know anyone there?"

"You should talk to your insurance company if you were in a crash."

"I wasn't. I need information for a case they handled years ago."

Sam typed something, eyes on his computer monitor. "Your insurance company will hire a lawyer for you. You don't hire someone yourself."

"Sam." I placed both hands on his desk so I was right in his face. "Stop. Listen. For five seconds. I'm not hiring an attorney. I want to ask about an old case the firm handled. If you know someone, it'd help me, because I might need someone who can dig around a bit."

His head jerked back. "Jesus. No need to get pissy. Let me see."

I straightened and exhaled. It almost felt good to be angry about something other than Marco's death.

"Hold on." He scrolled through the contacts on his phone. "Try Patrick O'Reilly. He's been there a hundred years."

"That's what I need. How do you know him?"

"He comes every year to Halloweem."

"He's a member?" I said, stifling a groan.

Halloweem is a yearly Mensa event held on Halloween in Chicago. I'd gone once with Danielle years ago when she'd been invited by Mensa Sam. The costume party was kind of fun. A lot of people dressed as puns or as characters from their favorite movies or shows. I was Faith from Buffy the Vampire Slayer—an easy costume, as all I needed were black leather pants and a black tank top.

A guy in the elevator had made a crude joke about holding a poster he had of Buffy and Faith with one hand. I'd skipped Halloween ever after.

Mensa Sam snorted. "Hardly Mensa quality. A friend got him in. But we stayed in touch. He sent me a few cases."

If he'd sent Sam cases, he'd probably earned some referral fees from them, so that should make him more willing to help.

I hoped.

59

"NOT SURE I CAN HELP," PATRICK O'REILLY SAID. "HOW LONG ago was it?"

I'd pulled up Patrick's firm profile photo on my office laptop. He looked a bit portly, and his jowls sagged, but it was clear he'd fit Conway and Flaherty's smooth good looks requirement when he'd been hired at the start of his career.

"The suit was filed twelve years ago," I said.

I'd already assured him I wasn't looking for anything confidential.

Attorneys can't share what their clients say without permission or reveal their work to anyone else. But I was only asking for information I could have learned from the court file, which would have been available to the public had it been where it ought to be.

"The paper file would be in off-site storage. I can only have it pulled at a client's request. But I can check our system," Patrick said.

He offered to call me back, but I said I'd rather hold, afraid the task would get put to one side as soon as we hung up.

After a minute or two, Patrick said, "Here it is. The plaintiff's firm was Johnson and Sandman. Individual attorney listed is Archibald Sandman."

I twisted strands of hair around my fingers. "Was he the lead attorney on the case?"

Though Johnson and Sandman hadn't had a website, I had learned about the named partner Archibald Sandman from lawyer databases. He'd retired five years ago and died of a heart attack two years after that. If he was the end of the line in my efforts to learn more about Alafair Halliwell's case, I was out of luck.

"Not necessarily. Our clerks enter into the case management software the name of whoever's listed on the Complaint."

The Complaint is the formal document that starts the lawsuit. Often the lead partner is listed on it whether or not that person expects to be working on the case on a day-to-day basis or at all. Depending on how Johnson and Sandman worked, Archibald Sandman might never have met Alafair Halliwell.

"So it could have been someone else," I said.

"Probably was," Patrick said. "Archibald wasn't a hands-on lawyer, to put it politely. Had good family connections, so he brought in business. But no one sent anything challenging to him. Or his firm. Nothing that required serious brain power."

He sounded a lot like Mensa Sam, though Sam would be appalled that I thought so given that he could theoretically prove his brain power with I.Q. test results.

"So all small cases?" I said.

"Strictly Municipal. And parking tickets."

The Municipal Division in Cook County oversees cases where damages are below $30,000. Mensa Sam's cases were mostly in Municipal.

I rocked my chair back and stared at the exposed metal ductwork running along my office ceiling. "Strange for a firm like that to have a med mal case."

"The woman must not have known better."

A lot of people think one attorney is interchangeable with another. Danielle had talked to a potential client recently who later told her he'd hired a cheaper attorney, one who would only charge him $1,000, to defend a murder.

"When he ends up in jail for natural life, I'm sure it'll console him that he saved money," Danielle said. "What does he think, he's going to get Clarence Darrow for $1,000?"

For med mal, though, the attorney gets paid based on a percentage of what's recovered for the client, and that percentage is set by law. So on top of getting a less experienced attorney, the person is paying as much as someone who has the best lawyer in the state.

"What about Johnson?" I said. "Sandman's partner?"

"That's Judge Johnson now. Will County."

I hadn't had any cases in Will County, so I didn't know the judges there. Danielle might.

I typed Judge Johnson into a search box and found his official court website. "His bio doesn't mention the firm. And I searched before, and there was no website for it."

"It wasn't around long. Johnson was let go from his previous firm—not enough business—and he was running for judge. It was his third run, and he finally got elected, so Johnson and Sandman ended up being sort of a placeholder. He left, and Archibald continued on under his own name."

"And he kept this Halliwell case?"

Keys clicked in the background. "Looks like it. No—wait. He kept it, but after five years, Sullivan's office added an appearance. Whole case closed a year later."

Matt Sullivan was a well-known Chicago personal injury attorney. It wasn't unusual for a lawyer with little trial experience to bring in someone like him as the case neared trial. Ironically, that often resulted in settlement.

I asked if Patrick could hold for a moment and quickly

scrolled through my timeline for the gap in Tabacchi's resume. There it was. It corresponded with the check paid to Alafair Halliwell and to the time Johnson and Sandman had existed.

"Did Johnson and Sandman have any associates?" I asked Patrick.

One of the main things Jacey had told me about Tabacchi, in addition to his many women, was that he was terrible with money, and the most common reason lawyers get in trouble is money—specifically, stealing a client's money. If Tabacchi had worked at Johnson and Sandman and represented Alafair, maybe he'd done something shady with Marco's settlement payment.

"Can't recall. Probably. Neither one was a fan of hard work."

I stood and paced between my desk and Danielle's. "Does Edward Tabacchi ring a bell?"

"Isn't he an alderman?"

"Was," I said. "He's running for Comptroller."

"That's probably why I recognize the name. Sorry, it's too long ago to remember if I knew him as an attorney."

I thanked him anyway and hung up.

The timeline couldn't be a coincidence. It couldn't.

60

ON MY LAPTOP, I OPENED THE PHOTOS I'D TAKEN OF THE CHECK Marco had written to settle with Alafair Halliwell. When a plaintiff's personal injury attorney settles a case, the check is typically made out to the plaintiff—the injured person—and the plaintiff's attorney's law firm, plus any medical care providers who treated the plaintiff but agreed to wait until the end of the lawsuit to get paid.

The attorney gets everyone to sign the check and deposits the whole amount in what's called a client trust account.

The attorney is supposed to immediately cut checks from that account. One check goes to the plaintiff's firm for the attorney's fees, other checks go to doctors or hospitals if there are any, and the remaining amount goes to the plaintiff.

If the plaintiff's attorney does everything right, the balance in the trust account should be zero for all but the brief time it takes those checks to clear. Attorneys aren't allowed to earn interest on any money that sits in a trust account.

Marco's check was made out to Alafair Halliwell and Johnson and Sandman. There were no medical care providers listed.

On the back was a signature of Alafair Halliwell that matched the one on the settlement release. The writing underneath it looked less like a signature and more like a series of indecipherable interconnected swirls. No lawyers had signed the release.

As I enlarged the swirls, Danielle came in and plunked her briefcase and a Venti Starbucks cup on the credenza. The scent of mocha Frappuccino filled the office, and chimes played as Danielle's laptop opened.

I stared at the writing. The swirls might start with a capital E, but the letter could as easily be a B, F, I, K, P, R, S, or Z. The rest of the letters were nothing but squiggles. It was tempting to see it as a purposeful attempt to hide the lawyer's name, but I'd seen stranger signatures.

What I needed were independent examples of Edward Tabacchi's and Alafair Halliwell's signatures. I needed Alafair's because the signature on the settlement release could have been forged along with the one on the check.

There was no signature on any page of Tabacchi's campaign website. I wondered if there'd been one on the site he'd had as alderman.

"Is that what he was hiding?" I said aloud.

Danielle spun her desk chair around to face me. "What?"

"I think Ed Tabacchi might have represented Alafair Halliwell when she settled with Marco."

I filled her in on what I'd learned and showed her the settlement release, check, and the timeline.

She stood behind me and studied each document over my shoulder. "It's a lot to hang on a gap in a resume and an illegible signature."

"A pretty coincidental gap."

She leaned against the credenza. "So Tabacchi settles, and around the same time, Alafair calls Marco. You're thinking she was complaining she hadn't gotten paid yet and that Tabacchi 'borrowed' the funds?"

"Or stole," I said.

Danielle had defended an attorney who had told his client the other side had settled a case but not yet paid. The attorney cashed the settlement check and paid his own bills. Six months down the road, when times were better, he paid the client what she was owed, saying the money had finally come through.

Of course, he didn't pay her interest on the money he'd "borrowed," and borrowing was against the law regardless.

It would have required some finagling for Tabacchi to do the same because he wasn't a named partner in Johnson and Sandman, so his bank might have questioned why he was depositing the check. On the other hand, if the check cleared with no problem, it might not have raised a flag.

"He would have had to forge Alafair's signature," Danielle said.

I enlarged the signature lines on the settlement release. "The one on the release doesn't look hard to copy. She wrote evenly with big letters. Or maybe she never saw or signed the release at all and never knew the claim against Marco settled."

Danielle shook her head. Her pearl earrings caught the sunlight through the window and stood out against her black and silver hair. "But then why call Marco to say she hadn't been paid?"

"Maybe Tabacchi told her the court dropped Marco from the case and she called because she was mad at Marco and wanted to have her say."

Danielle held up her hand. "Lot of maybes. Let's not get too far ahead. You don't know it was Tabacchi who represented Alafair. And would she really have been pissed at Marco? She had one office visit with him. Maybe she called to thank him for settling early or apologize that he'd gotten sued at all."

That fit with what Will Halliwell had suggested about his

aunt. I sat back in my chair, dropping my hands to my lap. "Thanks for raining on my parade."

"Here to help." Danielle smiled. "I'm not saying you're wrong. But don't leap to conclusions, or you might miss something else. There's always another side."

"Spoken like a true defense attorney."

"I had the same standards as a prosecutor."

She was right. As any attorney knows, the facts are never exactly what your client claims, or what anyone does. The truth is somewhere in the overlap and gaps.

———

I tried calling Will Halliwell and got voicemail. He returned the call when I was slicing pre-cooked chicken breast to add to stir-fry. Lauren had come over for dinner. So far, she'd managed to chat with Cora Smith about negotiating a package deal on chiropractic treatment, but she hadn't learned anything new.

I explained to Will that I was looking for something with his aunt's signature and why. He promised to see what he could find.

"I appreciate it," I said. "I know I'm a stranger asking for a lot of favors."

"It's all right," he said. "If someone defrauded my aunt, I kind of want to know about it."

After we hung up, I coated a pan with a coconut oil blend and filled Lauren in on my fruitless attempts to find something online that Tabacchi had signed.

"I figured the best place to find his signature is his office," I said.

Lauren finished slicing a pepper and moved on to a fresh garlic clove. "How would you get in?"

"I can't. People are there all hours. But his home office—"

Lauren handed me the plate of sliced vegetables and minced garlic. "You're sure he has one?"

"Yep."

In my research I'd learned that the Tabacchis and their son lived in a townhome that was one of five that had been carved out of the John Dawes House. Dawes was a prominent businessman and physician in Chicago's gilded age. Located about a mile and a half north of the Chicago River in the neighborhood now known as the Gold Coast, his was one of the few mansions that still existed from the building boom era after the Chicago Fire and before the Great Depression.

Unlike the more famous Glessner House, the Dawes House never attained landmark status, but there had been a few articles about it over the years. One was written after the Tabacchis moved in, and it mentioned they had a home office in a turret room.

"But he's not going to invite you to visit him," Lauren said.

I stirred the vegetables and meat, careful not to let the oil splatter on the stove. "His wife might."

It was what I'd talked with Danielle and Joe about, and I was hoping Lauren could work some magic to make the whole scheme come together.

Ariana Tabacchi was an executive of the Royal Albert hotel chain, which had been started by her great-grandfather. Like a lot of politician's wives she also served on non-profit boards and did a lot of entertaining.

As best I could tell from my research, her family connections and ability to connect with others were a large part of how Ed had become an alderman. Like a lot of men, he'd married and gained someone to manage his social calendar, and she'd married and added to her workload.

"So you're thinking, what, you'll offer to volunteer for a charity?" Lauren said after I explained my reasoning. "How does that get you in her home?"

The smells of garlic and red pepper filled the kitchen area. "Concerts are a great way to raise money. A house concert at the John Dawes House would be a big draw."

"The Harmoniums," Lauren said.

I shook my head. "Not The Harmoniums. I don't want Ed Tabacchi to guess I'm involved. But Joe and Danielle could do it. I'd come along as Joe's assistant, made up different, and look around."

For over a decade before I joined them, Danielle and Joe had played and sung together, mostly blues and jazz. They still did shows as a duo.

Lauren took out plates and silverware and set them on the kitchen island. "I thought you wanted answers before Eric's tuition is due. You can't organize a concert overnight."

"No, but I'm thinking you could sell her on a small gathering to bring people into the fold."

I was less concerned with the tuition deadline, which it was clear I couldn't meet, and more concerned with figuring out what had happened before Tabacchi, if he had been the murderer, could cover all his tracks.

"*I* could?" Lauren said.

The small event had been Danielle's idea. She'd been on the board of a non-profit that did job training for homeless teenagers. To help potential donors understand their mission, the board members each invited a small group of friends and colleagues to their homes for an informal wine and cheese evening. No donation required to attend, and no commitment, just an understanding that it was to hear about the organization.

"Ariana goes to all those high society charity events you love. You must know someone in common."

Those types of events, the ones that get attendees' photos in local newspapers and on social media, are good for Lauren for client connections. Plus she loves wearing cocktail dresses or evening gowns and making her date wear a tux.

Lauren rinsed romaine and spinach leaves for our salads. "I'll try. But say she totally buys it and you look around while everyone's paying attention to the music. What if you get caught?"

"It's not like I can be charged with breaking and entering. I'll be an invited guest, just one who was snooping."

At least, that's what I told myself.

61

WHILE LAUREN WORKED ON GETTING AN INTRODUCTION TO Ariana Tabacchi, I decided to go see Detective Sergeant Beckwell. My official purpose was to tell him what I'd learned about ChiTown and ask how I could have the possible financial fraud looked into.

We met in his office, a small interior room with a window overlooking a larger section of the police station. He wore a light gray suit today with a dark gray tie and white shirt.

He agreed I'd been right to request a forensic accounting on ChiTown and set the wheels in motion for a criminal investigation of the finances.

"Isn't there a chance it's connected to Marco's death?"

"We'll coordinate. If anything's uncovered that looks connected, I'll know," he said.

I told him what else I'd learned about Dr. Vujic and Tabacchi, including my theory about Tabacchi and Alafair Halliwell.

"Edward Tabacchi's accounted for the night Marco died," he said.

"You looked into him?"

He leaned back in his desk chair. "Ms. Davis, the police actually do investigate."

"I didn't mean that the way it sounded. I just never realized he was a suspect."

The detective waved his hand. "Not a suspect. But you and others indicated Mr. Ruggirello had no interest in politics and it was out of character for him to attend the fundraiser for Mr. Tabacchi. We looked for a personal connection between the two. And found none beyond the neighbor who invited Mr. Ruggirello."

"I've just told you what the connection might be."

"Maybe. Regardless, we learned that Mr. Tabacchi was campaigning the night of Mr. Ruggirello's death."

"The entire night?"

The detective sighed, put on his reading glasses, clicked a few keys, and looked at his computer monitor. "The time of death is estimated to be between six and eleven PM. Mr. Tabacchi was at a Cub Scout spaghetti dinner—before that, I didn't know anyone still had those—from four to five-thirty p.m. After that, he shook hands with commuters at the Belmont L station. Aides were with him the whole time. He took them out afterward for drinks and was home with his wife by ten."

I found a Brown Line map on my phone.

"Belmont is six stops from Damen," I said. "He could have taken the train to Marco's when he was done with the Meet 'n' Greet. There are back steps. He could've gotten in and out and right back on the L."

The detective folded his hands in front of him on the desk. "There was no 'in and out.' Tabacchi would've had to overpower a man half his age, make him drink soda or rum laced with drugs, clean up any sign of struggle without it looking cleaned up, and take the L six stops back without anyone realizing he was gone."

I shook my head. "He didn't need to overpower Marco or

struggle. He could've visited for a bit, slipped something in the soda, gotten Marco impaired, and then mixed in the rum and encouraged him to drink the rest."

"Which still takes time, and he's accounted for the entire evening."

"By his aides. But his former employees used to lie for him about where he was and who he was with. Why wouldn't the current ones?"

The detective frowned. "Your information's a decade old. And it's one thing to lie on the phone when he's seeing multiple women—at a time when he was single, you're telling me. It's another to lie to the police about a murder investigation."

"Right, but did you say 'Hey, your boss is suspected of murder' or just ask where he was?"

The detective pulled off his glasses, his expression a mix of impatience and kindness. "Ms. Davis, I feel for you. You suffered a terrible loss. But this is the end. The investigation is closed. Don't let Mr. Ruggirello's death take over your life. Even if you learn something we didn't—and I don't see that happening—you can't bring him back. For your own well-being, and his son's, let it go."

I recognized the danger Detective Beckwell was warning me of. I'd seen it in my own mother.

But I couldn't let it go. I wouldn't.

————

Unfortunately, getting an introduction to Ariana Tabacchi wasn't as easy as I'd hoped. Lauren struck out, and so did Joe when he went through his list of contacts.

Finally I remembered Ikenna, the bartender from the Barry Calvin cocktail party. Joe and I went to the Saturday matinee of a play he was in at Lifeline Theater and hung out in the L-shaped waiting area afterwards until Ikenna appeared from back stage.

I introduced the two men and drifted away, pretending to study framed photos and faded news clips about past productions. Joe explained that he'd heard about Ariana Tabacchi's charity and wanted to help raise awareness for a local literacy organization a past client had been involved in that coordinated programs throughout Illinois, Indiana, and Wisconsin. Literacy was one of Ariana's most cherished causes, and this program was struggling to get funding with all the state budget cuts.

Ikenna texted Joe two days later. He'd talked to an actor who also ran a catering company that worked regularly for the Tabacchis. That person got Joe a meeting with Ariana.

By promising to use his network to get people to the event, making a substantial donation himself, and agreeing to have his "assistant" arrange everything so there was no extra work for Ariana, Joe was able to arrange a wine and cheese event at the Dawes House featuring his jazz/blues duo as entertainment.

The date was three weeks down the road. I wished it could be sooner, but I planned to use the time to follow up on other avenues. If I could help it, I'd rather not infiltrate the Tabacchis' house.

In my efforts to find Tabacchi's signature I discovered that prospective aldermen needed to file a Statement of Candidacy, which had to be signed. Those weren't available on the Internet, so I tried City Hall. The clerk there sent me to the Chicago Board of Elections in a separate building.

But I had no luck there. Tabacchi's Statement was too old to be stored on site, and regardless, I'd need to file a Freedom of Information Act request to get it. While under state law the city is required to make an initial response within five days, the administrator kindly told me with paper records that old the initial response was likely to be along the lines of "we'll start looking" and the actual records would be provided "who knows when."

All the same, I filled out and emailed a request.

My efforts to find an old case file where Tabacchi might have signed a motion or complaint were also stymied. The electronic docket allowed searching by party name or case number, but not by attorney.

Through general Internet searches I found Edward Tabacchi's name on an appeal. The original case was twenty-one years old, which brought me back to the musty-smelling Twelfth Floor of the Daley Center where I requested the file be pulled from off-site storage, despite feeling uneasy about the paper trail showing me looking into Tabacchi's past. If Edward Tabacchi had been involved in the break in to my office and the mugging, he was already aware of me. I'd just need to be extra careful everywhere I went.

The investigator in our suite had more luck. He found me names of staffers from Tabacchi's aldermanic days, specifically ones who'd been there when Tabacchi had opted not to run again. The timing of that coincided with when I thought Alafair had called Marco.

Though it might be fruitless to hide my identity, I once again became Cat Davis gathering information for an article.

It was akin to locking your screen door in the summer hoping to keep out burglars. Someone who really wanted to get in wouldn't be stopped, but there was no reason to make it easy.

62

Two former staffers of Alderman Tabacchi talked with me on the phone, but I didn't learn anything beyond material for my article. While I was waiting to hear back from a third, I finally got in touch with two ex-Vujic Chiropractic employees I'd been trying to reach.

One talked to me on the phone and the other answered email. Neither admitted to being Dr. X, but both echoed the complaints about how Dr. Vujic worked people to death and skimped on bonuses.

Both said they wouldn't be surprised if Vujic billed for treatments that hadn't been performed, but both denied doing that themselves. I doubted they'd admit it if they had, as that would be fraud.

Neither had met Marco or knew anything particular about Hazleton or Dr. Vujic's past.

Lauren's efforts to learn about Vujic Chiropractic were more fruitful. She called me at nine-thirty Thursday night—eight days before the event at the Tabacchis' house was scheduled—to tell me she'd had dinner with Cora Smith.

By the time I got downstairs to her condo she'd already poured wine into stained glass goblets and set out a marble cheeseboard with pickles, liver mousse pate, brie, and crackers that she set on the wrought iron table.

"Thought you had dinner," I said.

"I did. But I bet you didn't."

I didn't deny it. While I found it easier to eat than I had the first weeks after Marco's death, big meals or anything beyond finger food still made my stomach seize up.

A little chill had crept back into the air, and we used it as an excuse to turn on Lauren's gas fireplace though it was May and she had all her windows open.

"Cora Smith has a son graduating college next year," Lauren said. "I told her how many business people I meet being a broker, and she suggested drinks after the visit to pick my brain about his job strategy. And of course I said sure, and that maybe I knew people who could help him."

I didn't bother to ask how Lauren had gotten Cora to open up. Most people think the key to having a lot of friends and being popular is being a great talker, and for some it is. But it also works to ask about the other person and be an engaged listener, as Dale Carnegie would attest if he were still alive. Lauren was adept at both and could switch approaches as needed.

I spread some brie on a cracker. "And?"

"After we finished dinner—I suggested we make it dinner since I had a long drive home—she told me Dr. Vujic and Marco supposedly really hit it off. Don't get upset, but they actually went out for dinner."

I stopped eating in mid-bite. "When?"

It shouldn't be my focus, but if it was recent it had to overlap with when Marco had been seeing me.

"Early December. But Marco told her they couldn't date because of the ongoing investigation."

I got a sinking feeling in my stomach. "Cora's sure it was December?"

"Yeah, it happened after a site visit Marco made, and she's convinced Marco was trying to get the inside scoop by dating Victoria. So convinced that she followed them, then followed Marco home 'in case she needed to know where he lives.' That's a quote."

I drank some of the wine, barely registering its dark, slightly spicy flavor.

Marco's and my first real date, when he'd taken me to the play, had been the first weekend in December. But we'd texted and talked a lot during the week leading to it. I wished he'd told her he couldn't date her because he'd met someone special, not because of an investigation.

"He probably only went out with her to see if she'd say anything related to the investigation," Lauren said, reading my mind. "Or it was just a friendly dinner, not a date, a way to ease tensions and try to get her alone."

"Which sounds like he was trying to manipulate her. Doesn't make me feel a lot better."

Marco and I hadn't slept together by then, and I'd never had issues with guys I was involved with having women friends anymore than I expected them to be upset because Joe and I were close. But I still felt bad.

Lauren refilled my wine glass. "Don't you think she was doing the same? Trying to get in good with him to get Hazleton to ease off on the clinic, or else mentally taking notes on everything he said to use it against the company?"

"Probably," I said.

The reality is if there's a lawsuit or might be one, any time you deal with someone on the other side you're watching what you say or do because it might affect the case. Marco hadn't been the lawyer, but he'd been the company representative, and it's not like Victoria Vujic hadn't known that when she had dinner with him.

"And let's not miss the big point here," Lauren said. "Cora knew exactly where Marco lived."

63

I THOUGHT ABOUT CALLING DETECTIVE BECKWELL WITH WHAT Lauren had learned. But he'd already heard about Cora saying threatening things about Marco, once to Jerry Hernandez and once to Kassie Frampton. I didn't think a third time would make that much difference. It was more ominous that she'd followed Marco home, but it wasn't as if she couldn't have found his address through a quick Internet search.

Having already stretched the detective's patience, I didn't want to push him to the point of not listening to me if I found something that truly indicted Cora or anyone else. Lauren said she'd keep cultivating the friendship with Cora.

The following Sunday evening I met former Tabacchi staffer Dan Himmel for drinks. We sat along the river at the same place I'd taken Jacey Wilcox.

A middle-aged man with thinning brown hair that circled the back of his head, Dan had been the assistant to Edward Tabacchi's right hand man during his aldermanic years.

One of my main questions was whether Marco and Tabacchi ever met, but I hadn't found a good way to get an answer with the other two staffers, which was why I'd asked to meet Dan rather than talking by phone.

Maybe in person I'd get a better sense of how to move the conversation in the right direction. If I could find a way to work it in I planned to show him a photo I'd gotten from Eric of Marco when he'd been a new doctor.

I'd refused to tell Eric why I needed it. I didn't want to get his hopes up.

Dan ordered a glass of beer, or a plastic tumbler of beer, actually, as the establishments along the River Walk didn't use glass. I drank Ginger Ale. I didn't want to risk missing anything in a haze of alcohol.

For about thirty minutes I went through questions for my potential article. After that, I nudged the conversations toward insane work situations, remembering the stories Jacey had told me and hoping for something similar.

All Dan shared was that Tabacchi hadn't known how to create a Word document and had always required his staff to print out emails for him to read, then dictated responses for the staff to send. Sometimes they'd spent hours a day doing that.

I told him about an awful experience my first week at the large law firm. The firm had thousands of attorneys nation-wide, so if Dan asked anyone there now about "Cat Davis," it would be believable that no one remembered her.

As the sun dropped lower in the sky, Dan ordered a second beer and I finished my soda. The breeze from the east grew cooler, and I still hadn't come up with a graceful or subtle way to ask about Marco. I had learned, though, that Dan hadn't seen or talked to Tabacchi for seven or eight years.

I straightened my shoulders. I couldn't waste any more time. "I need to know if a doctor came to see the alderman toward the end of his term."

"A doctor?" A shadow crossed Dan's face, and he looked down at his beer. "What's that got to do with your article?"

"Nothing." Dancing around the issue had gotten me nowhere with the first two staffers. It was either take a chance or give up. "I can't tell you why I'm asking, but I have a serious personal reason for wanting to know."

Dan glanced over at a fleet of bright green kayaks speeding along the river. "Serious how?"

"Someone I love might have died because of it."

He bit his lip but didn't say anything.

I scrolled to the photo Eric had sent me and passed my phone across the table.

Dan studied the photo. In it, Marco looked to be in his late twenties or early thirties. His hair was short and cropped close to his head so you couldn't see its waviness, and his expression was serious. This was Marco the surgeon, or almost-surgeon, a man I'd never met, not really.

I'd spent ten minutes looking at it myself the night before. I wished I could go back in time and know Marco from then until now. At least I'd have had years rather than months.

I explained about the fundraiser Tabacchi had at Marco's building, and how Marco had attended though he had no interest in politics.

The phone shook in Dan's hand. He set it down. "A doctor came to see Ed. They sat closed in his office for a long time, and Ed left right after. A week later he told us he'd decided not to run again. Whether the doctor was the man in this photo, I can't say for sure, but it could have been."

I stared at the phone lying on the table. Dan linking Marco and Tabacchi seemed too easy.

"And you're telling me this why?" I said.

Dan looked away. A small yacht docked at a restaurant across the river.

"I saw a piece on the local news about Marco Ruggirello's death and it showed his photo," Dan said. "He looked familiar, but I didn't know why. A few days later, it hit me that he might have been that doctor. But I wasn't sure. The police never contacted me, so I figured there was no connection."

I gripped the sides of the table. "What? Why didn't you call them?"

"And say what? I think this doctor who died might be a person who visited my boss over ten years ago?"

"What would it have hurt?"

Dan took a long slug of beer. "You can't seriously be asking that. I still work for the city. The 'former' in front of alderman doesn't mean Ed can't get me fired."

"Okay, so you told me now. Why aren't you worried about the same thing?"

Dan slammed his cup down, sending drops of beer flying over the table and my phone. "Of course I'm worried. But if somehow that visit might relate to murder, that matters more than my job, doesn't it?"

"No question."

The timing didn't prove Marco had forced Tabacchi not to run for alderman again, but if I was right that Tabacchi had cheated Alafair Halliwell that must be what had happened.

I thanked Dan, wiped my phone with a napkin, and stowed it in my purse.

He stood and motioned toward the table. "You've got this, right? I need to get home."

"Yes. Thanks again. If I can help it, I won't mention your name."

He sighed. "If it comes out that Ed was mixed up in the doctor's death, my name will come out. But I guess it won't matter then."

––––––––––

Now I truly regretted my earlier visit to the detective. If I hadn't yet gone to see him, I could have added this information from

Dan plus what Lauren had learned and made a case for him to reopen the investigation.

Danielle shook her head when I told her the next morning in our office, pointing out that Dan hadn't been sure it had been Marco until I'd asked him leading questions. To make it worse, when I'd done some digging about Dan I'd learned he'd made a lot of donations to one of Tabacchi's primary opponents and had volunteered for that woman's campaign. It was possible he'd told me what I wanted to hear, hoping it might smear Tabacchi.

I followed up with Will Halliwell, hoping for an original signature from Alafair. But he'd had no luck. My call to the court clerk about the file I'd requested also got me nowhere, as it had yet to be located.

It added to my suspicion that someone was ensuring any files Tabacchi had handled disappeared, but my experience as an attorney convinced me that bureaucratic incompetence was an equally likely explanation.

I paced my office, jaw clenched in frustration. The reality was, people didn't sign documents anymore. What would have been simple in my Gram's heyday was a real challenge now when emails were the accepted means of business communication, e-signatures stood in for handwritten ones in most courtrooms, and no one sent handwritten letters.

As far as Ed Tabacchi went, everything was riding on searching his office, which for all I knew was under lock and key.

On that point at least, I knew how to prepare.

64

I CONSULTED A FRIEND FROM MY THEATER DAYS WHO WAS NOW the Technical Director at one of Chicago's larger theaters where he oversaw set construction and safety. Over the decades, he'd built sets and handled props for hundreds of productions at small and storefront theaters.

While technically none of that related to breaking and entering, he'd often repurposed and refurbished old furniture, cabinets, and other items. He'd also organized a fair amount of guerilla theater and gaming in his twenties, making use of boarded and padlocked vacant buildings. Most important, I'd known him since I was nine, and he was willing to bend a few rules for me without asking questions.

Armed with a set of skeleton keys, a tension wrench, a lock pic, and a paperclip bent into an L with a paintbrush holder fixed on one end to make it easier to work with, I practiced in the back room of the theater where my friend worked.

I worked until I could unlock doors and get into locked desk drawers and file cabinets. I also practiced on file cabinets in the suite after hours, accompanied by Joe or Lauren because I didn't want to be alone there.

Mensa Sam's cabinets were the easiest. In all of them, though, it wasn't that hard to feel the lock pins and create the tension needed to release the locks.

Door locks challenged me more, but I got better and better. I told Danielle and Joe to play long and loud because I wasn't particularly quick or quiet. I kept dropping the tools.

By the Wednesday before the concert, I felt nervous but ready.

———

On Thursday morning I sent the detective an email telling him what Lauren and I had learned about Vujic Chiropractic and Tabacchi, though I didn't share our plans for the next evening. He responded with his usual comment about the investigation being closed, but he told me the investigation into ChiTown Property was progressing, and he didn't add his usual advice about stopping my efforts. Either he'd gotten tired of warning me or he was starting to think he might've missed something after all.

I hoped it was the second reason, but I'd read too many studies about how often people misread tone in emails and had seen it too often myself in litigation to have any real hope.

———

Earlier in the week, Lauren and I had hunted for information on the layout of the Tabacchis' townhome. I'd hoped to access building plans through the City of Chicago. Both the original conversion from the John Dawes mansion and a later remodel had required permits. But it turned out that for safety reasons, and because the architect has the intellectual property right in the design, those types of plans aren't available to the public.

At the Harold Washington Library, though, I found prints of

articles, complete with photos, on the conversion and later remodels, including the one Ariana Tabacchi did when she and Ed married.

Between the articles and information from a real estate agent Lauren knew who'd handled two of the other townhomes in the Dawes House, Lauren and I made a rough sketch of the layout of the Tabacchi home.

It was one of five four-story adjoining townhouses. The ground floor, with an open kitchen, dining area, living room, and powder room, was its largest floor.

The second floor was slightly smaller, though its larger bedroom and bath spanned 500 square feet, the size of a small studio apartment. The smaller bedroom also had an en suite bath. A stairway between them led to the third floor master bedroom and bath. It was in the shape of a circle, as it formed the base of a turret.

Rather than the stairway inside continuing, there was a bend in the hall that led to a wide cast iron spiral staircase. It led to the top floor, another circular room in the turret, this one with sloping ceilings and a skylight.

It made for a beautiful home office. In the latest photos, a large antique partners desk dominated one half of the room along with antique file cabinets, and a credenza. Beneath the skylight stood a group of armchairs around another Art Deco table, bookcases, and closets. With all of those furnishings, there was still plenty of open floor space.

Sliding glass doors beyond the armchairs led to a wide balcony that melded into the exterior fire escapes for the other townhomes and overlooked the interior courtyard garden.

The townhome had originally belonged to Ed's wife. It had been in her family for decades. County property records showed she'd transferred it to joint ownership three years after they married, which explained how a man who'd been a general practice attorney and alderman but now had no current visible means of support could afford it.

Nice deal if you can get it.

If I were unafraid of being caught, I might have considered trying to get into the office from the courtyard, as fire escapes led from the courtyard to each balcony. But I wasn't keen on adding breaking and entering to my resume and ending my career.

65

For the concert, I played the role of Catherine, Joe's assistant.

When we arrived, I stowed the extra appetizers in the gleaming SubZero refrigerator. It was to be a casual evening, as casual as one in a two-million dollar townhome can be, so I set wine, liquor, and mixers on the granite counter and cheese and other appetizers next to festive paper plates and cocktail napkins on the Art Deco era dining table. Despite my sweating hands and fluttering heart, I couldn't help admiring its lacquer finish and alternating dark and light wood grain.

Guests gathered in the sunken living room that looked larger than my entire condo.

Had anyone asked, I would have given my last name as Dee, but no one did. I didn't expect them to. With most professional and business people, anyone who appears to be an assistant is invisible unless something goes wrong.

To play the part, I'd worn narrow legged black pants and a bright red ruffled shift from H&M, pieces very different from my business clothes. I'd pulled my hair into a ponytail and applied deep red lipstick that matched the blouse.

Subtle use of three blush shades gave me sharp cheekbones I didn't actually have. False eyelashes and shimmery eye shadow—something else bought for the event—made my eyes stand out.

I got my nails done at a salon, something I'm opposed to on moral grounds because professional men are never expected to do it and it unnecessarily sucks up women's time and money. The nails were short, though, for ease with the lock picking tools that filled my small purse.

Lauren wasn't attending the event—she had her own assignment—but she'd added huge dangling gold-tone earrings from Wal-Mart to my outfit. We hoped my overall look signaled I didn't have money. Another reason I hoped most guests, and their hostess, would look right past me.

To my relief, Ed Tabacchi had a campaign event elsewhere that night, as he did almost every night, and a few questions by Joe revealed that the son was gone for the weekend. Joe and Danielle were tasked with keeping an eye out for an early return of either and watching Ariana.

I'd felt pretty sure I could fool Tabacchi since he'd only met me briefly, but I hadn't been in a play in nearly twelve years, so I was relieved he was out. My skills might not be quite what they once had been.

About thirty minutes in, Joe and Danielle took out their guitars. During the second song, I saw someone go into the ground floor powder room. I asked a woman I'd seen chatting with Ariana Tabacchi earlier if she knew where other restrooms were, putting urgency into my voice and clutching my purse. She nodded toward the stairs. I already knew, but I wanted cover in case anyone was watching me.

I climbed quickly and quietly above the second floor, where a legitimate guest would use one of the bathrooms, and the third, with the master bedroom suite. I heard no sounds from any of the bedrooms, and all the doors were closed.

The spiral staircase was narrower than it had looked in the magazine photos, and each step barely had space for my foot. I paused, slipped on lightweight cotton gloves, and gripped the iron railing to keep from losing my balance.

At the top, the door to the office was shut, but the handle turned easily. I pushed it open gradually, intent on minimizing creaks. The guitar music and vocals from downstairs ought to cover any noise, but there was no such thing as being too careful.

Joe's warm, resonant voice carried easily to the top of the stairs. I hoped he had equally sharp eyes. If Ed Tabacchi appeared or Ariana headed for the stairs, Joe was to end the song and let Danielle play the next without him, then text me. My phone was on vibrate in my pocket.

I left the lights off. Rays from the nearly setting sun came through the windows to the west, and a little bit more from the skylight above.

To the east sliding doors led to the balcony and fire escape. That area was darker, and the steps zigzagging down the side of the building from it already were in shadows.

Once my eyes adjusted, I studied the room. There were no paintings on the walls. It would have been hard to hang them, I supposed, given the curves, though a built-out closet provided a few flat walls that were empty. Had there been a painting with a safe behind it, it would have done me no good. I knew nothing about getting into safes.

The closet revealed nothing other than office supplies and two men's suits in dry cleaner plastic bags that smelled of chemicals.

The antique partners desk had a leather desk chair on one side and two smaller armchairs on the other.

As I approached, I breathed in a rich, faint tobacco scent that suggested a previous owner had smoked a pipe. Or maybe many pipes. A Logitech mouse sat on top of a stack of notepads, a heavy three-hole punch next to it. I wondered how often Ed used it. Not too many people put pages in actual physical binders anymore, though Dan had told me Ed was well behind the curve on technology, so maybe he did.

Beneath all of that was an old-style desk blotter with a paper appointment calendar printed on it with a small square for each day of the year. The appointments were written in abbreviations.

Most looked related to the campaign. The event Marco had attended was noted as "Fndrs Coff Linc Squ Zith 6 pm." The night Marco died said "Cub Sct Din Lakeview, Shk Hnds after Belmont."

Nothing else appeared on either date.

Unlike in the photo, the office had no file cabinets. But both the credenza and the desk had deep drawers that might hold files. Two of them were locked.

I started with the unlocked drawers in the credenza, using the flashlight function on my phone as I rifled through. My heart rate quickened when I found the Tabacchis' tax returns, but they were unsigned drafts, the versions businesspeople send off to their accountants for electronic filing.

The credenza also contained papers relating to Tabacchi's son's college applications and records. He was a film major at Columbia College in downtown Chicago. But he'd started as a biology major at a university out of state, and had attended community college before that. If only there had been financial aid forms, I might have found a signature, but no such luck.

I tiptoed to a heat vent and put my ear to it to be certain I was still hearing both guitars and both Danielle's and Joe's voices.

Crouching at the desk again, despite my fumbling the paperclip, the shallow drawer opened. My jaw ached from gritting my teeth while working the lock. Pressure started building in my head. Normally I'd take an Advil, but it was in my purse, which held nothing but my lock picking tools.

No help for it now.

The drawer contained blank checks for Ed's and Ariana's joint account and their separate personal checking accounts, plus tuition statements for their son.

Nothing with a signature.

I got into the deep desk drawer more quickly, but it wouldn't be long before Joe and Danielle would need to take a break. People don't want to listen to music forever, and fingers on guitar fretboards get tired and sore.

The hanging files were stuffed with paper, mostly relating to old real estate deals.

Pain increasing with every movement of my eyes, I skimmed the real estate documents, all of which related to Ariana's real estate holdings, not Ed's.

It occurred to me I'd stupidly assumed the office was Ed's, but Ariana was the one with the demanding job. This entire office might be more hers than his. Knees aching, I sank to sit on the floor for a moment and stretch my legs in front of me, back against the credenza. My head pounded.

The room had fallen silent.

I crawled on hands and knees to the heat vent. Only the murmur of conversation rose from the first floor. My heart gave a little jolt, but if Ed had come back, I'd be hearing Danielle singing alone, not silence. At least I hoped that was true, as I still needed to go through all the drawers on the front side of the desk.

I clicked on my phone, breathing deep to avoid the nausea its light triggered. I sent two quick texts:

Still looking.

Ed show up?

Return texts came in immediately:

No sign yet. Taking a break.

Ready if you need me.

Bracing one hand against the wall, I got to my feet and made my way to the sliding door to the balcony. I opened it, letting in a rush of warm air. It loosened my muscles and eased my head pain a fraction.

I scanned the room again. Something about the partners desk bothered me. In the faint light from the skylight and windows, I studied the leather desk organizer and the pens and pencils and paper clips in it, the yellow notepads, the heavy metal three-hole punch, and the old-fashioned desk blotter with its paper appointment calendar.

The mouse, unconnected to anything.

A jingle from a children's show ran through my head: Which one of these is not like the other?

I stepped closer and shone the flashlight over it. A plain black mouse that would work with any computer or laptop, yet there was no laptop or computer in the office. And it sat on the desk in the home office of someone with an old-fashioned three-hole punch and desk blotter.

I snapped a photo, making sure my cloth gloves were in place as I crossed the room. On hands and knees again, I crawled under the desk and shone my flashlight above my head. There it was. A power strip mounted on the underside of the desktop and a shallow shelf large enough to hold a laptop bolted next to it.

66

I HAD TO LIE ON MY BACK WITH THE PHONE ON THE FLOOR SHINING its light up. When my arms got in the way of the beam I worked by feel. Finally I got the drawer to slide out and retrieved a plain black laptop.

I didn't remember anything distinctive about Marco's, and I'd never seen it open. This one's home screen showed a snowy mountain scene. I checked my phone and, mentally crossing my fingers, typed the password Mirabel had given me long ago for his online bank account.

The entry field shook. A message advised me the password was wrong. I took a deep breath and slowly typed the password again.

The Windows music played, and the laptop unlocked.

I snapped a photo of the laptop and called Detective Sergeant Beckwell. I got his voicemail.

In a hushed voice, I explained where I was and what I was doing, then I sent a group text to him and my friends with the photo.

A folder labeled Old Matters required a password, too, but it was the same one that had opened the laptop.

The folder contained an html file and PDFs. With each new screen I opened, I photographed, texted, and read as quickly as I could. The pain in my head worsened with each movement. I considered taking the laptop away, but I not only wanted to finger Tabacchi, I wanted to know what had happened to Marco, and the police might never let me read the contents.

Plus, music was playing from downstairs again, my friends were all around me, and I'd left the message with the detective. I could call 911 if Tabacchi returned home.

One PDF included three pages of Alafair Halliwell's bank statements. A year and two months after Marco had signed the settlement release there was a deposit to Alafair's account of $23,000, $5,000 more than Marco had agreed to pay.

The file also contained a copy of the front and back of a canceled check from Ed Tabacchi to Alafair Halliwell for $23,000. It matched the date in the bank statement.

The html document had multiple dated text entries. I wasted minutes trying to email it to myself, but the laptop wasn't connected to WiFi.

The most recent entries were listed first, and it started with one from the Monday of the week Marco had died:

Tabacchi still stalling, claiming needs to plan exit strategy. Told him I'll go public next week. Don't want to spend first week at Quille's dealing w/this but when I explain she'll understand.

I touched the screen with my gloved fingertips, tracing each word as I reread it, my eyes blurring with tears. As much as I'd wanted to believe in Marco, underneath I'd feared he had chosen to leave me, especially after I realized how much I hadn't known or understood about him.

But this made it clear. He'd meant to be with me, and he hadn't abandoned his son.

An entry in January of this year was the last one before the entries shifted to the earlier timeframe:

Can't believe it. Tabacchi's running for Comptroller. Happened to see it when I was flipping channels. Should never have started skipping the news but who'd think he'd take the risk. Does he think I forgot? Changed my mind?

The pounding in my head intensified. I paused to listen at the heat vent. Both Joe and Danielle were singing. Still, it was foolish to stay here too long, especially with a full-blown migraine threatening.

I skipped over a dozen entries to read the earliest two:

Got call from Alafair Halliwell. Claims she was never paid for settlement. Attorney told her I didn't pay because I'm short of cash.

Tabacchi admitted to "bookkeeping snafu." Doesn't want his firm to know. Offered me fee.

Told him no, he needs to pay his client, pay her extra, or I'll report him and his firm. Still insists a bookkeeping error, is "looking into" what he can do. Told him he should not be practicing, should not be alderman.

I snapped a photo of both and texted it, then closed the file. It had started as I'd guessed, and I shouldn't waste any more time looking for details.

I hit X to close the entire folder, as footsteps rang from the metal interior spiral staircase.

I slammed the laptop shut and darted for the sliding door, pulling my gloves off and stuffing them in my pocket as I did.

The overhead light blinked on.

"Who's there?" a male voice said.

67

THE VOICE LACKED TABACCHI'S BOOMING QUALITY. MAYBE IT WAS another guest who'd wandered up. I spun, blinking in the light, thoughts racing as adrenaline coursed through me.

I told myself I'd be fine. It was like an improv.

The young man who'd entered was tall and stocky, with sharp eyes and the same ruddy complexion as Ed Tabacchi.

Rather than backing up as a guilty person would, I stepped toward him. "I'm so embarrassed, but I had to sneak up here and see the turret room. I saw photos online and, like, it's so beautiful."

I didn't like making myself sound vapid, but it was what came to mind, and if it would get me out of the situation it was worth it.

"Who are you?" Waves of garlic and red wine floated toward me as he spoke. Migraines make me hypersensitive to smells, but fortunately neither of these made the pain worse.

"Catherine. Joe's assistant? The musician?" I said, borrowing the lilting sentence endings Jacey had used. I forced myself not to glance toward the laptop. Hopefully the son would think it belonged to one of the Tabacchis. "Who're you?"

"Ed Tabacchi. Eddie. This's my house."

It was his stepmother's house, but I wasn't about to argue the point. I also noticed he didn't say "Junior," though obviously that was part of his name. I wondered if that said anything about his relationship with Ed Senior.

With effort, I kept my breathing steady. It was important not to show distress. "Fabulous house."

Eddie crossed the room. "So what do you assist Joe with? What's your job?"

"Oh, whatever he needs," I said, adding a nervous giggle that wasn't at all false. "Tonight I set out the wine and cheese, helped carry his guitar?"

"An all-around Girl Friday," Eddie said.

"Uh, sure," I said, as if uncertain of the reference. 25-year-old Catherine Dee wasn't a movie buff. Eddie obviously was, which made sense since he was a film student.

He inched closer. "Why were you looking around in the dark?"

The sliding door was to my right, and Eddie stood between me and the partners desk to my left. My pounding head made it hard to think clearly.

I still didn't want that laptop disappearing before the police arrived, and I wasn't sure if Eddie posed a threat.

"Sorry, migraine." I rubbed my forehead as I imagined pushing away the pain and locking it in a box, an exercise that usually dimmed it a bit. From experience, I knew it would roar back later, but if there was a later I'd be grateful. "When it hit I turned out the light, then I was about to step outside for some air."

I hoped I wasn't explaining too much, a trademark sign of a lie.

It didn't matter. Eddie headed for the laptop on the corner of the desk, keeping his body between me and the office door.

I fumbled in my pocket for my phone. My fingers tangled in a glove that had gotten wrapped around it.

Eddie opened the laptop.

I held my breath, hoping it had logged out when I'd closed it. If it had, even if he and not his father had stolen it from Marco, I might be able to convince him it had been on the desk when I'd come in. His father or stepmother could have found it and left it out to ask questions about later.

The screen showed the folder icons.

I lunged for the door, ignoring the pain the sudden movement caused to shoot through my forehead, but Eddie was too quick. He grabbed my arm and yanked me against him.

I heard a loud snick and he pressed something metal against my neck.

"What—what are you doing? Are you crazy?" I said, still hoping to pull off the innocent act.

He nodded toward the laptop. "Put in the password."

"I don't know what you're—"

Sharp pain on the side of my neck cut off my words. Blood trickled down my skin and my heart hammered. I didn't know how close his switchblade was to a vital artery. The smells of body odor and sweat—possibly mine or his or both—assaulted me, intensifying my migraine. My stomach churned.

"I'm not an idiot," he said. "I've been trying to unlock that laptop for weeks. You're here, and now it's open."

I prayed my friends had called 911 on getting my texts or that Detective Beckwell had seen them and heard my voicemail. Surely he'd come if he had.

I slowed my breathing, trying to show no fear, as if I were dealing with a vicious dog. "The police know I'm here."

He laughed. "Right. And your name is Catherine Dee."

The faint sound of sirens came through the open sliding glass door, but that meant nothing. Northwestern Hospital and three fire stations stood within a mile of this house. Sirens were part of the white noise of the neighborhood.

From the corner of my eye, I tried to see the balcony beyond the glass doors, but with the light on in the room, I couldn't see anything but darkness.

"What is the password?" he said. "For the Old Matters file?"

"I don't know," I said. Maybe I could buy time to figure out a plan by pretending to try different passwords. "I tried the one that unlocked the laptop. It didn't work."

His fingers tightened on my arm. "Then I guess you're no use to me."

68

MUSIC STILL DRIFTED IN FROM DOWNSTAIRS.

"Whatever's on that laptop," I said, gesturing toward it, "a good defense attorney might find a way around it. But a dead body in your dad's office—"

"It's my stepmom's office, and mine, and you broke in. I came upstairs after hearing a noise, confronted an intruder, and knifed her to protect myself."

"No one will believe that," I said.

"No? I'm betting you have some tool you used to break in. I'll say I thought it was a knife. Knife on knife."

Despite his confident tone, as he spoke, his whole body leaned toward the laptop, making it hard for me to keep my balance. It was as if he were drawn to it like metal to a magnet.

"Let me try some passwords," I said. "I have some ideas."

His arm felt sweaty and hot against mine. "What ideas?"

"Marco's son's birthday."

"Tried it."

Of course. He could have found that on social media, tried all sorts of combinations based on Marco's family members' names, birthdates, where they went to school, or any of the other personal details everyone now shares with the world. I needed something that wasn't out there.

I searched my mind for non-obvious security questions I'd filled out for my own online accounts. "His first pet's name. His favorite childhood toy. His best friend in high school."

"Right. You know those things."

"I do," I said, shocked my disguise had worked so well. Though Eddie hadn't met me at the cocktail party, only his father had, and I looked much different now than in any of my online photos. "I'm Quille. Quille Davis."

"Quille? Marco's girlfriend?"

"Yes."

Beyond Eddie I thought I detected a shift in the shadows on the balcony. I hoped it wasn't only the wind or wishful thinking on my part.

"Let me try a few different ones," I said.

He pushed me toward the desk. "One better work."

Stage fighting bears little resemblance to real fighting, but it does give you ideas, and I'd taken a few classes to get better at it.

Moving so fast it caused agony in my head, I bent over the keyboard, planted my hands on the desk, and ducked my head away from the knife. Shouting "Now," I forced my voice from diaphragm as if I were on stage, aiming to project all the way to the balcony.

As I yelled, I shifted my weight left, swung my right leg sideways and back, and hooked Eddie's legs right above the ankle. He pitched forward, his upper torso slamming onto the desk. A whoosh of air rushed from his mouth.

It was the perfect move, except I hadn't considered how the weight of his body in motion would affect me. Off-balance already because I was on one foot, I fell sideways.

My right temple smacked the front of the desk drawers on the way down. One intense, sharp pain momentarily blotted out the migraine, and my vision went black. I curled in a ball as tiny purple sparks exploded in front of my eyes.

Fighting nausea I rolled, hoping it was away from Eddie.

A hand grabbed my ankle and burning pain slashed the back of my calf. I yelled out and flailed my other leg. My foot connected with flesh, and I heard a muffled shout.

My vision cleared, but the pain in my leg seared, making me dizzy and nauseated. The room revolved around me. The floor felt sticky with blood from my leg.

Lauren, clad in black, was dragging Eddie by the feet away from me. She'd been down in the courtyard watching to send an early signal if Edward Tabacchi Senior returned. As I'd hoped, she must have climbed the fire escape to back me up on getting my texts.

Eddie still clutched the knife and he flipped onto his side and twisted toward Lauren, slashing wildly. I couldn't make my injured leg work properly, but I gripped the leather chair and pulled myself to my knees. Straining, I grabbed the three-hole punch from the desk. I swung it, connecting with Eddie's shoulder. I hit him again as the office door flew open, momentum landing me on top of him as Danielle and Joe charged toward us.

Eddie squirmed away and rolled under the desk, howling but still clutching the knife. Joe grabbed me and dragged me toward the armchairs. Lauren followed us, but Danielle dove under the desk after Eddie. A second later the switchblade flew out, skidding across the floor toward the office door.

Joe lunged for the desk, but Danielle emerged. Eddie didn't. She'd managed to handcuff one of his wrists to a leg of the massive desk.

Ariana Tabacchi, her hair falling out of her chignon, appeared in the doorway as sirens blared outside.

69

I heard Detective Sergeant Beckwell yelling at Danielle and Joe somewhere downstairs as paramedics got me bandaged and onto a stretcher and carried me down the metal staircase.

He walked beside me as I was taken through the living room. "I'll come to the hospital. We'll need a statement." His voice sounded harsh, but he touched my shoulder and added, "You'll be all right."

"Then what?" I said, careful not to move my throbbing head, though the pain in my leg was nearly overriding it.

"We'll see if you found a killer."

———

I needed surgery to a tendon in the back of my leg. I was in the hospital for three days and in a rehab facility for two weeks after that.

My mom dosed herself heavily with tranquilizers and tried to ride with my dad to Chicago to come see me. After half an hour though, she had a full-blown panic attack and my dad had to take her back home. She did insist that he continue on without her, though, despite that no one was available right away to come and stay with her.

Both Mirabel and Marco's mother, Rosa, came to see me and thank me, and his brother, Hector, called from Alaska to say the same and to ask about my injuries and treatment.

Danielle babysat my cases and, when she visited, filled me in on the developments in the case against the Tabacchis.

Eddie had never been fingerprinted in his life. So, unlike Edward Senior, his fingerprints hadn't been on file or available for the police to check against those in Marco's apartment.

When he was booked for the assault on me, it turned out his prints matched some found in Marco's apartment, including a partial on the bottom of an unopened can of Diet Chocolate Fudge Soda that had been in Marco's refrigerator.

My photo of the guy at the bar at Sociale matched one of Eddie's friends who had a previous conviction for theft.

To get a chance to plead to lesser charges he cooperated with the prosecution. Under oath, he stated that Eddie had paid him to follow me, break into my office, and steal my handbag. He claimed he'd never meant to hurt me in the Pedway.

Eddie was charged with attempted murder of me. In connection with Marco's death, he was charged with first degree murder.

Edward Senior was charged as an accessory after the fact. The prosecutor told me that charge might be changed to murder if evidence showed Edward helped plan what his son had done.

There was no evidence Ariana Tabacchi had known about her stepson's actions or her husband's connection to Marco.

When questioned separately, all three family members stated Ariana rarely used the turret office. If she had, it seemed unlikely she would have guessed the laptop belonged to Marco, as there was no evidence she'd known anything about Marco's and her husband's interactions.

The document entries showed that Marco met with Ed Tabacchi several times, pushing him to withdraw from the Comptroller race. Tabacchi begged Marco to let the primary play out, saying he wasn't the favored candidate and if he lost, he'd never run again, but at least he wouldn't need to tell his wife what he'd done.

I had no doubt that if Marco had exposed him, despite that he'd finally paid Alafair an extra $5,000 over what he owed her, he'd have been disbarred and, even in Illinois, probably wouldn't have been the people's choice to handle their money.

Marco had agreed to wait to see what happened with the primary, not wanting to make life hard for Tabacchi's wife and son. Even after Tabacchi won, he held off on going public, wanting Tabacchi to resign rather than see him exposed publicly, but he'd given him an April 30 deadline.

Edward Senior eventually confessed and pled guilty to being an accessory as part of a package deal. The State's Attorney's office reduced the charges against Eddie to second degree murder, plus assault and battery against me.

Edward said when he'd declared his candidacy the previous year, he'd hoped Marco might have decided over a decade out of politics was enough. He'd thought he'd been right about that when he heard nothing from Marco during the early months of his campaign. He hadn't known Marco now avoided news and politics due to his sobriety program.

After Marco confronted him, Edward had told his son. Eddie interned in his father's office and handled his computer issues. Edward Senior claimed he'd hoped his son would learn a lesson from it and also might be able to convince Marco that his dad had become a good man.

It was Eddie's idea to reach out to Marco's neighbors, supposedly as part of that effort.

After hearing about Marco's death, Edward suspected his

son had been involved but didn't want to believe it, so he didn't contact the police.

Despite the scar left on my leg and my continuing limp, part of me felt sympathy for Edward Senior. It would be hard to turn your own son in for murder.

As part of his plea deal, Eddie confessed. He'd learned about Marco by following the social media posts of everyone in his life. He'd also tracked down articles and guest blog posts Marco himself had written about the alcohol treatment program he'd gone into and how well it had worked for him.

The week after both her stepson and husband pled guilty, Ariana Tabacchi filed for divorce.

70

Hazleton's investigation of Vujic Chiropractic continued, so far as I knew. It no longer mattered to me.

Lauren kept dating the man she'd met in the course of trying to help me, and he found the real reason they'd met worrisome. He urged her to refrain from bringing criminals to justice in the future.

Almost as soon as the Illinois Attorney General's investigation into ChiTown Property Management began, Charlene Garfield got an attorney and turned herself in. She made a statement that after her longtime business partner disappeared, leaving the country, she discovered he'd embezzled money from a major account.

Wanting to protect her company's reputation, she'd replaced the money from her personal funds. But over the next months she discovered more and more areas where he'd stolen.

She started shifting money around herself trying to plug the leaks as she figured out the extent of it. She'd meant to make every account whole, and by the time she realized she couldn't, she'd been afraid to go to the authorities knowing she'd be charged.

The amounts stolen from Marco were relatively small, and Charlene had replaced most of the money. I transferred the account to a different management company and made sure statements would go to Mirabel and me regularly.

Even with the corrected figures, there was no way Marco could have paid Eric's tuition.

I could see, though, where he might have convinced himself he'd find a way. He could have planned to apply for a line of credit on the six flat to pay both the building repairs and tuition. He never would have qualified, but he might not have realized that.

The life insurance company agreed to pay, and Mirabel and I persuaded the school to put Eric at the top of the waiting list.

I finally started sleeping in my bed again because when I got home from rehab, it hurt like crazy to climb steps.

For years before dating Marco, I'd slept alone, and it had never bothered me. I'm a natural Starfish sleeper, arms and legs splaying everywhere, and when I got serious enough about anyone to spend nights together, it always challenged me to adjust. It was Marco being gone that was hard, not being alone, and whether I slept in the futon or here, Marco was still gone.

Still, that first night home I hesitated at the foot of the bed.

Finally I retrieved lavender oil from the care package Marco's brother, Hector, had sent me, put some on my wrists, and crawled into bed.

———

In mid-July we learned another student had withdrawn, so Eric could start at St. Sebastian in the fall. That news corresponded with me finishing my formal physical therapy. I still had exercises to do at home.

My doctor promised my lingering limp would disappear eventually and the scar would fade almost all the way.

Carole closed Café des Livres for a private party. She grouped half a dozen small round marble-topped tables together and set out plates of cured meat and cheeses to start, including my favorite, a triple cream goat cheese with a truffle rind.

Lauren had brought three bottles of red—a Pinot Noir, a Cabernet, and a Malbec—for herself, Carole, Joe's girlfriend, and me. Carole uncorked the first Malbec and poured it. Joe opened one of the whites he'd brought and poured it for himself, Mirabel, and Marco's mother, Rosa.

Mirabel gave Eric a sparkling water.

He wore a tank top and shorts and sat straight. His eyes, though not as lively as they'd been when I'd met him, didn't have shadows under them anymore, and his hair had grown a little longer and curlier, looking more and more like Marco's.

Carole lifted her glass. "To Quille, for uncovering the truth. And surviving despite her foolishness."

"I had a lot of help," I said. "With the surviving, not the foolishness."

"You were all foolish." She rested her hand on Eric's shoulder. "But I forgive you because you made life a little better for this young man."

After the meat and cheese course came coq au vin, made by Carole, and lasagna, made by Rosa. It was an evening of laughter and conversation about everything other than death and intrigue.

After dinner Joe, Danielle, and I stood together near the windows and sang Amazing Grace in Marco's memory. I choked up, missing a few notes. Carole joined in with a fourth part, a nice alto that could double as a tenor. I hadn't known she could sing, yet she wove around our voices expertly and filled in whatever I couldn't.

She smiled at me, probably reading the surprise in my face at learning something new about her.

When we were done, Eric hugged me.

"Thank you again," he said. "And not just for the insurance money."

"You're welcome," I said. "But it was for me, too. I wanted both of us to remember your dad as the happy person he was."

Carole disappeared and returned with an almond pear tart with vanilla gelato—my favorite of her specialties.

Joe raised his glass. "To Marco."

"To Marco," I said, and squeezed Eric's hand.

———

"Any ideas?" I said, scanning the section of the cemetery marked Block 8V by a two-foot worn stick in the southwest corner. The writing on it was so faded we'd had to get within inches to read it.

Joe took out the folded printout from the office. He wore jeans and an olive green T-shirt, the most casual I'd seen him since he'd left theater. Since he'd entered the finance world, we usually met after work.

We thought it would be easy to find the grave, but there were so many, and every winding road and row of plots looked like the next.

"Maybe the center," Joe said. "Look for an angel statue."

The graves were so close together you couldn't help walking over them, though I would have rather not. Despite finding the statue, we walked along four rows, peering at every flat headstone, before finding it.

If we'd stopped at my parents' house to get my mother and dad, they would have easily found the grave. My mother could probably find it in her sleep. But I wasn't quite ready to come here with her. I didn't know how I'd react to seeing Q.C.'s headstone for the first time after all the years avoiding it and resenting her.

We found it at last. Raised markers had no longer been allowed by the time Q.C. was buried, though the older parts of the cemetery were filled with them. Hers was a simple flat stone with the words Beloved Daughter And Sister above her name and the years of her birth and death below it.

The air smelled of dry grass and wilting flowers.

A finger-sized plastic doll with blond hair sat on the corner of the stone. My mother left a different toy every week. The groundskeeper, who'd known our family forever, gathered them periodically and donated the ones that survived the weather well enough.

"I never understood before how hard it was for my parents not knowing what happened. Who killed her." I held a rose in my right hand, which hung at my side, careful to avoid the thorns.

Joe bent to brush dirt off the word Sister on the worn gravestone. "Quille, you're not thinking —"

"If the police hadn't focused so much on my parents —"

"That doesn't mean over thirty years later with all of one crime solved as experience you could do it." Joe straightened and we stood side-by-side again.

"But what if I could? Maybe not tomorrow or next month or even next year. But sometime down the road. What if I could solve Q.C.'s murder?"

"Dangerous. Too dangerous." Joe sighed and squeezed my free hand. "But I'll be right there with you if you try."

"Thank you." I set the rose under the name Q.C. Davis. I hoped she was resting in peace. But I didn't see how she could be.

———

Start reading the next Q.C. Davis mystery The Charming Man today.

AFTERWORD

Quille as a character floated around in my mind for a long time before I wrote The Worried Man. She shares some obvious aspects of her life with me – mainly that she's a lawyer who also devotes herself to creative efforts. Other parts of her life, the most troubling ones, draw from my experience but are very different.

So I'll start here –

The most heartbreaking part of Quille's story to me is that she grew up feeling like an inferior replacement for a sister who was killed not long before she was born, whom her mother named her for.

A family in my neighborhood when I was growing up inspired that last detail. The real story, to the extent I remember it accurately, is that a neighborhood child died young. His parents, no doubt in the depths of grief, changed his brother's name legally to be that of the deceased boy.

Even as a kid I felt this awful mix of sympathy for the parents and anger at them, imagining how their living son must feel. I didn't know him personally, but that incident never left my mind. I found it so upsetting that I couldn't bring myself to give Quille quite that backstory. So I changed it to naming her for a recently deceased sister. That struck me as something parents might see as a tribute to their lost daughter. Understandably, Quille feels in her sister's shadow, but it's not quite as extreme as the parents changing her name.

The other challenging part of Quille's family history is her mother's depression.

For that, I drew only a small amount from my life. Luckily, my mom and dad supported whatever I aimed to do as a child and teenager. And I remember coming home from school and talking to my mom almost every day during that time. She listened, sometimes shared stories of her life, and gave great practical advice.

When I got older, we had a lot of differences, and our relationship became difficult. What I didn't grasp was that part of the disconnect came from my mom's own struggles. She'd always been a bit of a worrier. But as she aged and tried to cope with tragedies that came our way, her anxiety grew. In later years, she became depressed, and I'm sad to say that none of us realized it until it was extreme. I simply thought my mom, due to our differences, decided she didn't care about me.

I still remember the first time, a few months after a new treatment started working, when Mom called me and asked, "How are you?" I teared up. And had no idea what to say or where to start. My mother hadn't asked how I was in years. So many years that I couldn't even recall how long.

A few years later at a writer's conference a fellow author told me about her memoir. Her mother suffered from clinical depression all the author's life. She talked about feeling ignored, uninteresting, and valueless as a child because her mother almost never focused on her. The author's life revolved around her mother's illness.

And I thought about how many years I had when my mom was there for me. Yes, it was hard to more or less lose maternal support in my late twenties and through my thirties. But I experienced so much of my earlier life when my mom wasn't just there, she conveyed in word and deed that I could achieve whatever I wanted. That she believed in me. It made it easier to get through the later decades when our relationship changed.

So I borrowed from my adult experience and what I learned about children of depressed parents for Quille. But I also gave her Gram because she needed someone to encourage her. I saw Gram as helping Quille develop confidence and, probably more important, connecting with her emotionally so that Quille could in turn form close friendships and other relationships.

That mattered to me because I love reading novels where the main character joins together with a small group of friends or allies to defeat an outside evil.

Whether it's supernatural, such as in horror and occult fiction, or human, as in so many of my favorite mysteries and suspense novels, I like the main conflict to come from that outside force. There's nothing wrong with books that explore deep interpersonal conflicts. But I prefer those to be subplots, as they are in the Q.C. Davis mysteries.

Probably that's because the mystery genre, for me as a reader and author, is all about imposing order on the universe. In real life, the bad guys aren't always caught. And even if they are, it can't undo the wrongs done. In fiction, though, the sense of closure and justice offers a little healing. A little help getting through to the next day, to a better time.

On a lighter note, while I was never a professional stage actress like Quille, from age sixteen through my mid-twenties I made some of my money playing folk and bluegrass music and writing my own songs. Thus my choice to start each book with a quote from a song. (The one at the beginning of The Fractured Man is from one I wrote myself.) Also, similar to Quille's choice about acting, at some point I realized I didn't love music, singing, and performing enough to pursue it for a living. (Writing, on the other hand, I've never been able to stop doing.) Occasionally I do still miss singing with others on stage, especially doing harmony. So I let Quille leave her acting career but sing in an a cappella group for fun and a little profit.

I could write more about Quille, but I'll save it for future author's notes.

See you in the next book, **The Charming Man.**

ABOUT THE AUTHOR

In addition to the Q.C. Davis Mystery Series, which includes The Worried Man, The Charming Man, The Fractured Man, The Troubled Man, The Hidden Man, and No Good Plays (A Q.C. Davis Mystery Novella), Lisa M. Lilly is the author of the Awakening supernatural thriller series. Books in that series have been downloaded over 100,000 times.

A resident of Chicago, Lilly is an attorney and a member of the Alliance Against Intoxicated Motorists. She joined AAIM after an intoxicated driver caused the deaths of her parents in 2007. Her book of essays, *Standing in Traffic*, is available on AAIM's website.

She is currently working on the next Q.C. Davis mystery. She also hosts the podcast Buffy and the Art of Story.

ALSO BY LISA M. LILLY

Q.C. Davis Mystery Series

The Worried Man

The Charming Man

The Fractured Man

No Good Plays (A Q.C. Davis Mystery Novella)

The Troubled Man

The Hidden Man

No Good Deeds (Short Story for Readers Group members)

No New Beginnings (Short Story for Readers Group members)

The Awakening Supernatural Thriller Series

The Awakening (Book 1 in The Awakening Series)

The Unbelievers (Book 2 in The Awakening Series)

The Conflagration (Book 3 in The Awakening Series)

The Illumination (Book 4 in The Awakening Series)

Made in the USA
Monee, IL
17 August 2022

11751345R00201